# BORDER BADLANDS

## DEREK FEE

MIST MEDIA

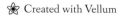 Created with Vellum

*For Aine, Bobbie and Sean*

## CHAPTER ONE

Brian Lennon wiped the sweat from his brow. His heart had been pounding since leaving his home in Creggan close to Crossmaglen. The only lights on the road to Inniskeen were from the isolated farmhouses he passed. He drove slowly and carefully. This was not a place to get lost. Although he had spent all his twenty-nine years living in the borderlands of Armagh and Monaghan, the area around Inniskeen had such a plethora of small lanes and so few signposts that he was grateful he had GPS to keep him on track. The night was dark and forbidding. The light from his car illuminated the bare trees that lined the road. Their outstretched branches were like arms reaching out to envelope his car and him. A shiver ran down his spine. He told himself everything was going to be okay but didn't really believe it. The man he was about to meet was probably the only person who could help to extricate him from the mess he now found himself in. Still, something didn't feel right. He was about to turn back when the robotic voice of the GPS announced that his destination was one hundred metres on the right. He turned into the narrow path. Away to his right he could see two dark shapes set against the skyline.

The lane ahead was rough and overgrown. Why had the man arranged a meeting in this godforsaken place?

Lennon drove slowly up the lane. He could see that the shapes were in fact two buildings set side by side. The larger building on the right was a rundown traditional farmhouse. It had been derelict for some time as the roof had fallen in and there was no glass in the windows. Next to it was a small two-storey structure with galvanised cladding, which he recognised as a barn. There was no sign of life. Should he stop and turn around? No. Without this meeting, he stood to lose everything his parents and grandparents had worked for. He really didn't have a choice. He stopped in a cobbled farmyard, shut off the engine and left the car. The silence was total and eerie. He walked towards the farmhouse and pushed open the front door. The sound of creaking hinges reverberated through the empty building. Inside, he saw broken furniture strewn around what had once been a living room. Although it was early January, he didn't feel cold. The radio weatherman had announced that it would be unseasonably warm over the next few days. He shivered nonetheless.

A sound outside caused him to turn quickly. Damn it. Why couldn't they have met in daylight? He heard the sound again and was sure that it was coming from the barn. He walked the twenty metres to the galvanised barn. A large double door hung loosely on its hinges. He pulled one door and it creaked open. It was pitch-black inside. 'Hello,' he shouted. 'Anybody here?' His words echoed back at him. He walked forward a few steps into the barn and the door creaked shut behind him. He found he was having difficulty breathing. A scuffling sound directly in front sounded like a rat. He hated rats. It was time to beat a retreat.

He was almost at the centre point of the barn when an arc light went on and dazzled him. He put his hand up to shield his eyes. The whole interior was lit up and he saw that a number of men were standing around the edges of the barn.

Each man was dressed in a blue boiler-suit and wore a bala-clava. Each held a wooden pickaxe handle in his right hand. Without a word being spoken, they moved towards him. He lost control of his bowels. 'Ah lads, please, no.' He held up his hands as the blows began to rain on him.

LENNON LAY INERT on the ground in the centre of the barn. The six men who had beaten him to death sauntered out without looking back. A minibus with its engine idling had pulled up beside the dead man's car. A heavy-set squat man climbed out of the driver's seat and took two sacks from the trunk of the minibus. He opened the first sack and the men passed in a line dumping their bloodstained pickaxe handles and gloves. When all six sets had been collected, he closed that sack and tied it up. He opened the second sack and the men peeled off their boiler-suits and balaclavas and deposited them in the sack. The last man in the line dropped in his boiler suit and a bloody mobile phone. As soon as they were finished, some of the men lit cigarettes and wandered around the farm-yard. No one spoke.

The squat man dumped the sacks in the trunk and slid open the door to the rear of the minibus. He then entered the barn, took out his mobile phone and photographed the badly beaten body. He dismantled the lights and stowed them in the rear of the minibus.

The men climbed in and took their places.

'Well done, boys.' The driver passed a bottle of whiskey into the seats behind him. The lights of the minibus ran over the dark shape of the barn as it turned back towards the road.

# CHAPTER TWO

J ust prior to the meeting of the PSNI Brexit Task Force, Detective Superintendent Ian Wilson picked up his cardboard place card and swapped it with that bearing the name of a colleague at the opposite end of the table from the chairperson. Wilson then took his new seat and watched as his task force colleagues trooped into the room and took their appointed places. A series of documents had been set before each chair. On top was a list of the members and their ranks, directly beneath was an agenda for the meeting and beneath that was a discussion paper on the challenges the PSNI would face when the United Kingdom withdrew itself from the European Union. The members of the task force had been asked to read the discussion paper before this inaugural meeting, but true to form Wilson hadn't bothered. It wasn't because he didn't consider Brexit a threat to the PSNI. He'd been around the last time there was a hard border on the island so he was aware of the consequences. Peace had led to a certain amount of complacency, but he knew the people who had created the Troubles were still out there waiting for an opportunity to unleash round two.

Wilson totted up the cost of gathering together a deputy

chief constable, two assistant chief constables, assorted chief superintendents and superintendents and a couple of up-and-coming chief inspectors. Assigning weekly salaries to each, assuming that the meeting would last two hours and dividing the total weekly salaries by twenty caused him to emit a low whistle. Brexit wasn't going to be cheap. It was safe to assume that similar task forces were meeting all over the UK. Local councils, police authorities, chambers of commerce, Uncle Tom Cobley and all would be setting up groups to examine the impact of Brexit on their particular activities. Wilson marvelled at man's ability to waste money on useless exercises.

He wondered which idiot in HR had decided to appoint him to the Brexit Task Force. He assumed they had employed the dartboard method when selecting appointees. It was the only conclusion that made sense. He had a well-established reputation for never reading papers, for never contributing to discussions and whenever possible for excusing himself from meetings.

All eyes turned as the conference room door opened and DCC Royson Jennings strode towards the head of the table. One of the ACCs was instantly on his feet to pull back a chair for the DCC. If you're going to lick arse at a meeting, best to get your lick in first so that it would be remembered. Wilson looked up to heaven. He wasn't keen on alien abduction, especially if it included elements of probing, but right at that moment he would have gratefully positioned himself for the tractor beam rather than watch colleagues, many of whom he respected, humiliate themselves by crawling up the DCC's arse.

A silence had descended on the room and Wilson noted that Jennings was staring directly at him. Jennings turned and whispered to the ACC who had played usher. Although Wilson couldn't hear the comment, he felt it concerned him and was of the nature of 'What is that sod doing on this important task force?' The ACC looked confused and shuffled some papers in the hope that the DCC's question might be answered in them. All their blushes were removed when Wilson's mobile phone indicated the arrival of a message. There was trouble and he was required urgently. Chief Superintendent Yvonne Davis was on her way to HQ to stand in for him and DC Harry Graham would meet him downstairs with a car. Wilson signalled to the ACC, who left the hot seat. He displayed the message and begged the indulgence of the DCC. Davis would be a more than suitable replacement. The look of gratitude on the face of the ACC was a joy to behold. Wilson was equally elated as he could see a real possibility that his boss would be co-opted in his place. It was one of those win-win situations he was always hearing about. The ACC relayed the message to Jennings. Wilson stood and nodded at the chairman before striding towards the door. He was gratified by the look of envy on the faces of his colleagues.

# CHAPTER THREE

Harry Graham was sitting in an unmarked pool car when Wilson exited HQ and sat into the passenger seat. 'Where's the fire, Harry?'

'We're going south, boss.'

'How far south?'

'Farther south than usual.' Graham engaged the gear and turned the car towards the exit.

'Give me the full story.'

'The details are sketchy, but it involves murder. The chief super told me to pick you up and take you to a location in Monaghan.'

'That's outside our jurisdiction.'

Graham didn't reply.

'Where exactly in Monaghan?'

'Small townland called Inniskeen.'

'Never heard of it.'

'Neither have most people. I looked it up and it's a spot on the map: one pub, one church and one shop. Don't worry, we've got a set of coordinates, which I've already put into the GPS, and we'll be met there by representatives of the Garda Síochána.'

'How far?'

'About an hour via the A1 towards Dundalk and then country roads.'

'And all you know is that it involves murder?'

'That's it, boss.'

They joined the motorway and headed south.

'Any news of Rory?' Harry asked.

'Nothing, I don't think Rory wants to be found for a while. I checked with his parents and they haven't any idea where he's gone. I think he's had enough of the PSNI.' Wilson leaned back indicating that the conversation was over. He was still angry with himself for not managing Rory Browne properly. He was partly to blame for Browne taking on a private investigation that almost got him killed and he'd received a rap over the knuckles for his lack of managerial skills. Browne had been suspended awaiting a full enquiry but had decided to tender his resignation instead. Wilson had done everything in his power to dissuade the young man from resigning. Browne was a good copper who had made an honest mistake. There was no way he would ever work in the Murder Squad again, but the PSNI needed people like Browne. Before vanishing from Northern Ireland, Browne had given detailed video evidence of what had happened between him and the serial killer Vincent Timoney. Wilson was trying to fill the vacancy, but the bean counters saw the resignation as the perfect excuse to cut the complement by one. The new policing mantra had been employed as a defence: do more with less.

It was a fine day and Wilson tried to appreciate the weather as they drove south. In Northern Ireland, Wilson was a policeman with jurisdiction throughout the province. As soon as he passed an unmarked line in the road they were currently on, his jurisdiction would end and he would become a tourist, which made him wonder what exactly they were heading into.

Graham took a sharp turn to the right just outside

Dundalk and the first signpost they saw pointed to the quaintly named Hackballscross. After another ten minutes, they encountered two garda patrol cars blocking the entrance to the lane identified by the GPS as their destination. Harry pulled in behind them and he and Wilson exited the car. They showed their warrant cards to the uniformed officer at the entrance to the lane and signed in.

'The building on the left,' the officer said as she lifted the crime scene tape and allowed them to enter.

Wilson surveyed the scene as he walked up the lane. The buildings ahead looked derelict except for the police activity. He noted an old farmhouse on the right and a barn on the left. The location was remote and there were not many occupied dwellings in the vicinity. It was a fine place to carry out a murder. A Toyota Corolla with a Northern Ireland registration was parked in the middle of a cobbled yard. They headed for the barn.

Harry pulled back the barn door to permit Wilson's entry.

The building was empty except for the body lying in the centre and a group of men, some wearing garda uniforms, standing to the right of the open door.

'Glad you could join us, Ian.' Detective Chief Inspector Jack Duane detached himself from the group and strode towards Wilson.

'I should have known,' Wilson said. Duane was the Garda Síochána's Northern Ireland man.

'It's good to have my old friend on a case with me.' Duane hugged Wilson. 'Haven't seen you since your return from Nova Scotia.'

'I'm beginning to regret coming back.'

'This case could be our swansong,' Duane said.

'How so?'

'Brexit, man, you guys will be a third country in the future. All the cooperation we've built up will be in the toilet. I always figured that you and I would go out like Butch Cassidy and the Sundance Kid.'

'And you'd be the Sundance Kid, of course. Anyway, they were shot to pieces in Bolivia as far as I remember.'

Duane tapped the side of his nose. 'That's the official version. I heard they got away and lived happily ever after.'

'I don't see that in your future. You remember Harry Graham?'

Duane nodded.

'What have we got here?' Wilson asked.

'He's one of yours. That's why we put the call in.'

'I saw the car outside.'

A uniformed garda inspector approached them.

'This is DI Daragh Flynn from Dundalk,' Duane introduced the new arrival. 'He's officially in charge of the murder scene. Daragh, this is DS Ian Wilson and his sidekick is DC Harry Graham.'

Flynn extended his hand. 'I'm supposed to be the senior investigating office here, but it appears that Dublin has different ideas,' he said, looking at Duane.

'We all obey our betters,' Duane said. 'Even if we don't agree with them.'

'Do you have a name for the victim?' Wilson asked.

Flynn produced his notebook. 'The car is registered to a Brian Lennon with an address in Creggan in County Armagh.'

'Any sign of a pathologist?' Wilson asked.

'The state pathologist is on the way,' Duane said. 'He's an obnoxious old fart and nothing at all like the beautiful Professor Reid you usually deal with. But we don't need a pathologist to tell us that this poor bastard has been beaten to death.'

'This place is pretty remote,' Wilson said. 'How did you discover the body?'

'Phone message to Dundalk Garda Station at three o'clock this morning,' Flynn said.

'What are you thinking, Jack?' Wilson asked.

'Looks like a punishment beating gone wrong,' Flynn interjected.

Wilson and Duane looked at him. 'Punishment beating gone wrong my arse,' Duane said. 'The man was murdered pure and simple.'

'If they wanted him dead, they could have put a bullet in his skull,' Flynn said.

'If they did that,' Duane said. 'Then a fool of a policeman wouldn't believe that it was a punishment beating gone wrong.'

'What do you want from us?' Wilson said.

'The genesis of this crime lies in the north,' Duane said. 'Since his car is parked outside, it's safe to assume that Lennon was lured here on some pretext or other and then murdered. The crime scene investigators will be arriving from Dublin shortly. Let's wait and see what they come up with. We need to get all the PSNI has on Lennon and his associates. If I'm right, we're going to be interviewing suspects on your side of the border. We have no jurisdiction up there, so Brexit be damned, we're going to have to work together.'

'That's the first time I've heard you admit you don't have jurisdiction in the north,' Wilson said.

Both men laughed.

Flynn's face wore a puzzled look.

Another of the uniforms joined them. 'The pathologist has arrived.'

'We'll let him get on with his job,' Duane said. He put his arm around Wilson's shoulder. 'I'm reliably informed that there's a reasonable restaurant in Hackballscross and I've been up since seven and haven't had my breakfast. I think you should join me. Harry can keep an eye on things here.' He turned to Graham and slapped him on the shoulder. 'Can't you, Harry?'

'Yes, sir,' Graham confirmed.

## CHAPTER FOUR

W ilson was briefly introduced to Dr James Kelly, the State Pathologist of the Irish Republic. He expected to find an individual whose presence befitted the post but was disappointed. The physician was not so much obnoxious as condescending. Kelly was perhaps unlucky to have been born with a permanent sneer on his corpulent face. The meeting was perfunctory, and Wilson was happy to join Duane in a garda car and head back in the direction of Hackballscross.

The small crossroads hamlet was undistinguished and counted only a few houses in an otherwise rural scene. The bar/restaurant that Duane had been recommended was totally out of character with the bleak surroundings. The building was imposing, and the cut-stone entrance resembled a round tower. A large rectangular building next door had the appearance of a dancehall. Duane led the way into the bar and ordered the largest breakfast available. Wilson stuck to a coffee. He had felt elated at being freed from the Brexit Task Force but now wondered if he had simply jumped out of the frying pan into the fire.

Duane chose a table in the corner of the room and selected the seat facing the door and the bar. 'Sorry for landing this one on you, Ian,' he said when they were seated. 'But the boys we're going to be dealing with require the attention of the top guns and not idiots like Flynn. His idea of an investigation and mine would turn out to be totally different.'

'So, there's no possibility that it was a punishment beating gone wrong?' Wilson smiled.

'That's what they want us to think. Who's worried about a kneecapping in which the victim loses so much blood he dies? How many perpetrators of kneecapping have we put in jail? The punishment-beating-gone-wrong scenario means we don't have to look for a motive.'

A waitress headed in their direction carrying a tray with Duane's breakfast and Wilson's coffee. The policemen stopped talking and waited until she was out of earshot before continuing.

'Do you have an idea who might be behind this murder?' Wilson asked.

'You know the way the big banks and the car manufacturers are making their plans for a future outside the EU?'

Wilson nodded. He had long ago suffered Brexit fatigue.

'Well, the boys on both sides of the border are also preparing. They see some commercial possibilities in tariff differences between the north and the south. The local criminal organisations are ready to reap the rewards of political folly.'

'From our side, we're more worried about violence erupting again.'

'It's a very real possibility. The headbangers are still out there, but for the moment their concentration is on making money.'

It seemed to Wilson that Duane knew more about those headbangers than he was prepared to divulge.

'We need to know what your Intelligence people have on Lennon,' Duane said while munching a well-cooked piece of bacon. 'My guess is that it won't be much, if anything at all.

We have nothing on him and that makes me wonder why someone wanted him dead.'

'Motive doesn't rank high in this area.'

'That was true once but not anymore. These country boys are just like their city cousins. They don't have much of a market for drugs and prostitution, but they're very concentrated on what advantages they do have.' Duane mopped up the yolk of his eggs with a piece of toast and gulped down the end of his tea.

'Shouldn't we get back before Dr Kelly leaves?' Wilson asked.

'I try to spend as little time as possible in the company of that prick.' Duane pushed his empty plate away. 'What's he going to tell us anyway? That Lennon was beaten to death sometime last night. We'll check the cameras on the main roads for traffic during the relevant hours, but there'll be nothing. Why? Because the perpetrators won't have used the main roads. They know every back road in the area and there are no cameras on those.'

'You don't think we'll get them.' Wilson finished his coffee.

'How did the trip to Nova Scotia go? Did Reid pass muster with your mother?'

'The trip was great, even if the weather wasn't. Reid more than passed muster. By the time we left, you'd have thought they were mother and daughter.'

'I envy you, Ian.'

'You were there once.'

'So were you, and people like you and me always screw it up.'

'Let's get back and see what the prick has to say.'


KELLY HAD ALREADY DEPARTED when they arrived back at the crime scene. Arrangements had been made to transport the body to Dundalk in order to carry out an autopsy. Time of death was estimated at between ten and midnight. A large CSI wagon was parked at the entrance to the lane and Wilson could see four technicians in white plastic suits moving around the farmyard. The investigation would follow the well-worn procedure. Graham and Flynn joined Wilson and Duane.

'Someone will have to tell his people,' Duane said.

'I have no part in this,' Wilson said.

'Not exactly true. My big boss has been speaking with your big boss and you and I are going to be working on this together. The email confirming it is in your inbox as we speak. We get to ride forth one more time.' Duane smiled. 'You'll handle the relatives. I'll arrange for the identification.' He turned to Flynn. 'Give him the address.'

Flynn took out his notebook, wrote down an address and handed the page to Wilson.

'Just like Butch and Sundance,' Wilson said. 'And we know how that ended.'

## CHAPTER FIVE

Detective Sergeant Moira McElvaney stood in front of 25 University Square and looked at the plaque on the wall identifying the building as the home of the Faculty of History, Anthropology, Philosophy and Politics of Queen's University, Belfast. Her boss should have been standing beside her. They had allowed for a two-hour Brexit Task Force meeting but hadn't planned for Wilson's ad hoc rush to Monaghan. Thus, she found herself alone to take a meeting with Professor Michael Gowan, whom she had never met. One Moleskine notebook had been saved from the inferno that had consumed the rest of Jackie Carlisle's legacy to the people of Northern Ireland. The notebook had been in cypher and Gowan had a reputation within the university community as a code breaker. A decent amount of time had passed since Wilson had deposited the notebook with Gowan, and although the book was unlikely to assist them in confirming their theories regarding Carlisle's death, one never knew what little gem it might drop into their laps. Moira was directed upstairs by one of the dragons on the ground floor that operated as gatekeepers. She located Gowan's office and knocked.

'Come in.'

Moira entered and found herself in a comfortable office large enough to house a desk and a seating area in which tutorials could be held. Bookshelves covered the walls and sagged from the weight of the tomes they supported.

Gowan stood and extended his hand. 'Detective Sergeant McElvaney?'

'Yes, I'm sorry I should have shown you my warrant card.'

Gowan sat. 'Please take a seat.'

Gowan was bald at the front and had an excess of grey hair at the rear of his head. He was short and wore a thick sweater that had seen better days. He had a jovial face and Moira guessed he would be popular with his students.

'Will Superintendent Wilson be joining us?' he asked.

'He's been called away urgently. I'm afraid you'll have to put up with me.'

'There's no pain in that. Are you a graduate yourself?'

'BA Sociology at Coleraine.'

'A good school. I'm sure you're busy, so let's get to the point.' He removed the black Moleskine notebook from his desk drawer. 'First, let me return this notebook with my apologies for the time I took to accomplish the task. My schedule was seriously affected by a bout of illness.'

'Nothing serious, I hope?'

'Serious enough to keep me out of work for six months, but I'm well on the road to a full recovery. Thank you for asking.' He took out a folder and laid it beside the notebook. 'Mr Carlisle's code was not that difficult to break. I simply identified the vowels and then made assumptions regarding the consonants to try to make sense out of the sentences. It's a tried and tested method. The contents you will have to judge for yourself. It seems to me that Jackie Carlisle was attempting to write a story about a series of characters without names but with functions. For example, there is the Queen, the Judge, the Lord, the Mogul, the Politician and even the Policeman. The story of these characters is interspersed with an attempt to fashion a political philosophy. I consider his writing crude and naive. Given his inner thoughts, I think it not a bad thing that we live in a parliamentary democracy.'

'How so?'

'Carlisle favoured oligarchical rule. I met him on several occasions. He was a very presentable demagogue with a considerable constituency.' He pointed at the folder. 'I've transcribed the contents of the notebook. I got the impression from Superintendent Wilson that he didn't have much faith that the notebook would have any bearing on his investigation. Having read it, I think it may help. Carlisle displayed many of the characteristics of a psychopathic narcissist. People like him don't stick a syringe into their arm and kill themselves, even if they're in pain. Carlisle felt he had role to play. So, despite what the coroner might have said, I don't believe he died by suicide. Read the text. It may be the ramblings of a second-rate politician, but I suspect there's something in there that can help you. It depends what you want to discover.'

Moira picked up the notebook and the folder. She stood up. 'I think I might have enjoyed studying with you.' She took a business card from her pocket and handed it to Gowan. 'It's been interesting. If you think of anything else, don't hesitate to call.'

'I may be an old fart, but I know a clever young woman when I see one. Good luck with your investigation.'

# CHAPTER SIX

Sir Philip Lattimer entered the conference room at the Merchant Hotel and saw that Helen McCann had already installed herself at the head of the table. The meetings of the Circle were traditionally held at Coleville House Lattimer's ancestral home, and consequently he had always claimed the chair. He was not at all pleased with either the new location or the apparent change in chairmanship. His first reaction was to complain, but then he remembered the indignity inflicted on him the last time he had threatened McCann. Without commenting, he sat in the chair to her right. He hadn't seen her for several months and noticed that she had shed weight that she didn't really have to spare. Her normally beautiful face had thinned and, while her cheekbones were more prominent, the overall look detracted from her beauty. He glanced at the rear of the room, where a stranger loitered. Lattimer recognised the type. He had hoped that dispensing with Sammy Rice would enable them to concentrate on the business aspects of the organisation they had built, but the sight of this thug with a bushy beard and an overgrown mop of hair wandering around disquieted him. The man elicited a feeling of unease. He felt he had seen him before but couldn't remember where.

'He's with me, Philip,' McCann said without looking up from the papers she was examining.

'I assumed so,' Lattimer replied.

'Also, I've asked Daniel to join us. We need some new blood in the group.' She closed the report she'd been reading. 'You've put on weight, Philip. It doesn't suit you. I'd advise cutting out a few of those business lunches. Or, at the very least, the post-luncheon brandies.'

'The weight is an unfortunate consequence of one's business obligations.' Lattimer was still trying to digest the news that his son Daniel would be joining the Circle. The brat hadn't said a word to him. He should be part of the decisions made by the Circle and not simply a recipient of instructions relayed by Helen McCann.

Lord Glenconnor entered the room accompanied by DCC Jennings. McCann stood to greet the new arrivals, air-kissing the old lord. They hadn't had time to take their seats when Daniel Lattimer entered the room, ignoring his father's sharp look. There was a warm embrace between the young man and his future mother-in-law.

McCann sat and looked at the four men. 'Good afternoon, gentlemen. Thank you for attending on such short notice. I don't have to introduce Daniel Lattimer, who I am delighted to welcome as a permanent member of our little group. You'll see I've distributed a copy of our financial standing.'

'I think Helen should be congratulated on the rise in our investment portfolio,' Philip Lattimer said. 'We've consolidated our position in the province.'

'Thank you, Philip, but I didn't come here to discuss our financial position,' McCann said. 'This group was formed to tackle existential threats to our province. And we are facing one now.'

Balderdash, Philip Lattimer thought. The Circle had been

created to influence every aspect of life in the province. Their members held top positions in political life, business and the professions. They were the real rulers of the province. He'd never been happy about their foray into criminality. The liaison with the Rice family and with Jackie Carlisle was convenient twenty years ago, but now it was time to move on. Thankfully Rice was no longer on the scene and the gangsters who replaced him were more interested in money than politics. McCann was living in the past. She was a zealot like her dead husband.

'We must prepare for the next phase in the evolution of Ulster. The Union is under severe threat and we must be prepared to use all our resources, financial and physical, to maintain our connection with Great Britain,' McCann continued.

Lattimer saw the concern on the faces of Glenconnor and Jennings. Their existential crisis was their own. Glenconnor peddled Circle influence as effectively as himself, and Jennings' ambition could only be satisfied by using their political connections. He wondered whether McCann was losing her grip. His gaze returned to the man at the back of the room. Who the hell is he and what part is he playing here?

'We must preserve ourselves at all costs,' McCann concluded.

'What exactly are we talking about?' Jennings asked.

'There are people in this province who would hand us over to the Republic. We cannot allow that to happen. It isn't a question of demographics anymore. There are Lundys in our midst and we must be prepared to eliminate them.'

Lattimer concluded that Helen McCann had lost her marbles. It would explain her loss of weight and her strained features. He wondered what had pushed her over the edge, and what he and the others sitting around the table were going to do about it.

There was silence in the room as the men around the table

digested the meaning of what McCann had just said. Carlisle's murder hadn't been an aberration. It had been a template for the future. Anyone or anything that threatened Helen McCann or her husband's precious legacy was going to be dispensed with. Lattimer didn't think that the other members would be up for that and hoped they would stand with him to prevent her from going rogue. But he wasn't prepared to voice his opinion just yet. The thug at the rear might be more than McCann's bodyguard. He'd always known that she represented the 'dark' side of the Circle. Despite the brains and the sophistication, she was closer to the Rices and Carlisle than she was to him and his lordship. The Rices were dead and so was Carlisle and she had a hand in their deaths. Carlisle had been one of them but that hadn't saved him. They had all looked the other way while the McCanns dragged them into crimes they would not normally countenance committing. It was clear that she now intended some form of assassination of those she felt were selling Ulster down the river. In that case, no one was safe.

McCann looked at each face around the table. Aside from Daniel, they were a spineless lot. Her late husband was worth ten of them. But she was here to provide them with a spine. They thought of the Circle as a boy's club. A more focused version of the Masons or the Orange Order. She saw it as the most potent force for maintaining the status quo in the province. The silence around the table said more than any words could. She would let them assimilate the new truth. Ulster had to look after itself. The time for depending on the lily-livered in Westminster was over. Maybe the province would have to be washed in blood again before it could rise pure and safe. If that were the case, she would play her part. She was ready to die for what she believed in. But there were others who would die with her. Old Lattimer and Glenconnor had passed their sell-by dates. She had no doubt that they were not ready for what might lie ahead. But they knew too much.

She smiled. 'I can see that my reading of the situation comes as a shock to you. What I'm really saying is that we must be prepared for every eventuality. The financial strength we have built up over the years will be applied to ensure the continued prosperity of the province. And we will secure the backing of our friends across the water by diverting funds their way. Now, if you will permit me to close the meeting, I'm rather tired.'

Lattimer, Glenconnor and Jennings left the room but her future son-in-law remained.

'You look tired,' Daniel said.

'I'm not sleeping well.' Nobody in the Circle knew about the abortive attempt on Wilson's life. Why couldn't Brennan have succeeded? Instead Wilson was still chipping away at Carlisle's death. 'I often get bouts of insomnia. It goes with the territory.'

'You should take better care of yourself. We want you front and centre at the wedding.'

'I've arranged for Kate to be appointed Attorney General for Northern Ireland as soon as the post is vacant.'

'That's quite a wedding present.'

'Does she ever mention Ian Wilson?'

'Why do you ask?'

'I wonder whether she still has feelings for him.'

'No, she never mentions him.'

'He killed my grandchild.'

He slid his hand across the table and covered her left hand. 'Kate told me she had a miscarriage.'

'He caused it. He killed that child, and I'll always hate him for it.'

'Let it go. You have important work to do.'

'You're the future of this organisation, Daniel. And I'm not saying that just because you're my future son-in-law. I know you're a believer. You can carry a plan through. I think the Judge would be proud of you.'

'I'm as true a believer as you.'

# CHAPTER SEVEN

Creggan is a small townland situated on either side of the Newry Road about two kilometres north of Crossmaglen. Nobody is sure who coined the phrase 'bandit country' for this area, but its reputation for violence is such that there is a large police presence in a town of 1,500 inhabitants. Wilson wasn't happy with his charge from Duane. He knew the man too well to doubt that he would find the email from the chief constable when he opened his computer back in Belfast. He also expected to be told that the Garda Síochána would be in the lead for the duration of the investigation. Lennon might be a resident of Northern Ireland, but the murder took place in the Republic and there was no indication that the perpetrators were from Wilson's side of the border. He had enough on his plate already without having to play second fiddle to Duane.

Graham had insisted on inserting Lennon's address into the GPS, meaning Wilson had to endure the voice of the computer instructing them to make every turn. They continued along the Newry Road, passing the collection of houses that constituted the village of Creggan, before turning left down a long laneway that led into what appeared to be empty countryside. The GPS gave up on them and was constantly 'recalibrating'. Eventually, Wilson insisted that the apparatus be switched off. After two kilometres of laneway, they arrived at a series of farm buildings. Graham stopped in front of the house and he and Wilson exited the car and made their way to the front door.

Graham's knock echoed back at them, but there was no sound of movement inside. Graham tried the door and found it unlocked. Wilson nodded and they both entered, directly into the main room. On the left, there was a range with cupboards to one side and a Welsh dresser to the other. A wooden table and four chairs sat in the centre of the room and a well-worn couch was against the wall to the right. There was a writing desk in the corner. The space could have been a time capsule from the 1950s. They moved to the rear of the house, where they found two bedrooms and a bathroom. The array of male toiletries on the cabinet above the sink indicated that Brian Lennon had been in residence. If that were the case, Wilson was sure that he lived alone. They would have to ascertain where his next of kin lived in order to transmit the news of his demise. Wilson returned to the main room and was about to open the front door when he heard a car outside. Through the window he saw it was a police car and took out his warrant card. He exited the house with his warrant card exposed. Graham followed close behind him.

The two policemen in the Land Rover remained where they were. The driver exited when he saw Wilson approaching with his warrant card.

'Detective Superintendent Ian Wilson,' Wilson said. 'And this is my colleague DC Graham.'

'Sir,' the constable saluted. 'The neighbours reported strangers at the house. Sorry sir,' The officer pointed at the label on his stab vest. 'Constable Locke from Crossmaglen, superintendent. Can we be of any assistance?'

'Only if you know the owner of this house.'

'It's our job to know the owners of every house in our area.

This house belongs to Brian Lennon. Since there's no sign of his car, I don't think he's at home now.'

'That's probably because he was beaten to death in Inniskeen in County Monaghan last night.'

'Holy God, we didn't hear.'

'I don't think it's been announced. It'll probably be on radio and TV this evening.' As they left Inniskeen, they'd passed a truck bearing the legend 'RTÉ News' on its way to the crime scene. 'Any idea where we might find Lennon's next of kin?'

The second policeman had alighted from the Land Rover and joined them. He was younger than Locke by a good ten years. Locke informed him about Lennon's murder.

'Lennon lived alone,' Locke said. 'His father died a few months ago and his mother's been dead a good wee while. He has no direct family so I suppose his cousin over in Crossmaglen would be the next of kin. He's Barry Lennon and he runs a local butcher's shop.' He took out a pen and paper and wrote down the address.

'Did you know Lennon well?' Wilson asked.

'As well as I know anyone else,' Locke replied.

'Was he the kind of man who'd be liable to get himself beaten to death?'

'I wouldn't have thought so. He was a quiet wee lad, kept to himself, especially after his father died.'

'Any political affiliations?'

'Not that I know of.'

'Were his family connected?'

'I don't think so.' Locke looked around. 'I think you should be asking my superiors these questions, sir. We're a bit out of our depth. We're just two local officers responding to a call.'

'I know, but in my experience, officers like you know a hell of a lot more about what's going on locally than your superiors.'

Locke smiled. 'I've heard about you by reputation, sir. You

might have a point, but I doubt my chief super would agree with you.'

'Thanks for your time, constable. Given the situation, I think you should hang around and arrange to have the house secured. We'll go back to Crossmaglen and have a word with Barry Lennon.'


THROUGHOUT THE TROUBLES, the notorious town of Crossmaglen conjured up comparisons with Tombstone, Deadwood and Dodge City in the 1870s. Fifty-eight police officers and one hundred and twenty-four soldiers were killed in south Armagh during that period, many in Crossmaglen itself. The town, however, looked as peaceful as any other when Graham parked directly outside Lennon's shop on North Street. It was a fine January afternoon with fluffy white clouds skipping across a blue sky. The butcher's shop front was freshly painted yellow and there was an array of fresh meat on display. Two elderly ladies were in conversation with a man behind the counter wearing a white butcher's uniform with a white plastic hat set at a jaunty angle. The conversation stopped abruptly as soon as Wilson and Graham entered the shop. The two women stared at the policemen and quickly concluded their business.

Wilson often wondered whether he had PSNI tattooed on his forehead. He had no doubt that they had been recognised as 'peelers'.

'What can I do for you gentlemen?' the butcher asked.

'Barry Lennon?' Wilson asked removing his warrant card.

'Aye, there's no need for the card.'

Wilson introduced himself and Graham. 'I understand that you're Brian Lennon's cousin and possibly his next of kin.'

'Ah Christ!' Lennon said. He came from behind the counter and put the 'Closed' sign on the door. 'Come into the back room.'

They entered a small room at the back of the shop containing a roll-top desk with a laptop computer on it. A captain's chair was in front of the desk and there were two wooden chairs against a back wall. 'Is it bad?' Lennon flopped into the captain's chair.

'The worst,' Wilson sat on one of the wooden chairs and Graham took the other. The butcher was more powerfully built than his dead cousin. Given that most of Brian's face had been beaten it was impossible to tell if there was a family resemblance. Barry's face was round with smooth cheeks. Wilson assessed his age as somewhere between thirty and thirty-five. He had dark blue eyes and a head of curly black hair in which grey had not yet appeared. 'Your cousin was beaten to death in a barn in Inniskeen in County Monaghan last night. The Garda Síochána is investigating the murder and we've been asked to assist on this side of the border. I'll be passing along your name and coordinates in relation with the identification of the body.'

'His father is only a few months in the grave. Who in God's name would want to kill a poor bugger like Brian? He never did anyone any harm.'

'I think the answer to that question will occupy the Garda Síochána for the foreseeable future. Did he have any enemies locally?'

'Not that I know of.'

Wilson was aware that Barry Lennon had been weaned during a time when the residents of Crossmaglen and the police were not on the best of terms. He couldn't shake the feeling that Lennon was holding something back. 'Nobody gets beaten to death on a whim. And nobody gets lured to an out-of-the-way derelict barn without there being an ulterior motive. Your cousin's murder was planned and executed, and you're not the first one to tell me that he didn't have an enemy in the world.'

Lennon shrugged his shoulders.

'Was Brian involved with a woman?'

'I don't think so. He was serious about someone about two years ago and it might have led somewhere if his father hadn't got ill. There's been nothing recent, as far as I know.'

'What about money? Did Brian owe anyone?'

'Have you been to the house?' Lennon asked.

Wilson nodded.

'They lived like church mice. I often brought them up a bag of steaks or a leg of lamb. They were proud people. They wouldn't have borrowed money to save their lives.'

'How big is the farm?'

'A hundred and fifty acres give or take.'

'Who gets it now?'

'I have no idea. My uncle passed it to Brian before he died. Apparently, there are some tax advantages in doing so. I don't know whether Brian made a will. I'd be surprised if he did.'

'So, there's no inheritor?'

Lennon shrugged his shoulders again. 'If there is no will I suppose the farm will be auctioned off. We've family all over the world and all of them will get a piece. It'll be sad to see one of the last Lennon properties going on the block.'

'Why is that?'

'On your way into town, you would have passed a sign with the name of the village on it. The Irish reads *Crois Mhic Lionnain*, which is Gaelic for Lennon's Cross. The Lennons were the big family here at one time. Most are gone now.'

Wilson stood. 'We'll want to speak with you again and I'm sure so will the Garda Síochána. They'll be in contact with you.'

They walked back into the shop.

'Harry,' Wilson said. 'Give Mr Lennon one of your business cards.' He turned to Lennon. 'Maybe you'll find the name of the family solicitor and pass the information along to DC Graham.'

Graham produced a business card, which Lennon took and deposited into a pocket in his butcher's apron.

'Is there any chance you'd sell me a leg of lamb?' Graham asked. 'It's always better in the country.'

Lennon took a leg from the window, wrapped it up and handed it to Graham.

Wilson shook his head.

'I have to pay,' Graham said.

'Twenty quid.'

Graham handed the money over.

Wilson extended his hand. 'I'm sorry for your trouble.'

Lennon shook. 'Thank you.'

Graham followed suit and they exited onto the street.

'What do you think, boss?' Graham asked.

'I think we're going to have to wade through a lake of bull-shit before we nail someone for killing Brian Lennon.'

# CHAPTER EIGHT

Moira looked around the squad room. She and Siobhan O'Neill were alone. In the rear, the ghost of Peter Davidson shared a joke with Harry Graham. To the side, the phantom of Eric Taylor was superimposed on O'Neill and directly behind them an apparition of Rory Browne stared back at her. She didn't need to pinch herself to know that the old days were gone. Davidson was sunning himself by the pool in Spain, and last week she'd attended Taylor's retirement party. The boss had confirmed that HQ was trying to steal Browne's post. He was fighting hard to keep it, but austerity was going to win the day. Moira felt like an old-timer hankering back to the past, but she missed the banter and the camaraderie of the group she had joined several years before. The PSNI, like every police force in the country, was the victim of savage cuts. She thought the mantra 'do more with less' should be engraved above the badge on their caps. It had more relevance to the force now than 'keeping people safe'. Whoever said the past is another country knew what they were talking about.

She turned back to her computer and looked at the video footage once more. She willed the screen to produce some magic, to give her a much-needed breakthrough in the investigation into the body incinerated in the boot of a BMW at Helen's Bay. The charred remains were still in a steel drawer at the mortuary. If the boss was right and the remains are those of Mickey Duff, they would remain unclaimed. It had looked like there could be a break in the case when Browne had received an email to say that a drone had been active over Helen's Bay on the day the BMW was torched. Moira had followed up that lead and procured the video. The date and time were good, but the drone was flying further out to sea than they'd hoped and had caught only a peripheral view of the action on land. As soon as the car exploded, the operator had turned the drone towards the site, but he failed to catch the perpetrator except for a faint figure in one or two frames. Moira had a technician enhance the image, but there was no way to recognise the person. By the time the drone had flown over the area close to the explosion, the figure had disappeared. Wilson was sure it was Eddie Hills, the right-hand man of gang boss Davie Best. But no jury would accept the fuzzy, long-range image as identification. She was back at square one. There was no proof that the body in the morgue was Duff or that Hills was his killer. It was frustrating for her and Wilson that they could prove neither supposition. It was doubly frustrating that they might never be able to solve the crime.

Moira went to her browser and clicked on the icon for the *Belfast Chronicle*. The front page of the online edition was dominated by a colour photo taken earlier in the day. The Secretary of State for Northern Ireland was visiting Belfast. He was new to the job and was acquainting himself with the convoluted politics of the province. To assist in that process, he was meeting the great and the good. Standing next to him in the picture was a woman Wilson believed to be responsible for at least one murder and possibly several others. If he was right, she was also guilty of corruption and fraud as well as money laundering. Like Hills' guilt in the murder of Duff, it was largely supposition. Davidson had collected indirect evidence on Helen McCann's involvement in the murder of Jackie Carlisle, but it wasn't enough to get her in front of a judge. Both Maura's cases were, therefore, sources of frustration. In the photo, McCann was smiling as she shook the hand of the secretary of state. She was the epitome of the political power-broker. Leaders of the main political parties had pushed themselves to the fore of the crowd. Moira spotted Kate McCann standing next to her fiancé. At the rear of the group, Moira picked out a face that she thought she recognised. The man had a mop of curly black hair and a black beard covered most of his face. There was something familiar about him, but she couldn't quite put her finger on it. She looked at the breaking news section and saw that the body of a man had been discovered just over the border in County Monaghan. Although she hadn't heard from Wilson since he had departed in the early morning to attend the Brexit Task Force meeting, she didn't connect him with the discovery. After all, the find had been outside their jurisdiction. She went back to the photo and stared at it. Then she picked up her phone and called Belfast International Airport.


WILSON AND GRAHAM arrived back at the station just as darkness was falling. The lights were burning and there was an eerie quiet in the squad room when they entered. Moira and O'Neill had the appearance of a couple of troglodytes working away at their computers in silence. Wilson went to his office and switched on his computer. He brought up his emails and saw that Duane was as good as his word. Chief Constable Norman Baird's instructions were clear: the Garda Síochána was in charge of the investigation and Wilson was to assist as requested. Through the glass panel separating his office from the squad room, Wilson could see Graham imparting the news of their visit to Inniskeen. He stood, went into the squad room and sat in Browne's old seat. 'I see Harry has already told you about our little trip.'

Moira turned her computer around towards him. 'It's already on the wire. There are no details yet, but Harry says an RTÉ van was on the way to the scene as you were leaving. They'll probably have the name on the evening news, and it'll be in the *Chronicle* in the morning.'

'Jock McDevitt might have to burn the midnight oil this evening,' Wilson said.

'You might like to look at this photo,' Moira zoomed in on the *Chronicle* photo she had been examining.

'They're up the poor man's arse already,' Wilson said. He hadn't missed the fact that Helen McCann was front and centre. Nor that his ex, Kate, was there. He could understand how Helen, standing beside the man who for the moment directed the fate of the people of Northern Ireland, could think herself omnipotent and untouchable. She was probably right, but that was not going to stop him pursuing her. She had worked hard to surround herself with a cloak of invulnerability, but somewhere there was a gap in that cloak, and he would keep searching for it. Also, he didn't like having someone out there who had already financed a failed attempt on his life and who wouldn't hesitate to repeat the process.

'Look at the expression on his face,' Moira said. 'He's already beguiled.'

'She has that effect.'

'Did you notice the guy at the back of the group?' Moira asked. 'The guy with the beard. Do you recognise him?'

Wilson stared at the photo. Only a fraction of the man's face was visible. And the beard covered most of it. 'Maybe, but I couldn't be sure.'

'I checked with Belfast International,' Moira said. 'McCann arrived by private jet this morning and is scheduled to leave in a few days. She wasn't alone. She arrived with a female secretary and a male assistant. All three produced British passports and were waved through the VIP area. No one noted the names on the passports.'

'What are you thinking?' Wilson asked.

'Could the man with the beard be Simon Jackson?'

'When is that flight leaving?'

'They weren't sure.'

'Destination?'

'A small French airport called Mandelieu.'

'They're too cool for their own good,' Wilson said. 'Next time they might not be so lucky. We have a European Arrest Warrant out for Jackson. Let's get our French friends to check out the villa.'

'Easier said than done,' Moira said. 'No one knows the value of a European Arrest Warrant in the current political climate.'

'Do it anyway.' Wilson turned to O'Neill. 'Siobhan – Brian Lennon native of Creggan, County Armagh, I want everything we have on him. Let's start a whiteboard. Also let's have what we've got on Barry Lennon, a butcher in Crossmaglen. I've an instruction from the CC to assist in whatever way possible the Garda Síochána's investigation into Brian Lennon's death. Let's get on it.'

# CHAPTER NINE

Despite being mid-winter, it was a fine evening and Wilson decided to leave his car at the station and walk to his favourite watering hole. Total darkness had fallen, and the lights were burning as he strolled along the Shankill Road. He'd last taken this walk during the summer and that seemed a world away. It wasn't a question of the weather. Neither had it anything to do with the life that the tourists brought to the city. The Titanic Centre continued to draw in the visitors, and he had never seen the pubs and restaurants so busy. The difference was that there was an air of apprehension. The unasked question was on everyone's mind. Would the madness return? Were the politicians so venal and bound up in their ideological cocoons that they would let the unthinkable happen? No one wanted to go back to the bad old days, but most people recognised that that was a possibility. Wilson prided himself on the fact that he could gauge the feeling in the city. The carefree days of summer, when the whiff of uncertainty was cloaked by the sunshine and gaiety, were gone. The faces he passed mirrored the anxiety he felt himself. He loved this place, warts and all. He lifted his collar and burrowed into his coat. Just as he passed the Grand Opera

House, he saw a sight that lifted his spirits. Stephanie Reid walked as though she glided rather than touched the pavement. Her blonde hair was cut short and her head seemed to bounce along. He crossed the road, came up rapidly behind her and slapped her on the backside.

'Not in public please.' She didn't break stride.

'How did you know it was me? I was careful to stay behind you.'

'My peripheral vision is fine, thank you very much.'

They stopped outside the door to the Crown and kissed before they entered. Although their local pub was a mecca for tourists, a January evening was generally much quieter. They headed straight to Wilson's regular snug.

'Where are you parked?' she asked as soon as they were settled and had ordered their drinks.

'I walked.'

'I don't like the sound of that. I hope we're not in for another one of those nights.'

'No chance, it's been a while since I took the temperature of the city by padding its pavements.'

'And how did you find it?'

'There's something in the air that I don't like.' He told her of the apprehension he'd detected.

'There always Santa Monica. Although I'm starting to despair.'

Their drinks arrived and Wilson paid.

'So, what brought on this desire to feel the pulse of the city?'

He told her about Brian Lennon's death and Jack Duane's remark that they might not be able to work closely in the future.

'Who's doing the post-mortem?' she asked.

'The state pathologist, a guy called Kelly. I don't think he and Jack are friends.'

'I've met him. He's competent, but I don't think he's had a

chance to read *How to win friends and influence people*. But this is Jack's case, right?'

'Since it straddles the border, I've been instructed to assist in any way I can.'

'And something about the death is bothering you?'

'That any human being gets beaten to death bothers me. I'm also bothered by the fact that someone went to the trouble of murdering a young man from Northern Ireland by luring him to a derelict farm in the south. Someone is trying to muddy the waters.'

'But you and Jack will get them.'

'Of that I am not so sure.'

'I've had a tough day too so will we have a bite to eat in town followed by a few hours of listening to jazz, or will we have a burger and fries followed by the back seat in a cinema?'

'Let's opt for the bite and jazz. I think the sight of you and me cuddling up in the back row might cause the young people to toss their dinners.'

MOIRA THREW the remnants of her microwaved dinner into the trash. I need to get out more, she thought. Mike Finlay had continued his pursuit of her until he realised it was futile and since then no one had shown her the slightest bit of interest. That wasn't completely true. A visit to any pub in the city would lead to a bit of ogling from some barfly, but she was way beyond the age when a quick fumble in a laneway was her definition of either sex or the start of a possible future relationship. Every time she thought about men, a picture of Frank Shea floated across her mind. She was still in touch with Jamie Carmichael in Boston and Shea sent her the odd email with attached photo from Aspen or Barbados. Apparently, unlike her, Shea was making shedloads of money. Her mother was always quizzing her about her social life, and she had become an expert at deflection. Telling the truth about her lack of a social life might have led her mother to suggest a retreat to a nunnery. Moira had moved from her original garret to a modern one-bed apartment in the Titanic Quarter. One of the reasons for choosing the apartment was the existence of eight square metres of virgin wall in the living room. This wall was now half-covered with post-it notes connected with lines of red wool. It had become the nerve centre of the investigation into the death of Jackie Carlisle. She finished her regulation half-bottle of wine and put the stopper in. She picked up the file on the David Grant murder. That's where it had all begun. Grant and Malone had discovered the corruption that was lining the coffers of Sammy Rice and his partner, Carson Nominees. One of the murderers was dead, but the second was still missing. If he surfaced, they would be able to link Rice with the killings. But Rice had also disappeared. She couldn't yet connect Rice with Helen McCann but suspected the missing link would turn out to be Carson Nominees. But where was the proof?

# CHAPTER TEN

It was after ten o'clock when DI Daragh Flynn drove his Ford Mondeo onto the access road above Bessbrook Play Park outside Newry. He pulled up behind a black BMW 750 and exited the car. He opened the back door of the BMW and sat in.

'About time,' the man sitting in the rear said.

'You've done it this time, Tommy,' Flynn said. 'If the Lennon murder was a painting, your signature would be on the bottom.'

'Don't talk shite. I had nothing to do with that. Anyway, the death of a wee fart is a three-day wonder. The peelers have bigger things on their minds than worrying about some little nobody. This province is full of unsolved murders.'

'I'm glad you had nothing to do with it because they're bringing in the A-team this time. Jack Duane is up from Dublin and Ian Wilson is going to handle the northern side.'

'Duane is a trigger-happy donkey and Wilson is past his sell-by date. They'll fuck around for a couple of weeks before going back to their comfortable billets. I have twenty witnesses who'll say that I was at a darts match until midnight and I can't be in two places at the same time. In any case, I'm Teflon.'

Flynn was aware of Tommy Feeney's connection with terrorists and the political parties that grew out of them. 'That may be the case, but I wouldn't take Duane and Wilson so lightly.'

Feeney removed an envelope from his inside pocket and handed it to Flynn. 'What do you care? Just keep me informed of where the investigation is going and of when any raids are due to take place and I'll do the rest.'

Flynn took the envelope and put it inside his jacket without examining the contents. 'Have you worked out how we found the body so quickly?'

Feeney was silent.

'Someone called it in.' Suddenly Feeney was interested. 'I thought that might interest you. It would have been better for the killers if the body hadn't been found for another few days at least. And neither Duane nor Wilson is buying the suggestion that it was a punishment beating gone too far.'

'I don't give a shit what scenario they're buying. Someone calling it in is another matter.'

There was silence in the car.

'Someone in your organisation is unhappy,' Flynn said.

'Aye, maybe there's a wee rat hiding away in some corner or other. I'll find him, I always do, and I'll deal with him. Take my advice, Daragh, don't ever rat.'

Flynn started sweating. It always happened when he was in Feeney's company for more than a few minutes. He took a deep breath. 'I have plenty of reasons not to rat.' He patted the envelope in his breast pocket.

Feeney placed a huge hand on Flynn's shoulder. 'Sound man, keep me informed and everything is going to be hunky-dory.'

Flynn felt the weight of the hand on his shoulder. He reached for the door handle. 'I'll be in touch.' He turned and stared into Feeney's flat face. The bastard was giving him his

trademark evil smile. Flynn nodded and quickly slipped out
the door.

Back in his own car, Flynn found that his hands were
shaking and he had to put them on the steering wheel to steady
them. His mouth was dry and he needed a drink, but not in the
north. If he was stopped for drink-driving north of the border,
it might raise a red flag. The BMW was gone, and he was
alone looking down at the empty children's playground below
him. It had been a long road that had put him in the power of
an animal like Feeney. He remembered the first day he had
placed a bet on a horse. It seemed like an innocent enough
pastime. A few euro here and there on a horse or a dog. But
gambling had come a long way since those far-off days. The
plethora of online betting opportunities had drawn him in like
a magnet and before he knew it, he was betting on events as
obscure as the result of a Norwegian women's football match, a
subject on which he was completely ignorant. The few euro
became tens, then hundreds and finally thousands of euro. He
ended up squandering all his own money and maxing out his
credit cards and his personal credit before turning to the loan
sharks. They soon owned him and then they sold him to
Feeney. He fished out the envelope Feeney had given him and
flicked through the contents: five hundred euro in used twen-
ties. His debt with Feeney currently stood at over a hundred
thousand euro.

Flynn started the car and reversed back onto the main
road. There was a small pub outside Dundalk where he could
have a discreet drink. A tear ran from his right eye. He had
fucked up his personal life and he was in the process of
fucking up his career. It was all going to end in tears for him
and his family and there was nothing he could do about it.
There was always the chance of a big win that would get

Feeney off his back. But clearing his debts would be only one step on the road. The tears were flowing freely as he joined the main road from Newry to Dundalk.

CHIEF SUPERINTENDENT BOB RODGERS of the PSNI Special Branch exited the lift and walked into the first-floor parking lot of the apartment building. It was two o'clock in the morning and he had spent an enjoyable evening in the company of his mistress. It was a grandiose title for the woman his father would have called his bit on the side, but 'mistress' was an accurate description since he paid for her apartment and gave her a stipend sufficient to pay all her bills. Rodgers' support allowed a woman half his age to spend her life visiting the gym, the hairdresser and the nail bar. Meanwhile, his wife, to whom he had been married for thirty-five years and who was blissfully unaware of his bit on the side, could spend her days at coffee mornings or playing mahjong and watching her favourite soaps. What more could she want? His salary would not have been enough to cover the expenses relating to his double life but his salary was only part of his income.

The parking garage was in total darkness and before the doors of the lift closed, he pushed the white button set in the wall that would flood the space with light. Except this time it didn't. 'Shit.' He took out his mobile phone and brought up the flashlight app. He pressed the button and a beam of light emanated from his phone. He moved gingerly through the dark garage, taking care to avoid banging into cars on the way. The light cut a focused beam ahead and he followed it in the general direction of the place where he usually parked. He said a prayer of thanks as he arrived at his Lexus. The silence in the garage was broken by the noise of his car door opening automatically as the key approached. His father would have been astonished at a car door opening when the key came into its vicinity. He was about to climb into the driver's seat when he felt the muzzle of a gun pressing into his neck. The touch of the cold steel sent a shiver down his spine. So, this is the way it ends, he thought. It was the way he would have done it himself. He had a certain amount of professional respect for the man behind the gun. He'd heard nothing, suspected nothing. 'If you're going to do it, get on with it. If you have something else in mind, I'm all ears.'

'You've got a set of balls for a silly old fucker,' a voice behind his head said. 'That young pussy is going to be the end of you.'

Rodgers relaxed when he recognised the voice. The gun had not been removed from the back of his neck, but the odds of him being shot had reduced, although they weren't reduced to zero. 'I saw you were back in town. The beard and hair didn't fool me. They might not fool Wilson either.'

'You sold me down the river.' The pressure of the gun increased.

'You sold yourself down the river. Davidson was never a threat. We were taking steps to protect you.'

'You were going to throw me under the bus.'

'No, we weren't. Now, take that fucking gun off my neck.' The pressure from the gun reduced.

'I wanted to kill you. There would have been general rejoicing. But the boss says no. She thinks you can still be useful.'

Rodgers looked at Jackson in the light from his phone. 'Think ye landed on yer feet, ye silly wee bastard. Well, ye haven't. If she doesn't want me dead because I'm still useful, think about yerself. I bet that's how she feels about you too.'

'You could be lying dead on this floor and I could be upstairs doing a proper job on your young friend.'

'Piss off home, yer mistress is looking for you.' Rodgers sat into his car. 'The next time you put a gun to my head, pull the fucking trigger. Because if you don't, it'll be the last chance you get.' Rodgers started the car and turned on the high beams. The garage was flooded in light, but there was no sign of Jackson.

# CHAPTER ELEVEN

It had rained overnight as a cold front crossed Ireland from west to east. Wilson exited his flat and reluctantly began running in the direction of the Titanic Centre. There was a smell of ozone from the Lagan and there were whitecaps further out to sea. Dark clouds hung over the city, suggesting that a new bout of rain was holding off but not for long. The morning run was a ritual that helped him stay fit and acted as a time for meditation before the working day ahead. As he got older it was becoming more of a chore and removing himself from the warm clutches of his partner had been especially hard this particular morning. Reid had become a large part of his life: a part that he couldn't do without. The trip to Nova Scotia had only confirmed that conclusion. She and his mother had got on famously. The Parkinson's that made Victoria Anderson's hands shake was 'under control', although that didn't mean that the deterioration Wilson had noticed wasn't real. Reid had gone into doctor mode and she and Vicky connected in an intense way. Wilson's stepfather, Greg Anderson, had organised fishing and whale-watching trips and after two weeks there had been floods of tears on departure day.

While the trip underlined the fact that Reid was an essential part of his life, he also noticed that there were now a few more elephants padding around the room than normal. Sooner or later the questions those elephants represented would have to be answered.

For now, Wilson preferred to focus on work. He needed to find a strategy to get Helen McCann into the dock. He was going to need a lot more evidence than the smoking gun that the phone Davidson had retrieved from Belfast International represented. McCann's money and status would also be a substantial obstacle to bringing her to justice. He was still struggling to identify why she had decided Carlisle had to be killed. The man had a terminal illness. Why was it necessary to murder him?

The first spits of rain hit his face and he looked up to see that he was only a hundred metres from home. He had no recollection of turning and heading back, but the watch on his hand told him he had completed his usual run. He sprinted the last hundred metres and arrived in the vestibule of the building as the rain began to fall in stair rods.

After showering and shaving, Wilson joined Reid for breakfast.

'What's on the agenda for today?' she asked.

'Another trip to bandit country.' He gave his voice a quiver.

'You wouldn't have it any other way.'

'Would you mind giving Dr Kelly a ring? Ask him how the autopsy went.'

'You don't trust him?'

'I just like to have my own private pathologist look over things.'

'He might not appreciate the interference.'

'If you think you might be treading on his professional toes, just leave it.'

'You're in a good mood today.'

'I think I may have escaped from the dreaded Brexit Task Force. Jennings' face when he saw me at the table was priceless. He mustn't have bothered to examine the membership of the task force. Some poor bastard at HQ is going to pay for sticking the dart in my name.'

'No, I don't think your humour is related to your escape from the task force. Despite your prostrations, I think it's because you enjoy working with Jack.'

He finished his coffee and stood. 'I have to go. Leave the dishes and I'll do them tonight.'

'It's not a sin to have a friend.'

He bent, kissed her and headed for the door.

She looked at the breakfast dishes and then her watch. She'd have just enough time to clear them away.

THE DUTY SERGEANT said good morning and immediately pointed upstairs. Wilson went straight to Chief Superintendent Yvonne Davis's office; he knocked and put his head around the open door.

Davis looked up from the papers she was examining and motioned him in. 'You are officially off the Brexit Task Force, but I suppose you guessed that already. This business down south isn't a put-up job between you and Jack Duane is it?'

Wilson sat without being invited. 'Brian Lennon was beaten to death in a barn in Inniskeen in County Monaghan. He's a native of Creggan just outside Crossmaglen. Jack and I are of a mind that it didn't happen on the other side of the border by accident.'

'I saw the instruction from the CC. The Garda Síochána is in the lead.'

'The murder happened on their patch.'

'But you think the perpetrators are closer to home?'

'That would be my initial guess. Harry and I passed by the dead man's house on our way back to Belfast and I interviewed the man's cousin, who appears to be the next of kin. The motive wasn't money by the look of the house. They're small farmers and Lennon's father died six months ago.'

'So, it's political?'

'I asked Siobhan to run Lennon through the system. I'm about to check in with her. Someone at the scene mentioned it might be a punishment beating gone wrong. I saw the marks on the body and the objective was definitely murder. I think someone wanted to create a bit of confusion by committing that murder in the south.'

'Where do we go from here?'

'Harry and I will head back to Crossmaglen later. We'll have to get a picture of the victim and see if he pissed off anyone local. I want to speak with the family solicitor. The inheritance isn't going to make anyone rich, but we need to know who stands to gain.'

'What's Jack up to?'

'You mean Detective Chief Inspector Jack Duane?'

Davis sighed.

'He's not exactly a happy man. He was organising the processing of the scene by the garda CSIs and will probably be attending the autopsy. We didn't make any specific arrangements regarding our cooperation but that's something we must think about. I suppose we'll be seeing a lot of Jack over the next few weeks or months depending on how long the investigation is going to take.'

Davis moved a stray hair away from her face. 'Jack and I have put our relationship on hold.'

'I wasn't aware.'

'Richard and I are in counselling. The drug issue with our eldest was a wake-up call. We're trying to put the pieces of our broken marriage back together.' She looked away. 'It's not going so well.'

'Sorry to hear it.' He could see that she didn't want to continue the conversation. 'What about the replacement for DS Browne?'

'I'm pushing and the administration is pushing back.'

'I need the body. Harry, Siobhan and I are going to be on the Lennon business full time. Moira is on everything else. I still want to get the bastard that fried Mickey Duff. And there's the case that we can't talk about. Sooner or later we're going to have to go public with Jackie Carlisle.'

'Not yet.'

'I suppose we'll have to wait until you take your seat in HQ.'

'That was uncalled for. I understand your frustration but don't let it boil over. If you expose your hand too soon, they'll circle the wagons and the investigation will be killed.'

'We can't wait forever.'

'Then get the evidence.'

Wilson stood. 'Get me a replacement for DS Browne.'


DC Siobhan O'Neill was at the whiteboard when Wilson entered the squad room. There was a photo of Lennon at the top of the board. It was so fuzzy it could have been anyone. The face of the corpse in Inniskeen was pulped. The face that looked back at Wilson from the photo was not going to win a beauty contest. His eyes were too close together, his nose too big, his forehead too high and his jaw too weak.

'Where did that photo come from?' Wilson asked.

'DVLA, it's off his driving licence. So far, it's the best I can find. Mr Lennon didn't plaster the Internet with his photo. In fact, Brian Lennon has no Facebook profile, no Instagram account, no social media presence at all. I'm not even sure he has an email address.'

Wilson motioned Graham and Moira to join them. 'Let's hear what you've managed to discover.'

O'Neill stopped writing and picked up her notebook. 'Brian Lennon, born in Creggan on June 21st, 1990. His mother died four years later from a brain haemorrhage. Attended St Patrick's Primary School and St Joseph's High School. Left school after his GCSEs to work full time on his father's farm. Unmarried. His father died from lung cancer six months ago. I've checked with Intelligence and they have no file on him. I put in a request to Military Intelligence about possible political affiliation but that could take days, weeks or months to get a response. On the surface, it looks like he was just what it says on his driver's licence, a farmer.'

Wilson stared at the board. Lennon hadn't had much luck in his short life. There was no sign of a motive so far, but it was early days. It was possible that he had a life that was off the radar. If so, they would have to find out what it was.


WILSON WAS PREPARING for another trip to Crossmaglen when Moira entered his office and closed the door. 'I went to see Professor Gowan yesterday,' she said.

'You got the notebook?'

'It's locked in my desk. Gowan worked out the code and he transcribed the whole thing.' She held up the A4 file.

'And?'

'I've had a quick look. It rambles all over the place. It's part story, part crazy political philosophy. But if you look behind the story there might be something. There are no names only designations: the Queen, the Judge, the Lord, the Mogul, the Politician and the Policeman. Together, they aspire to control their country. They're an oligarchy that knows what's best for everyone else. The only person missing is the military man. There's a possibility that Carlisle had pretensions to literature. But he's never shown it before. I've just scratched the surface.'

Graham knocked on the door.

'Keep at it. It's all we've got at the moment.' He ushered her towards the door. He didn't have to tell her that he'd grasp at any little piece of evidence that would put McCann behind bars. 'Harry, we have to get to Creggan. I don't want anyone screwing around with Lennon's house.'

# CHAPTER TWELVE

A stout padlock had been fitted to the front door of Lennon's farmhouse in Creggan. Wilson had phoned ahead, and Constable Locke met them on their arrival. Wilson took the key, thanked Locke and told him he would be keeping the key for the duration of the investigation.

Their examination of the house the previous day had been perfunctory. This would be a proper search and, depending on the result, it might lead to a more detailed forensic search. They put on their surgical gloves before they entered.

Wilson was looking at the main room in detail. This time he saw the photos on the wall. He saw the picture of the Sacred Heart with the small electric votive light still burning. This was the place where Brian Lennon had grown up and probably spent over ninety per cent of his twenty-nine years. He examined the photos. The largest was taken on the Lennons' wedding day. The bride was dressed in white and the groom in an ill-fitting suit. Beneath was a photo of Mrs Lennon cradling a baby in her arms. On the side were photos showing the proud parents and their very young son. There were no photos of Brian Lennon as he grew up. The family had been broken when he was just four. There was nothing else in the room that spoke of a woman's hand. Everything was stark and utilitarian.

'I'll take the living room and the kitchen,' Wilson said. 'You do the bedrooms.' Graham moved to the rear and Wilson was left alone.

He always felt like an intruder when he examined the home of a victim. It was part of the job to probe into the person's life, but it sometimes revealed aspects of one's own life that remained under the surface. He thought about the lack of photos in his own apartment and resolved to put that right. He imagined the father and son who had lived here together and hoped that they might find each other again in the afterlife, if such a thing even existed. He came out of his reverie and moved to the writing desk. The top was littered with unopened envelopes and letters from farming suppliers. Lennon wasn't methodical in his filing. Wilson opened the envelopes and sorted the letters. All were bills requiring payment. There were three drawers directly below the writing surface. He opened the middle drawer and took out a series of files. One contained detailed annual accounts of income received, the second contained bills relating to the first half of 2018 and the third had documents relating to annual tax declarations. The careful filing was in marked contrast to the mass of bills on the surface of the desk. Wilson assumed that the files were the work of Lennon senior. He spotted a letter dated a year earlier with a letterhead of a solicitor based in North Street. He took out his notebook and copied down the name and address. He returned the files to the middle drawer and opened the drawer on the right. It contained only a stapler, a box of staples and a half-dozen pens bearing the logos of local businesses. The left-hand drawer held a cash box containing two hundred pounds in notes and twelve pounds and fifty pence in coins. A second box contained six medals awarded to Brian Lennon for Gaelic football. He replaced the boxes and closed the drawers.

The kitchen cupboards yielded cups, saucers and assorted utensils. The range was cold and a cup on the drainer contained the remnants of Lennon's last cup of tea. A couch dominated the living end of the room and was strategically located facing a television that could have been twenty years old. He could almost see the widower and his bachelor son sitting side by side on the worn seat on a cold winter's evening.

Graham returned from the bedrooms carrying a box. 'Only a wardrobe full of clothes and this underneath the bed.' He showed Wilson the contents of the box: Lennon's pornography collection. 'The second bedroom is full of bags containing the old man's clothes. I suppose he meant to throw them out but hadn't got around to it yet.'

'Nothing of a political nature?' Wilson asked.

'Not that I could find.'

'We'll let Duane decide whether we need to let Forensics at the place. Put the box back where it belongs.'

They were no nearer to knowing who Brian Lennon was and why more than one man had been willing to beat him to death. Wilson opened his phone and called Duane.

'Where are you?' Duane asked.

'Lennon's house in Creggan. Where are you?'

'Louth County Hospital. Kelly has just completed his autopsy.'

'And?'

'Not over the phone. Let's meet in an hour at the same pub as yesterday.'

Wilson reluctantly accepted the invitation. Duane was happy hopping back and forward over the border, but he wasn't. He started towards the door and noticed a 2018 calendar sitting on a chair. Several of the days had hand-written annotations. He picked up the calendar and rolled it up.

'The cousin was right, boss,' Graham said. 'They were living like church mice. Belfast people like me think that

Belfast is Northern Ireland, but it's not. Places like this are the real Northern Ireland.'

Wilson jammed the calendar into his coat pocket. 'And there are a lot of lonely farmhouses just like this one.'

'Where to, boss?' Graham asked.

'South again.'

DUANE WAS ALREADY SEATED at the rear of the pub. Wilson and Graham joined him and when the barman approached, they ordered tea.

'How did the autopsy go?' Wilson asked when they were alone.

'From the direction of the strikes,' Duane said. 'Kelly reckons that Lennon was surrounded by six men. His best guess from the shape of the bruises is that they were wielding axe handles. Lennon died from massive internal bleeding resulting from the beating. His death wasn't an accident. He was murdered. I'll have a copy of the autopsy report this afternoon and I'll pass it along. Anything from your side?'

Wilson briefed him on the visit to Lennon's house the previous day and the return visit that morning. 'DC O'Neill has been dredging up whatever she can find on Lennon, but there's not much. He doesn't appear to have interacted with us and Intelligence didn't have him on their radar. As far as we're concerned, he's clean.'

'We have no record of him either,' Duane said. 'We don't think he had any paramilitary connections. I also put the word out to our grasses. They've been slow to come back, which gives me a bad feeling in my stomach.'

'What next?' Wilson asked.

'I have the local uniforms knocking on doors in Inniskeen and the surrounding area. Maybe someone saw something out of the ordinary. In the meantime, the CSIs have been going over the barn and the house. There would have been some blood splatter on the attackers. We must follow the process. There was a pretty active IRA presence in this area during the Troubles and a lot of the heavy mob are still around. They're on your side of the border as well. So, if we decide to go that road, we might have to reconsider making your role more official.'

'Let's not go there yet,' Wilson said. 'I discovered the name of the family solicitor. He has an office on North Street in Crossmaglen, close to Barry Lennon's shop. It's strange that Lennon didn't know that right off.'

'They're a close-knit and closed-mouth lot around Crossmaglen. You'd best tread lightly until the picture becomes clearer.'

'And what are you going to do?'

'Talk with the CSIs and pray to God that they've come up with a lead.'

'What about the person who called it in?'

'I've listened to a recording of the call. He did a pretty good job of disguising his voice and the call was made from a mobile. If I'm right, that phone is probably at the bottom of Lough Neagh.'

'It'd help if we could find him,' Wilson said.

'I'm sure it would. We need your colleagues in Forensic Science Northern Ireland to give Lennon's house the once over.'

'I can just hear Davis's anguish when she sees the impact of an FSNI investigation on her budget.'

'It can't be avoided.'

'Did you contact Barry Lennon?'

'The butcher? Yes, he's coming in this evening to identify the body. He didn't sound particularly happy about it.'

'I got the impression that very little cooperation can be expected from that quarter.'

'Ah shit,' Duane said looking beyond Wilson. 'If it isn't your pal from the *Chronicle*.'

'Well, well, well.' Jock McDevitt, crime reporter with the *Belfast Chronicle*, pulled up a chair and sat down. 'What have we got here?'

'How did you find us?' Duane said.

McDevitt waved at a waiter and ordered a pint of Guinness. 'A guy I know on the *Louth Champion* clued me in on Brian Lennon's untimely death and the fact that he was a resident of our beloved province. The *Belfast Chronicle* far outweighs the *Louth Champion*, so we couldn't let them lead on such an important story.'

'I mean how did you find us in this pub?' Duane said.

'I think one of the gardaí at the crime scene got the impression that I had something to do with the PSNI. I think he misunderstood something I said.' McDevitt's drink arrived. 'Can I get you gentlemen anything?'

Duane and Wilson stood. 'No thanks,' Wilson said. He nodded at the drink. 'It's a bit early for that and we were about to finish up anyway.'

'I'm on my way over to Creggan myself after I finish this pint. Maybe I'll run into you again.' McDevitt turned to Duane. 'My friend from the *Champion* is looking for a quote from you. I don't suppose you'd like to give me something.'

'Aye,' Duane said. 'Fuck off.' He started for the door.

'Be careful in Creggan, Jock,' Wilson said. 'I don't think some of the people there will be too keen on getting the McDevitt treatment.'

'I'll walk on eggshells, Ian.'

# CHAPTER THIRTEEN

DCC Jennings waved CS Rodgers into the visitor's chair. He'd received a frantic call from him earlier to demand an urgent meeting and he'd agreed reluctantly. Rodgers had spent ten minutes ranting about his altercation with Simon Jackson. 'Something must be done about that fucker.'

Jennings sighed. There must be something in the air. McCann had been off the wall at yesterday's meeting. That wasn't just his opinion either as Philip Lattimer and old Glenconnor were also clearly shaken by her display. Now Jackson had gone beyond rogue by threatening to kill the head of PSNI Special Branch. Rodgers looked like he hadn't slept and if someone put the fear into Black Bob there had to be something behind it. Things were unravelling. McCann and Lattimer had become greedy. They'd gone too far when they sanctioned the murder of Grant and Malone. The bodies started to pile up after that, leading to the madness of trying to take out a detective superintendent of the PSNI. Not that he disagreed with McCann about the threat Wilson represented to their organisation. 'It's just hot air, Bob. He was only trying to put the frighteners on you.'

'You didn't look into his eyes.'

But I did look into McCann's eyes, Jennings thought. And I didn't like what I saw there. 'What would you like me to do?'

'Help me get the bastard before he gets me.'

There was something in the air. 'That might be over-reacting. What if I pass the message upstairs that the attack dog should be kept in check?'

'One of my mates had a German shepherd that was a bad one. It got ill and he was forced to bring it to the vet, who was an expert on dogs. As soon as the dog entered the vet's office, the hair on the dog's neck rose. The vet turned to my mate and said: "Get that fucker out of here and lock him in one of my kennels outside. Then go home and I'll deal with the dog. Because if I don't, that bastard is going to kill someone." That's the only way to handle a mad dog: kill it.'

'That's out of the question. Jackson is untouchable for the moment.'

'And what about me? Am I to wander around waiting for Jackson to pop up behind again and this time kill me? That's not my style. I've done everything that was asked of me and I also know where the bodies are buried. The people at the top should remember that.'

'No threats, Bob. That's the one way you can open the door to Jackson.'

Rodgers slumped in his chair. 'Good God, Roy. I feel old. I don't want to go out to a guy like Jackson. For old times' sake, get the bastard off my back.'

'I'm going to try.'

'Try my arse. Either you do it or I will.'

'I told you to stop talking like that. Keep that up and someone will wipe your slate clean. Don't put a gun to anyone's head. It's not a safe strategy.'

Rodgers stood. 'I'm going to disappear for a couple of weeks. And when I come back, I want to hear that there's no chance I'm going to meet Jackson in a dark garage again. Otherwise all bets are off.' He stormed out of the office.

He'll calm down Jennings told himself, but he didn't really believe it. Rodgers was scared and scared men do stupid things. He went into his private bathroom and sloshed water onto his face. If it was unravelling, what was he going to do about it? Jackson may be untouchable, perhaps Rodgers isn't.

MOIRA WAS ENGROSSED in Gowan's version of Carlisle's notebook. She knew that Carlisle had pancreatic cancer and now she was wondering if he might have been suffering from some disease of the brain as well. What she was reading was the equivalent of a brain dump, it was everything and it was nothing. It was either the ramblings of a diseased mind, or a very clever way of explaining the evil part of the life of a man not renowned for being evil.

She was already putting names to the characters he had created to tell his story. She might be wildly out, but she had to start somewhere. Carlisle was no George R.R. Martin, but he had adopted the fantasy genre to tell his tale. The mythical kingdom where the story was set was none other than Northern Ireland. The Queen would be Helen McCann and the Judge, her late husband. The Politician was presumably Carlisle himself. The other characters were not so easy to identify. Northern Ireland was full of lords so that could have been anyone. And she had no idea who the Mogul or Policeman might be. Together the group ran the mythical kingdom but not overtly. They controlled the kingdom by manipulating the many minions under their control. In the process they amassed tremendous wealth and exerted great influence even beyond the frontiers of the kingdom. To maintain their control, they bribed and corrupted and, when they needed to, they murdered. The group's original aim was to protect and preserve their kingdom, but as their power grew so did their corruption.

She had read the story with the intention of discovering a

motive for Carlisle's murder, but as she closed the file, she still had no idea where she was going with the investigation. She knew McCann had a hand in Carlisle's murder. Were the Lord, the Mogul and the Policeman also guilty? Much as she loved puzzles, she doubted her ability to crack this one.

# CHAPTER FOURTEEN

The office of Michael Coyle BCL was in a small two-storey building on North Street, Crossmaglen. Graham parked directly outside the door. 'This town gives me the willies,' he said as he cut the engine.

'Why is that?' Wilson asked.

'The population here don't fancy the police. Did you see the police station? It looks like Fort Apache. It wasn't built like that because steel barriers were the only materials available.'

'I could always bring Moira.'

'No, but I don't like it.'

Wilson understood Graham's misgivings. There was a lot of history here and most of it wasn't pleasant.

The two policemen entered the brightly painted building. A secretary was seated directly inside the front door.

Graham produced his warrant card. 'We have an appointment with Mr Coyle.'

The secretary picked up the phone and announced their arrival. 'He's with a client at the moment,' she said as she replaced the handset. 'He'll be with you shortly.'

Wilson and Graham sat. After a few minutes, a young man dressed in a pinstriped suit appeared from behind the secretary's desk and ushered a middle-aged lady to the front door. As her back disappeared, he turned to face Wilson and Graham, who had stood up.

'Detective Superintendent Wilson,' Coyle extended his hand. 'I saw you playing rugby when I was a kid.'

Wilson shook. That couldn't have been too long ago, Wilson thought, given that Coyle looked like he had recently celebrated his twenty-first birthday. But maybe that was just another sign that he was getting on himself.

'It was a shame you got injured.'

Wilson nodded. He'd heard that remark too many times. Why the hell didn't someone ask for the reason he didn't run like everyone else when he heard the shout 'Bomb'? 'This is DC Graham,' Wilson said. He noted that there was no handshake for Harry. He supposed there never was.

'Let's go through.' Coyle moved to the door behind the secretary and held it open for Wilson and Graham. 'We have a small conference room at the rear. Can I offer either of you coffee or tea?'

Wilson declined for both of them.

The conference room was indeed small, with eight chairs squashed around a heavy mahogany table. Coyle sat at the head and the two policemen took seats to his left.

'How can I help you?' Coyle wrote a short note on an A4 pad.

Wilson saw he had written down the date and the names of the policemen. 'You've probably heard that a young local, Brian Lennon, was found murdered yesterday,' Wilson said.

'I saw it on the television news last night. Terrible business. He was a nice man.'

'That's what everyone says. I noticed some correspondence from your firm at Mr Lennon's house and I was wondering whether you are the family solicitor.'

'We've done some legal work for the family. I suppose you could say that we are the family solicitor.'

'I understand that Mr Lennon's father died some months ago.'

'Yes, six months ago to the day. That particular family has been hard-hit by tragedy.'

'Did he leave a will?'

'He did. A rather simple one. He left all his earthly possessions, small though they were, to his son. What has that to do with Brian's death?'

Wilson ignored the question. He was there to ask questions not answer them. 'So, all of Brian Lennon's assets consist of the cottage and the farm in Creggan?'

'We are solicitors, not accountants. Brian may have had a mattress stuffed with fifty-pound notes in his cottage, but I have no information to that effect.'

'Do you know of any reason why someone would want to do Brian Lennon harm?'

'Absolutely not. Like I said, he seemed to be a pleasant enough young man.' Coyle removed a handkerchief from his pocket and blew his noise. There was more noise than action.

'Was the will probated?'

Coyle wrote a note on his pad. 'I hope we're not about to stray into areas covered by client confidentiality.'

'Both the clients I'm interested in are dead. I hardly think the issue of client confidentiality is applicable.'

'I run this office for my father,' Coyle said. 'He has the main office in Newry. I think you should talk to him.'

'We'll talk to him if we need to. If you handle the Lennons' business, you're the man we need to talk to in this phase of the investigation. Did Brian Lennon make a will?'

'Not to my knowledge.'

'What happens to the cottage and the farm then?'

'Assuming there is no will, the estate will be listed in *bona vacantia*. It means "ownerless goods" and it's a legal concept that's particularly associated with English law and is therefore found in most countries that have based their law on England.

Here, *bona vacantia* is dealt with by the Crown Solicitor as the Treasury Solicitor's agent.'

'Laymen's terms please,' Wilson interrupted.

'The assets will be estimated and if there is no direct heir, as in this case, they will be listed. If they are important enough, an heir hunting company will establish the heirs and their portion of the assets. The assets will be sold, and the money distributed in relation to the qualifications of the heirs. If no heirs are found, the assets revert to the Crown.'

'So, no one person benefits from Brian Lennon's death?'

'Apparently not, unless there is an heir that I don't know about.'

Wilson stood and extended his hand. 'Thanks for your time. I don't think we'll be bothering your father.'

Coyle smiled and took Wilson's hand. 'Would you mind signing an autograph for me? You were a big favourite of my father's when you played.' He handed Wilson his pad and a pen.

Wilson selected a fresh page and signed. It had been twenty years since he had pulled on a rugby jersey. He handed back the pad and headed for the door, followed by Graham. 'We'll see ourselves out.'


'WHAT WAS THAT ABOUT, BOSS?' Graham asked when they were seated in the car.

'For one, we can scratch out money as a motive, and without an alternative motive we might be up shit creek on this case. But that wasn't the most interesting aspect of the interview. Mr Coyle was definitely holding something back. He was fine talking about *bona vacantia* and the legal issues, but not so comfortable when it came to discussing the Lennons. There's something here that no one wants to speak about, neither Barry Lennon nor the family lawyer.'

'Where to now, boss?'

Wilson shrugged. 'We move on. If it's not money it might be love. Let's try and find someone who might possibly tell us the truth.'

OVER WILSON's varied career as a detective in the PSNI, he had worked dozens of cases and those he hated most were the motiveless murders. The old adage that the first forty-eight hours are the most important in any investigation is often true, especially when there are witnesses who can point towards a perpetrator, or when a bloody knife is left at the scene with clear fingerprints, or when a killer leaves his DNA all over the crime, or when there is a wealth of CCTV footage. The problem arises when there is no witness, no knife, no DNA and no CCTV. In such cases, the investigative team must stumble around like a man in a dark room. There might be some clues in there, but it takes time for your eyes to become accustomed to the gloom. In the meantime, you smash your knee against the table, your sense of frustration grows and you doubt your ability to solve the crime as the investigation runs into weeks, months or even years. The circumstances of the crime must be gone over again and again before you can nail the miscreant. That is the part of the job that Wilson knew he was good at. He would ferret out the information piece by piece until the golden nugget appeared from the heap of shit. Mickey Duff was a case in point. Wilson was sure that Eddie Hills had driven Duff to Helen's Bay, managed to get him into the boot of the car and then torched the car. Goodbye Mickey. The difficulty was that there wasn't a single piece of evidence to substantiate that hypothesis and Hills wasn't about to roll over. So Duff would stay in his locker for a few more months before being buried. He was afraid that Brian Lennon might suffer the same fate. He wanted to tell Graham to take him back to Belfast, but he knew that the answer to the questions surrounding Lennon's death wouldn't be found there. 'Let's have a word with the local priest.' Wilson got out of the car and went back into Coyle's office.

The secretary was startled by his return. 'Mr Coyle is busy.'

'Where does the local priest live?'

'Newry Road.' She scribbled an address on a post-it.

'Do you have a phone number for him?'

She hit some keys on her computer and added a number to the post-it. 'Fr Gallagher is his name.'

'Thanks.' Wilson took the note and went back to the car. He gave Graham the address and took out his phone.

The priest's housekeeper informed Wilson that Fr Gallagher was not at his residence but would be returning shortly and they were welcome to come and wait.

THE PAROCHIAL HOUSE was a fine two-storey building constructed of cut stone. As Wilson and Graham pulled into the driveway, a black Volkswagen Touareg followed them up the drive and parked directly behind them. Wilson climbed out of the car and saw a middle-aged man dressed in a black suit exiting the other vehicle. There was no sign of a clerical dog collar but that was the modern approach. He stayed beside his car.

'Superintendent Wilson.' The priest strode towards him hand extended. 'Joseph Gallagher, my housekeeper phoned me.'

Wilson shook. 'I hope I haven't interrupted something important.'

'No, I was on my way back.'

Wilson introduced Graham, who received a warm handshake.

'Let's get inside,' Gallagher said. 'I have a thirst on me and Mrs Given will have the tea ready for us.'

Gallagher was as good as his word and insisted that they

join him for tea and cakes. They hadn't had lunch and Graham attacked the cakes with gusto.

'You're here about poor Brian Lennon,' Gallagher said.

'You knew him well?' Wilson asked.

'I've been parish priest of Upper Creggan for the past twenty years. I know every family in the area.'

'Everybody I speak to tells me that Brian Lennon was a mild character without an enemy in the world.'

'I would have said the same,' Gallagher sipped his tea. 'Until I heard that he was murdered.'

'He hasn't been in trouble locally?'

'Good Lord no. Brian and Jim Lennon kept themselves to themselves like many of the folk around here. The poor boy was devastated by his father's death. Jim had the diagnosis and knew there was no cure. But even when we expect something, it's a shock when it arrives. Jim and Brian were as close as any father and son I've ever encountered. How did Brian die?'

'Badly, the autopsy was carried out yesterday and it was certainly murder. And a very nasty murder at that.'

'So, he didn't receive the last rites?'

'I very much doubt that a priest was in attendance.'

'It's a terrible thing to be sent to the next life without the benefit of a priest.'

'Lennon wasn't married or in a relationship, was he?' Wilson asked.

'No. I think he was going out with a girl at one point but nothing came of it. He was raised by his father, so I imagine he wasn't all that comfortable in the company of women.'

'There's very little chance then that his murder was occasioned by an angry husband or boyfriend.'

'Not a chance. I was Brian's confessor, and while I'm not about to break the seal of the confessional, I can tell you that his sins did not involve either the Sixth or the Ninth Commandments.'

Wilson finished his tea. He'd run out of questions. 'Do you

know of any reason why someone should want to murder Brian Lennon?'

Gallagher put his teacup down slowly. 'You'll not hear a bad word spoken against Brian Lennon in this parish.'

It was the second time that Wilson had noted a slight pause before answering. The first had been the previous day with the butcher. The basic lack of trust between the local community and the police was going to impede this investigation. 'Despite that, I think the motive for his death will be found here.'

'I pray to God you're wrong.'

Wilson stood. 'We've taken up enough of your time. Thank you for your hospitality.'

'It's nothing.' Gallagher ushered them towards the door.

Wilson noticed Graham stuffing two cakes into his pocket as he rose.

Gallagher stopped at his front door. 'I understand Brian is currently in Dundalk. Do you have any idea when his body will be released?'

'The Garda Síochána is in charge of the case,' Wilson said. 'I'll check with the senior investigating officer and let you know.'

Gallagher opened the door. 'I'd be grateful.'


'It's dangerous to be popular around here,' Graham said when they'd taken their places in the car.

'I was thinking along those lines myself. The man had no money and not an enemy in the world, and yet a group of men beat him to death. And even the priest doesn't want to tell us what everyone else is keeping to themselves. It's one for the books, Harry. Let's get back to Belfast. There's nothing more we can do today.'

At the end of the drive, Graham turned towards Newry to link up with the A1. A blue Hyundai fell in behind them.

Wilson turned the driving mirror towards him, took out his notebook and wrote down the registration number.

'What is it, boss?'

'Nothing much, Harry. I saw that blue Hyundai that's following us parked behind us yesterday at Barry Lennon's shop. I saw it again when we left Coyle's office and now it appears to be escorting us out of town. I'm interested to know who it belongs to.'

'It's a small place, boss. Maybe it's just a coincidence.'

'You know I don't believe in coincidences.'

# CHAPTER FIFTEEN

Jock McDevitt was sitting at a corner table in McEneney's Bar in Cardinal O'Fiaich Square. It was the kind of country bar he loved: all mahogany, shined brass and stuffed leather seating. He would own a pub like it if he won the lottery. He was with Padraig Keating, a stringer on the *Argos* and his new best friend for the duration of the investigation into the murder of Brian Lennon. Keating was one of those eager puppies who got a buzz from working with a big-time reporter from Belfast. McDevitt had already phoned in a story for tomorrow's *Chronicle* and made the most of the savage nature of the beating Lennon had received. That information had cost him fifty euro, which was paid to a uniformed garda of Keating's acquaintance. Keating had also managed to get a comment from the Republic's chief pathologist, and he had interviewed the deceased's cousin, Barry the butcher. The piece was salacious enough to induce the editor to put him on the front page. Of course, Duane and Wilson would prefer to carry out their investigation without the glare of publicity, but McDevitt felt it was his duty to ensure that the citizens of the province were informed of the darkness in their midst. He had a feeling that the case was a local one and therefore a molehill in the eyes of his editor. It was his role to turn that molehill into a mountain.

'Another one?' McDevitt asked.

Keating put up his hands. 'No chance, the guards have turned into demons since the new drink-driving law came into force. And I can't afford to lose my licence, even for three months.'

McDevitt took out a fifty euro note and slid it across the table. 'Maybe later.'

'Maybe.' Keating did a magic trick and made the note disappear.

Although working for a Dundalk rag, Keating had been born in Armagh, which almost made him a local – Keating insisted that only people born and raised in Creggan parish were considered locals in Crossmaglen. The locals don't like outsiders.

'What do you think happened?' McDevitt asked.

Keating looked around surreptitiously. There were only three other patrons in the pub, and they were at the bar. 'It's a local affair, which means we have to be super cautious. Asking too many questions could be very bad for your health.'

'Do you know anyone local who could give us a steer?'

Keating finished the dregs of his pint of Guinness. He shook his head.

'But you'll find someone.'

'I'll ask around. In the meantime, don't forget where you are. Keep a low profile. You told me that you're a big pal of Wilson. He might be your best source.'

McDevitt didn't think so. If the murder had happened on Wilson's patch, there would have been a chance. But with Duane in charge, Wilson would keep his own counsel. 'Keep your ear to the ground and keep me informed.'

Keating stood. 'I have to go. I'm due back at the office before I'm finished for the day.'

McDevitt motioned to the bar to refill his pint. There were

no Garda Síochána on his way home and the drink laws were not as draconian as those of the south. There was a story here somewhere, but he was damned if he knew where to find it. He was acquainted with all the characters in Belfast, but his knowledge of the players in south Armagh was sketchy. He would get an intern working on that in the morning. It would mean trawling through the local rags and the local court documents. His pint arrived and he handed the barman a five-pound note. 'Keep the change.'

The barman went to the cash register and returned with McDevitt's change.

'I said you could keep the change.'

The barman turned and went back to the bar. One of the patrons watched McDevitt as he took the first sip of his pint. It tasted all right, but McDevitt wondered whether someone had pissed or spat into it. He wasn't so endeared to the pub anymore. He lifted his messenger bag and left. He was sorry he had ever followed this murder up. Maybe he should leave it to the local rags. That way the only information that got out would be what the killers wanted people to know.

# CHAPTER SIXTEEN

W ilson allowed Moira to walk him through the convoluted story outlined in Carlisle's notebook. In the pantheon of fanciful tales, the story was at the top of the list. The events and the characters might have been a figment of Carlisle's imagination, a failed attempt at a fantasy novel or an attempt at redemption. Wilson wasn't in a position to choose. 'Bizarre,' he concluded.

'It all depends on how you look at it,' Moira said. She had read the contents of the notebook for a second time. 'The political philosophy stuff is off the wall. The idea that there are people who are born to rule went out with button boots. But what I don't like is his support for the deep state idea. The characters in the story are the leaders. They're supported by a whole group who subvert democracy by running the state for the benefit of an elite.'

'What's so new about that? It seems to me that's what we've got everywhere. How else could the one per cent protect themselves?'

'Yes, and I'm a simple detective sergeant. But the bones of this story are that a group has been manipulating this province for more than fifty years. They had been siphoning off state money and building up a war chest to be used if their view of the political direction of the province is challenged. They've corrupted politics, government, the judiciary and the police. They've murdered and stolen, and they believe themselves above the law.'

'It's a tale in a notebook written by an old disillusioned man.'

'What if it's not?'

'We have to have proof.'

'Maybe we already have it, but we haven't yet connected the dots.'

'Then I suppose we had better start.' Wilson leaned back in his chair. Carlisle's unlikely tale might have been the tip of the iceberg. The motive for murdering Carlisle had stumped him. Perhaps the notebook was only the opening shot. Carlisle was a sick man. Maybe someone was afraid that he would see that his misdeeds were threatening his place in heaven. That thought might cause him to seek salvation by unburdening his conscience. 'The David Grant murder has always bothered me. Big George Carroll identified the killers for us, and we tied Sammy Rice in as the paymaster. The killers' motive was money. But what about Rice?'

'He was one of the beneficiaries of a corrupt bidding process. The other one being Carson Nominees, which appears to have shut up shop.'

'Or morphed into something else. Then Rice is murdered, and a loose end disappears.'

'A very convenient murder.'

'I need to look at the interviews with Richie Simpson again. I know Simpson fired the shot that killed Rice, but I think somewhere he said that Carlisle had contracted the hit. But not tonight. It's been a long day. Fancy a drink?'

'I thought you'd never ask.'

.  .  .

'Do you intend to make an honest woman of Reid?' Moira asked as they began to unwind in the cosy atmosphere of the Crown.

Wilson was in the process of drinking a pint of Guinness and managed to spill some. 'There are only a few people who could get away with asking me that question,' he said when he regained his composure.

Moira smiled. 'And I'm one of them.'

Thankfully Reid wasn't present. She had called Wilson earlier to cancel the Crown in favour of supporting a colleague who was giving a speech at the university. 'The subject hasn't been broached,' he said. He had just about fended off Reid's plan to abscond to the US. He'd known her desire for change probably had something to do with the death of her mother and hoped that it would pass. It had diminished, but they were not out of the woods on the move to California yet. However, he wasn't going to discuss that subject with anyone, even Moira.

'How long have you two been together?'

Wilson raised his eyebrows. 'And how's your sex life?'

'Non-existent.' She sipped her vodka and soda. 'I've been living like a nun since I got back from Boston.'

'What about young Finlay?'

'Thank God, he's got the message and stopped bothering me.'

'Not a case of the lady doth protest too much?'

'Definitely not.'

'Nothing on the horizon?'

She didn't answer.

'Still thinking about that Shea character?' he said. 'Life is short. Don't waste it.'

'My husband got out of jail last year. He's been trying to contact me to explain why he beat the shit out of me. I know it's a cliché, but he found God in prison. Do a bit of GBH and the pearly gates open for you.'

Wilson ordered another round of drinks. 'It might give you some closure.'

'Don't worry, I don't think all men are like Alex. But I'm not ready to listen to excuses for what he did to me. Maybe down the road but not now. Anyway, how did we switch subject? We were talking about you and Reid and honest women.'

'I worry about you sometimes.'

'I'm not a child.'

'It's the job. We've lost McIver and Davidson and now Browne. It chews up people and it's getting worse. Austerity and the cuts are making the pressure greater. Even the public is noticing it. I can feel the atmosphere changing. The respect for what we do isn't there anymore.'

She touched her fresh glass to his. 'If we let it get to us, what happens then? Where is all this coming from? Is it the business with Duane or Helen McCann?'

'A young man is beaten to death,' he sipped his beer. 'I know the locals I've spoken to are hiding something. They don't trust me. Either that or they're afraid.'

'Don't they realise the hole they're digging for themselves?'

'I don't think so. And then there's Helen McCann. She thinks herself so far above the law that she can arrange the murder of a major politician like Carlisle using a corrupt Special Branch officer, and there's nothing we can do about it. Corruption is a virus. It infects everyone it touches.'

Jock McDevitt's head poked around the door of the snug. 'Evening, folks. Oh dear, by the looks on your faces the discussion is serious, which probably means I should piss off.'

Moira turned away and Wilson thought he noticed a slight blush on her cheeks. He wondered what had occasioned it. 'Not at all, Jock. Please join us. These after-work discussions can raise passions. What's the news from tomorrow's *Chronicle*?'

McDevitt rooted around in his satchel. 'Maybe you'll get

the opportunity to get the drinks in.' He produced a galley of the front page of the *Chronicle* and placed it on the table. The headline ran: 'Katherine McCann QC to be appointed Attorney General for Northern Ireland'.

Wilson and Moira looked at each other. They knew that their task of bringing Helen McCann to justice had just got that much harder.

'The rise and rise of the lovely Kate McCann. You should have kept your oar in there, Ian.' McDevitt laughed, but he was alone. 'I take it neither of you is happy for Miss McCann.'

Wilson picked up the galley and handed it to McDevitt. 'Put it away.' He ordered another round of drinks. He wished Reid hadn't decided to attend the lecture. This was the kind of news that could inspire a bender.

'I was promised the lead on the murder of Brian Lennon, but the editor thought the McCann story deserved the headline. By tomorrow, Lennon will be ancient news and the money I spent on the stringer from Dundalk will have been totally wasted.' He looked from Wilson to Moira. 'Okay, who's dog just died?' Nobody smiled. 'I was looking forward to a few drinks with some intelligent police officers, but I think I'll head back home and watch Netflix instead. I keep paying the subscription, but I never watch anything.'

The drinks arrived and Wilson paid for and distributed them. 'I'm off home after this round anyway. What about Linfield? Do you think they need a new coach?'

# CHAPTER SEVENTEEN

DCC Jennings' first reaction upon receiving an invitation from Helen McCann to dine with her was to refuse and claim pressure of work. But reason prevailed, and he accepted with grace. Somewhere in the back of his mind the ambition to reach the position of chief constable of the PSNI still existed. But his hope that the present incumbent would screw up royally had not been fulfilled. Norman Baird was going to see out his mandate as chief constable, or even have it renewed, and the fire of ambition that had burned in Jennings' breast had begun to fizzle out. Lately, he had been concentrating his mind on how to get away safely with his money and his skin intact. None of his heart's desires would be easy to attain. He had done the bidding of the Circle for too long. It was naive to think that he had not left a trace that some assiduous investigator could find. He thought about Wilson, who had been his nemesis since the day they first set eyes on each other. For some reason, the one had instantly recognised the other for what he was. He wished Wilson had been taken care of.

He had been directed to McCann's room and took a deep breath before he knocked.

'Good evening, Roy.' McCann was dressed in a silk evening dress that showed off her slim figure.

'Good evening, Helen.' Jennings allowed himself to be ushered to a table that had been set up in the centre of the room.

There were two plates covered by stainless steel plate covers. McCann sat and Jennings followed suit. At the nod from McCann, the waiter raised the covers, revealing two equal plates containing a portion of steak, some potato and broccoli. A second nod sent the flunky on his way out of the room.

'I know your reputation as an ascetic,' McCann said. 'So I didn't go overboard on the food.'

'What you've ordered is perfectly adequate.' Jennings was teetotal and took no pleasure in food.

McCann started on her meal. 'I need your help.'

Jennings cut a piece off his steak and transferred it to his mouth.

'Wilson has a piece of evidence relating to the Carlisle affair,' she continued.

'So I heard.' Jennings stopped eating. 'And you want it to disappear.'

'You've been so helpful in that regard in the past.'

And I might end up in jail because of it, Jennings thought. He allowed his thin lips to smile. 'It was a pleasure to be of service.'

'It's not my fault that you haven't made it to chief constable.' She had barely touched her food. 'It has always been the aim of the Circle to have a member in the highest office of the PSNI. You will obtain the phone for me.'

'I don't think the phone is your problem.'

'And what is?'

'Jackson is a loose end.' Jennings greatest fear was that Rodgers would crack. If he could arrange for Jackson's demise,

Rodgers would be eternally grateful. 'Perhaps you should consider eliminating him.'

'While Jackson was on the run, he made a video outlining the Carlisle operation. In it, he mentions Rodgers, you and me. This video has been placed in safekeeping with the instruction to release it if any misfortune should befall its maker.'

Jennings pushed his plate away. He tried to suppress his surprise. 'I wasn't aware of this recording. In the realm of evidence that can put us in jail, it far outweighs the phone. I think it would be more important to locate the place of safe-keeping and retrieve that recording. Jackson could be dealt with at the same time.' He could imagine the pleasure Rodgers would get from extracting that piece of information from Jackson. But that might entail going a bit further than necessary, which might lead to the video being made public. Jackson was no fool.

'You may leave Jackson to me. But in the meantime, you will get me the phone.'

'I'll look into it.'

McCann dabbed her lips with a white napkin. 'It was so nice of you to drop by.'

Jennings stood. 'Be careful how you handle a snake, they sometimes bite their handler.'

McCann opened the door and Jennings left. The fact that Jackson had made a video had shocked him to the core. Threatening people like McCann and Rodgers was a very dangerous manoeuvre. It was a further indication that things were beginning to unravel.

## CHAPTER EIGHTEEN

The craic in DJ Dave's Disco Emporium in Dundalk had been ninety. The DJ had been a bit shite, but the drinks were good, and Padraig Keating had lined up a couple of women for the future. He'd blown the fifty euro that McDevitt had given him, but there would be plenty more coming from that quarter. Fifty euro doesn't go far on a night's drinking. Keating stared at his watch as he staggered out onto Woodvale Manor. He fished around in his pocket and looked at the change in his hand. He had just enough for a taxi home.

'Spare some change, pal?'

Keating looked up and the change fell out of his hand. Standing in front of him were two large men wearing balaclavas. He tried to speak but no words came. The man directly in front of him punched him hard in the stomach. Keating doubled over and vomited on the ground, just missing the men's shoes.

'You're a dirty wee bastard,' the second man said, and Keating felt a blow to the side of his head that sent him reeling into the road.

The two men picked him up and half-dragged half-carried him off to the left and through some open ground in the direction of the Young Irelands GAA club. Keating got sick again and the men waited until he'd finished vomiting before continuing on their way.

'Please don't kill me,' Keating pleaded as they pulled him closer to the football pitch.

'Don't you worry your poor wee head,' the largest of the men said. 'We're not going to kill you. But you'll not be talking to that bastard from Belfast for a wee while.'

Keating didn't believe them, and he voided himself.

'He's shit himself,' the smaller man said.

'Matter a damn, they'll have to clean him up at the hospital.'

They dragged him into the centre of the pitch and rained blows on his head and body. The large attacker took his right arm, twisted it at an angle and broke it. Keating heard the crack of the bone snapping. They dropped him to his knees and the smaller man produced a revolver from inside his coat. He pointed the gun at Keating's head. This is it, the young man thought. The pain in his arm was excruciating. He wished he'd told his mother he loved her before he left home. He looked up as the man put the gun back under his coat. 'The next time,' he said and punched Keating one more time in the side of the head.

MOIRA FINISHED CLEANING her dinner dishes and went to the wall of her living room. She had managed to get a stock photo of the famous, or infamous depending which side of the sectarian divide you came from, Judge McCann. The photo showed him in his later years and depicted a stern-faced old Calvinist. Even though she abhorred his brand of right-wing politics, she could see the strength and charisma in his face. She had written 'The Judge' under the photo. Beside him was a photo of Helen McCann, which she had obtained from the *Chronicle*. It was a glossy portrait and McCann looked beautiful. She was more than twenty years the Judge's junior and could have had any man she wanted, but she had settled on him. Moira took a black marker and wrote 'The Queen?' beside it. Underneath a photo of Carlisle, she had written 'The Politician'. She drew three empty square boxes and put 'The Lord', 'The Mogul' and 'The Policeman' under them. She put large question marks in the centre of each of the boxes. If she was right, she had identified half the cast of characters. If she was right. There was a good chance that the rambling story in Carlisle's notebook was just that. In that case her wall and its interconnection to Carlisle's murder and those of Grant, Malone and O'Reilly might also mean nothing.

There were some givens. Jackson had murdered Carlisle and had phoned McCann as soon as the deed was done. He had absconded but had turned up in a photo taken in McCann's garden in Antibes. If McCann could sanction the murder of a friend, then how much easier would it have been for her to order the deaths of a few civil servants striving to do their jobs and expose corruption? Moira took one of her red balls of wool and connected the photo of McCann to the three murdered men. But they were killed on the orders of Sammy Rice. She connected a length of wool from a photo of Rice to the pin holding the photo of McCann in place. The wall was beginning to look like the map of the London Underground. She needed to find out how Rice was connected to McCann. On the surface, they inhabited different worlds. She turned on the desk lamp and opened the file on Grant's death. She had heard about police officers who became obsessed with a particular case and knew such situations generally ended badly. She started reading.

# CHAPTER NINETEEN

Another day, another dollar, Wilson thought as he entered Tennent Street Station. He was glad to leave the filthy weather outside, but inside it would be another day at the coalface trying to uphold what was rapidly becoming the crumbling foundation of policing in Northern Ireland. The general feeling was that if the politicians don't give a damn, why should the rest of the population bother. What country could survive two years without an effective parliament while its elected representatives squabbled over trifles? There was a political vacuum and meanwhile the province had attained the distinction of having one of the highest levels of poverty in the UK. It was on days like this that he understood where Reid was coming from when she suggested moving to California. He wanted to go even further and find a deserted island where they could hide from the madness.

The rest of the team was already at work when Wilson entered the squad room. 'Harry, you and I are heading south again. Duane has set up an incident room in Dundalk Garda Station and there's a briefing at ten. Moira, you and Siobhan will have to hold the fort.'

'That's what we do,' Moira said.

Wilson thought that she didn't sound so happy and she looked tired. 'The Garda Síochána is the force carrying this ball.'

'Until it's passed to us,' Graham said. 'Lennon might have been murdered in the south, but the case will eventually end up on our plate.'

'I agree,' Wilson said. 'But for the moment we play second fiddle.'

DUNDALK GARDA STATION is an imposing colonial-style, detached, five-bay, two-storey-over-basement building that was built around 1850 and started its life as a gaol. It is like many of the buildings that the British bequeathed to Ireland and the rest of the Empire. The Brian Lennon incident room was in a large conference room at the rear of the building. Four desks had been set up and a selection of young detectives manned the modern computer terminals. Wilson noticed that three of the four detectives were examining CCTV footage. Duane was at the top of the room talking with Flynn and both men were examining a whiteboard that had Lennon's photo on the top. Duane motioned them forward.

'Anything new?' Wilson asked.

'Divil the bit,' Duane said. 'We're nearly finished reviewing the CCTV for the night of the murder. I always knew we'd end up with nothing. There are so many unapproved roads in the area without a single camera on them and the locals know them all. Whoever murdered Lennon had the escape route already planned, and that plan didn't include being caught on camera. The question is where do we go from here?'

Flynn nodded to the two PSNI men and moved off to talk to the men at the terminals.

'Did you have a word with Barry Lennon when he came to identify the body?' Wilson asked Duane.

'We had him in for an interview after the viewing. I thought seeing the body would loosen his tongue, but he didn't bite. He was polite but firm. Brian was a nice lad who never harmed a soul. Barry has no idea why anyone would want to harm him.'

Flynn re-joined them. 'The lads are just about finished. They've gone bug-eyed from watching cars shooting up and down roads. They found nothing from the Inniskeen direction.'

'Nothing from the door-to-door either?' Wilson asked.

'Nobody saw or heard a thing for the whole night,' Flynn said. 'A spaceship could have landed and nobody would have seen or heard it.'

'Anything from our CSIs?' Duane asked.

Flynn shook his head. 'The grass around the edge of the farmyard was trampled, but there wasn't a clear boot impression. The tyre marks on the cobbles are consistent with a minibus. That's about it. Whoever killed Lennon knew their business. They left us nothing to work with.'

'We're running into a brick wall here,' Duane said.

'Lennon could have been the nicest man in the world,' Wilson said. 'But someone wanted him dead and had lots of help in arranging it. The pathologist says that six men beat the shit out of Lennon. They must have left something behind. There has to be more.'

'The forensic report will be issued tomorrow, but I've spoken to them and they found nothing,' Flynn said. 'I can order them back to go over the area again.'

'Good man, Daragh,' Duane said. 'Keep the boys at it and make sure that the results of the CCTV and the door-to-door enquiries are added to the file. And make sure a copy is sent to Detective Superintendent Wilson.'

'Absolutely, chief.' Flynn saluted and moved away.

'I have an office here. Let's pick up some tea and have a

chat. I'd prefer something stronger but circumstances are against it.'

'Not bad,' Wilson said after sipping his tea. 'I was expecting cat's piss.'

Duane had closed his office door and moved the two PSNI men into the far corner of the room. There was an outer office, but it was empty. Wilson put the move down to the fact that Duane was some kind of spook in his spare time.

'I need to talk to you guys alone. This station leaks like a colander. You're probably aware that An Garda Síochána and the PSNI have been launching combined operations against criminal gangs in this area over the past year.'

Wilson nodded.

'The object of the exercise is to close down the refining of agricultural diesel and the production of illicit alcohol. We're also trying to curtail the trade in contraband cigarettes. When the tax man doesn't get his cut, the hierarchy gets a boot in the arse from the minister.'

'I'm lost,' Graham said.

Duane sighed. 'Both jurisdictions provide diesel to farmers at a special price. In order to stop the farmers from selling on the diesel a red dye is added. That's why we term it "red diesel". A lot of red diesel is being stolen and a refining process is used to remove the red dye. Then the diesel is sold on the black market. It's ending up on the commercial market and the Revenue Commissioners are being bilked out of millions of pounds. It's the same with illicit alcohol. Vodka is being distilled illegally and then being labelled as the real thing. We've busted several refineries and distilleries, but whenever we hit, no one is ever present. We find some diesel, some vodka, lots of empty bottles and counterfeit labels. Within weeks the operation is up and running again.'

'Someone is giving the criminals information,' Wilson said.

'You should be a detective,' Duane said. 'Your Intelligence Branch and my people have been looking closely at everyone who was involved in the raids and they've worked out that the leaks come from here in Dundalk. That's why no one here knows that the next raid is planned for tonight.'

'And this relates to Brian Lennon how?' Wilson asked.

'Whoever wanted Lennon dead could have had him killed during a burglary at his home. Lennon could have been shot by accident. He could have died in so many ways. But we believe he was beaten to death by six men wielding axe handles. All those men are implicated in a murder, and it's certain that they belong to an organised crime group. Can you imagine the hold the leader of the gang has over them?'

'How will this raid advance our cause?'

'We're going to hit a diesel refinery and a distillery at the same time. That's going to have a serious impact on revenue. Consequently, someone is going to be very mad, which is going to result in pressure being put on the leaker.'

'It looks like a roundabout way of advancing our case.'

'We need to know on which side of the border the man responsible for Lennon's murder operates. We need him to expose himself.'

'What do you want from us?'

'Nothing. The raids are planned and will go ahead. If we're right, we'll net some of the bad guys, and if we're very lucky, one of them will squeal. If you want to ride along that can be arranged.'

'Not my game.' Wilson's phone rang. He looked at the caller ID. It was Jock McDevitt. He pressed the green button.

'Where are you?' McDevitt asked.

'Dundalk,' Wilson answered.

'So am I. I linked up with a young stringer from the local rag in Dundalk. He knows the characters around Crossma-glen. He was beaten to a pulp last night outside some nightclub in Dundalk. He's currently in Louth County Hospital. I think maybe you should talk to him.'

'Maybe his beating has nothing to do with Brian Lennon.'

'Then it's one hell of a coincidence.'

'And I don't believe in coincidence.'

'I'll meet you at the hospital entrance in fifteen minutes.' McDevitt ended the call.

'Jack, do you think you could find something for Harry to do for the next hour or so?'

'I'll take care of Harry. What's up?'

'I think McDevitt managed to get some poor eejit beaten up. He's in Louth County.'

'That little fucker is dangerous. I'll get one of the lads to drop you off.'

# CHAPTER TWENTY

M oira, who had no experience in international finance, was attempting to make sense of the maze that the owners of Carson Nominees had created. She was struggling to concentrate. She had woken up that morning with her head lying on her arms on her home desk. She had no idea what time she had fallen asleep, but she knew it had been late. That conclusion had been confirmed when she saw her face in the bathroom mirror. She looked like crap. She had quickly showered, dressed, grabbed her notes and headed for the station. Now she was feeling the lack of a good night's sleep. She scanned her notes from the Grant file. There was no doubt there was corruption and that Sammy Rice was up to his neck in it. Rice's bids were heavily padded so that he and his partners made windfall profits. One link that might lead back to Helen McCann were the bank guarantees provided to Rice by the shadowy Carson Nominees, which was incorporated in the Cayman Islands and had made regular payments to other companies incorporated there. Carson also had bank accounts in Panama and other secretive jurisdictions. The subsequent winding up of the company was unlikely to have been a coincidence. Three innocent men had been murdered to cover up corrupt tendering practices by some government departments. Carlisle had a deep connection with the Rice family's political activities going back decades. She was making progress, but this wasn't supposed to be her day job. The investigation into Carlisle's death, and the labyrinth it was exposing, was supposed to be off the books. She turned her attention to Mickey Duff.

Wilson had warned her off the direct approach. He'd already accused Eddie Hills of murdering Duff but didn't have a shred of evidence to back it up. Hills and his boss, Davie Best, were the new kings of the walk in Belfast. Moira had studied their files, but she hadn't had an opportunity yet to study them in the flesh. She was not usually rash but there's a first time for everything.

MOIRA ADJUSTED her eyes to the low light in the interior of Club 69. Cleaners were busy removing the detritus of the previous night's revellers and a tall, well-built young man in a white T-shirt and tight jeans that emphasised his fit body was stacking glasses behind the bar. She was suddenly aware that she hadn't had sex for months. 'Davie Best around?' she asked.

'Who's asking?' the hunk behind the bar said.

Moira produced her warrant card and the hunk started laughing. 'Piss off before someone gets annoyed with you.'

'That's no way to speak to the scum, Joey.'

Moira turned to face the man behind her.

'Moira McElvaney unless I'm mistaken,' Best said. 'And I rarely am.'

She had expected someone resembling the photo that was pinned to the first page of Best's file. It had been taken when Best was demobbed and he had looked cadaverous. The man standing before her now was a facsimile of the man in the photo, but Best had added bulk since then. 'How do you know my name?'

'It's my business to know.' Best pulled up a chair, sat down and appraised Moira. 'You're not bad looking. I might have given you a job ten years ago, but I don't even audition old skanks, so why don't you toddle off home.'

She noticed Hills entering the club and watched as he walked over to sit next to his boss. He was well-built and had a narrow white face that would put him in the frame for the part of an SS officer in a war film. His eyes were dark and dead. Her skin began to burn, and she felt uncomfortable and a little intimidated. And she didn't intimidate easily. These two men had created an itch that she had to scratch even though she was sure she would regret it. 'I wanted to have a look at Mr Hills in the flesh. I have a particularly good likeness of him that was taken from a drone over Helen's Bay on the day a BMW was torched there.'

Hills started to rise, but Best put his hand on his arm. 'You've overstayed your welcome DS McElvaney. I think you should leave. If we ever do have an audition for a skank, we'll give you a call.' Moira was about to protest but Best continued. 'It's non-negotiable. Private property and all that. I'm assuming your boss doesn't know that you're out on your own.'

'Be talking to you soon, Eddie.' She turned and strode to the door. When she got outside, she took a deep breath and exhaled slowly.

THE TWO MEN watched Moira as she left. 'I lied,' Best said. 'She can audition any day.'

'Does she have something or was that bullshit?'

'If she has something, it's not enough to get Wilson down here or to drag you into Tennent Street.' Best motioned to the barman. 'Two Americanos.' Business was good and he didn't need a red-haired bitch putting the wind up Eddie. Putting DCI George Pratley in the ground had disrupted their drug operation, but only for the few weeks it had taken them to put a new one in place. Wilson and his pals didn't seem to realise that the world is full of bent coppers and the money that floods in from selling drugs means there's plenty for all.

'I'm not going down for Mad Mickey,' Hills said.

'She was only blowing smoke. We'll find out what they have and then we'll see whether we have to react.' He looked at Eddie. They'd come a long way together. They'd survived Iraq and Afghanistan and they'd taken out Sammy Rice. 'The worst-case scenario is that you'll have to spend the rest of your life on the Costas with our friends.'

The barman deposited the coffees and disappeared.

'I burn easily.' Hills sipped his coffee.

Best would be sad to see Eddie go but business came first and his associates understood that. Everybody is replaceable. He wouldn't like it, but if he had to put a bullet in Eddie's head, he wouldn't flinch.

## CHAPTER TWENTY-ONE

W ilson's PSNI warrant card hadn't cut much mustard
with the receptionist at Louth County Hospital.
Padraig Keating was very unwell and was not receiving visitors
under any circumstances. Wilson had contacted Duane and
asked him to place a call to the director of the hospital. Like
magic, Wilson and McDevitt had been promptly permitted a
five-minute conversation with the patient.

Keating was a pitiful sight lying in his hospital bed. His
right arm had been set and he was in plaster from his fingers to
his shoulder. His face was puffy and bruised and his jaw had
been wired. His chest had been strapped and he was breathing
with difficulty. He was drugged to the eyeballs and his mind
was living on another planet while his body healed. Wilson
didn't feel good about bothering the young man.

'Padraig lad.' McDevitt moved close to Keating's ear.
'What happened?'

Keating made a garbled reply.

'What did he say?' Wilson asked.

'I think he told me to fuck off.'

'Maybe we should come back later.'

McDevitt looked down at the young man who had closed

his eyes. 'I don't think it had anything to do with the nightclub. It's much too professional for a random beating. I shouldn't have involved the lad.'

'No, you shouldn't.' Wilson pulled McDevitt away by the arm. 'Later, Jock.'

McDevitt allowed himself to be moved towards the door of the ward. 'The *Chronicle* will pay your medical expenses,' he said as he retreated.

'I don't think the medical expenses are at the top of his list of wants. What he really wants is you and me out of here.'

They went to the nurse's station. Wilson flashed the warrant card again without saying it was a PSNI one. 'Any idea what happened?' he asked.

'I only know that he was found in the centre of a GAA pitch,' a young nurse with a name tag announcing her as Sorcha said. 'I know he doesn't look it, but he's been lucky. The doctor doesn't think there are any internal injuries. The guards were here last night but weren't able to get anything out of him.'

'Thanks.' Wilson pulled McDevitt towards the lifts. 'You've caused enough trouble for one day. Why don't you get back to Belfast and find some other way to get yourself on the front page?'

'Come on, Ian. I was only doing my job.'

The lift door closed on them. Wilson turned and faced McDevitt. 'Maybe you should think about how you do your job. That poor lad in there won't be right for months. Police officers get paid for putting our lives on the line, it's in the job description, but that lad was probably reporting on flower shows until he had his head turned by a big-time crime reporter from Belfast. Now, he's in for a lengthy hospital stay and a bit of rehab with that arm. I hope your piece in the *Chronicle* was worth it.'

'I feel bad for the kid, but I don't make the rules,' McDevitt said as they alighted from the lift. 'It wasn't me who beat him up. But it's obvious that we touched a nerve.'

'What did he put you on to?'

'Nothing definite, but he was asking around about Lennon.'

'I've been asking too, but nobody has tried to punch out my lights.'

'You're the law. Putting you in hospital will only bring a half a dozen others like you to town. They'll use a completely different strategy on you.'

Wilson didn't say that he was sure they were already using that strategy. They exited the hospital and stood in the entrance

'It's bigger than just topping someone,' McDevitt said. 'I could smell it yesterday. I'm drawn to crimes like this as a bee is to honey.'

'Go back to Belfast, Jock. If you stay here, there's a good chance you'll be the next one in a hospital bed.'


DUANE AND GRAHAM were enjoying a cup of tea in the incident room when Wilson returned.

'Young man name of Padraig Keating,' Wilson said as he joined them. 'He had the shit beaten out of him last night outside a club called DJ Dave's Disco Emporium. He was found sprawled in the centre of the local GAA pitch. Your guys brought him in.'

'I'll bet there was a girl involved,' Duane said.

'I don't think so. Keating is from south Armagh and works for the local newspaper here. McDevitt hired him to help point out the local characters in Crossmaglen. Keating was very professionally beaten. There's no major damage but enough to leave a mark and issue a message.'

'Is he saying anything?' Duane asked.

'Yes, he told McDevitt to fuck off. I guess he won't be

saying much about his attackers when he is able to speak. He'll have some cock and bull story ready by then, and it might even involve a girl.'

'But you're sure it doesn't.'

'It's too much of a coincidence that Keating got beaten shitless the same day as he was seen around Crossmaglen with a man whose face appears regularly in the *Belfast Chronicle.*'

'Then we need to follow up. Flynn!' Duane motioned Flynn over. 'We have a little task for you and the lads.' Duane told him about the events of the previous evening. 'There were a couple of uniforms at the hospital so there's a report. I'm willing to bet that they've written it off as a row over some biddy or other. There's got to be some CCTV outside the nightclub.' He nodded at the men sitting at the computer terminals. 'Send a couple of them over to DJs and pick up whatever footage is available. Get me a couple of shots of the guys doing the beating up.'

'What if it was a row about a woman?' Flynn asked.

'It doesn't appear that Keating gave as good as he got so it's GBH or ABH at least. It's our job to nail the bastards. Tell the lads to ask around if anyone saw what happened.'

'Can't we let the uniforms follow up?' Flynn said.

'Our lads are unoccupied for the moment.' Duane said. 'There's a chance it's related to our case, so let's give them something to do. Get to it'

'Yes, chief.' Flynn went and spoke to two of the detectives, who immediately left the room.

Wilson waited until he, Duane and Graham were alone. 'There's nothing more that you need to tell us Jack, is there?'

Duane drew an X with his finger on his heart. 'Cross my heart and hope to die. You know what I know. And the invitation to tonight's shindig still stands.'

'You're a consummate liar, Jack.'

'Boss,' Graham said. 'Siobhan was trying to reach you about that car registration you asked her to check. The owner of the car is a Mary Rose McCluskey with an address in Crossmaglen.'

'Shit,' Wilson took his phone from his pocket. 'I had to switch it off in the hospital and I forgot to put it back on again.'

Duane was looking at Wilson.

'I noticed the same car dogging us yesterday,' Wilson explained. 'I know Crossmaglen is a small town, but I like to cover all the bases. If there's nothing more to do here, I think we'll have a word with Mrs McCluskey.' He turned to Graham. 'Tell Siobhan to find out what we have on her.'

Graham drifted off, speaking into his phone.

'I need to get back to Dublin,' Duane said. 'Then they want me to lead the raid later. Flynn will be in charge until I return.' He winked at Wilson.


FLYNN WAITED until Duane had departed for Dublin before he left the station. He went immediately to Kennedy's and ordered a double whiskey. He downed it in one gulp and his hands stopped shaking. He ordered a refill. The money Feeney had given him had vanished in one afternoon of racing. His luck was out but like every gambler he believed good fortune was just around the corner. Meanwhile, his life was heading into the toilet at supersonic speed and there appeared to be nothing he could do to stop it. His wife had packed up and taken their two sons to her parents' farm in Tipperary. He cradled his whiskey. Feeney was getting brazen. Although he denied killing Lennon, Flynn didn't believe him. Feeney was known to suffer from fits of pique or madness and was liable to get up to mischief. There was a strong possibility that he was also behind the assault on Keating. Flynn couldn't imagine what might be next. Duane was no fool and neither was Wilson. It was only a matter of time before they would have Feeney in the frame for killing Lennon. How long would it take them to expose him as Feeney's man? He could go to them and tell them everything he knew. But maybe he wasn't the only officer in Dundalk taking money from Feeney. In that situation, he would soon be dead. There wasn't a jail in Ireland, north or south, where he would be safe. He had dipped his toe in a pool and been pulled in by the biggest crocodile. Escape was going to prove tricky if not downright impossible.

# CHAPTER TWENTY-TWO

Wilson and Graham grabbed a quick pub lunch before heading for Crossmaglen. Wilson was already getting dizzy with the crossing and crisscrossing of the non-existent border between the two jurisdictions. He sometimes had to check which side he was on. Leads were thin on the ground. The murder of Brian Lennon had been carefully planned and executed. Therefore, there had to be a motive. Graham parked outside a two-storey detached house in Ard Ros. The Irish tricolour was flying on a flagpole in the garden.

Wilson rang the bell and a middle-aged woman answered the door. He held out his warrant card in his right hand. 'Mrs Mary Rose McCluskey?'

The woman nodded and her face hardened. 'Aye.'

'I'm Detective Superintendent Ian Wilson and this is DC Graham. May we come in?'

'No, you can't. State your business.'

Graham stepped forward. 'Are you the owner of a blue Hyundai Kona?' He gave her the registration.

'Yes.'

'We noticed this car several times yesterday following us on our business around town,' Graham said.

'My husband was driving the car yesterday, but I doubt very much that he was following you. From the cut of you, you're from Belfast. You don't understand a small town like Crossmaglen; you can't go on your messages here without running into the same people three or four times.'

'Is there any reason why Mr McCluskey might be following us?' Graham asked.

'Perhaps he thought you looked suspicious. Maybe he thought you were casing the place.'

Wilson smiled. 'What's your husband's name and where can we find him?'

'Michael's at work.'

'And where does he work?'

'At Feeney's Builders Providers out on the Newry Road.'

'Thank you, Mrs McCluskey,' Wilson said. 'You've been very helpful.' He saw from the worried look on her face that she hadn't intended to be.

Graham proffered one of his business cards. 'Perhaps you'd ask your husband to contact us.'

She looked at the card like it was something she had found on the bottom of her shoe and shut the door in their faces without touching it.

'Nice lady,' Graham said as they made their way back to the car.

'Sarcasm is the lowest form of wit.' Wilson opened the passenger-side door.

'Feeney's Builders Providers?'

'Why not? I'll bet Mrs McCluskey is on the phone to her husband right now and he won't be there when we arrive. But let's go there anyway.'

THE ENTRANCE to Feeney's Builders Providers was through a large cast-iron gate that led to an open parking area. The shop took up one side of the yard and there was what appeared to be a storage and collection area on another side. There was a gatehouse between the car park and the storage area. Graham parked between a pair of trucks; one had the name of a local plumber stencilled on it while the other advertised an electrical services business.

'There's the Kona, boss.' Graham pointed to an area that was reserved for the staff's vehicles.

'Let's see if I'm right about Mrs McCluskey.' Wilson ambled towards the entrance of the shop.

Once inside, they found a typical builders providers with shelves of building, plumbing and electrical materials laid out in aisles. At the far end of the large building there was an area devoted to electrical appliances. To the left of the entrance, there was a counter behind which two men and one woman wearing black T-shirts bearing the company logo were serving a group of men in overalls. On a second storey behind the serving counter were a series of doors that Wilson thought might lead to offices.

Graham flashed his warrant card at the older of the men behind the counter and he detached himself from his customer.

'I'm Detective Constable Graham and this is Detective Superintendent Wilson. We'd like to have a word with one of your employees, Michael McCluskey.'

'I'll get the manager.' The man disappeared upstairs and through a door, closing it behind him. He returned two minutes later, accompanied by a short well-built man sporting a bushy red beard.

'Can we move to the end of the counter, gents?' the new arrival said. 'By the way I'm Con Coleman, the manager.' There was no handshake. 'How can I help you?' he said when there were out of earshot of the customers.

'We'd like a word with one of your employees, Michael McCluskey.'

'Michael is out on a delivery,' Coleman said.

'When do you expect him back?' Graham asked.

'He's on a long run, could be late. What's Michael done this time?'

'We'd just like to have a wee word with him,' Graham said.

'I know most of the peelers around here. You guys are new.'

Graham took out a business card. 'Maybe you'd give Mr McCluskey a message that we'd like to talk with him.'

Coleman took the card and looked at it.

'Have you worked here long?' Wilson asked.

Coleman's eyes darted from Graham to Wilson. 'Forever, I'm one of the old stock.'

'Is Mr Feeney around?' Wilson asked.

'He owns the place. He doesn't involve himself in the day-to-day running of it.'

'He leaves that to you, right?'

'Too damn right. It a big business to run.'

'Thanks,' Wilson said. 'Don't forget to pass the message to Mr McCluskey. We're anxious to talk to him and I think he should make himself available as soon as possible. We wouldn't like to get the feeling that he doesn't want to talk to us.'

Coleman put Graham's card into his shirt pocket. 'I'll make sure he gets back to you.'

'They must have got him out as soon as his missus called,' Graham said as they exited the shop.

'They didn't bother, Harry. He's still in there. They've just put him somewhere we couldn't see.' Wilson took out his phone and called O'Neill. 'Add Con Coleman to your list. I want everything we have on him.'


'MICHAEL, you have the brains of a louse.' Coleman's face was as red as his beard. 'You were told to be careful and you used a blue car. You should have taken a company van.'

'What are we going to do now?' McCluskey asked.

'We're going to knock up a delivery schedule that covers the areas where they saw you yesterday. We'll talk to the customers tomorrow.'

'How will I explain the use of the Hyundai?'

'The company van was giving gyp and we had to have it looked at by a mechanic. The deliveries were urgent, and you had to use your private car.'

'I'm sorry.'

'I didn't like the look of them two blokes. That Wilson is too bloody cool.'

'Mr Feeney is going to be pissed.'

'Don't worry about it. We should have realised that we were dealing with a different breed of peeler. The mistake is mine not yours and I'll stand up for it. Get busy on preparing the paperwork to cover yesterday's deliveries. I want you ready to talk to those bastards first thing tomorrow.'

# CHAPTER TWENTY-THREE

DCC Jennings had already established that Yvonne Davis was the enemy. For whatever reason, she had fallen under Wilson's spell. It would give him immense pleasure to destroy her, but he'd already received the message from the chief constable that she was to be treated with kid gloves. Someone at the top had decided that CS Davis was going places. Possibly into his job when he vacated it. Now he needed her to cooperate with him. He had mulled over McCann's instruction to retrieve the incriminating mobile phone. There was a time, when he was more junior, that he could slip unnoticed into evidence lockers, rifle through supposedly locked filing cabinets and surreptitiously remove items or files that the Circle, or his political masters, needed to disappear. Tampering with evidence was one of his skills. It was a different matter for the DCC to be unnoticed as he interfered with boxes of evidence or filing cabinets. He was still of the opinion that getting rid of Jackson was preferable to retrieving the stupid mobile phone, but he knew McCann of old and she would not rest until she felt totally safe. The phone was in the possession of Ian Wilson, which was a major obstacle. Even though he was the DCC of the PSNI and had spent his life developing the mystique that nothing was beyond his power, he'd decided he needed Davis to get the phone for him. There was a plan B, but he had shelved it for the moment.

'Please sit down, chief superintendent,' Jennings could see the apprehension on Davis's face and a wave of pleasure passed through him. It happened with all his underlings when they were called to a personal meeting. 'Thank you for coming so soon.' She looked tired as well as apprehensive. 'I was wondering how the investigation into the Lennon murder was going. The CC is concerned that we should actively contribute to the Garda Síochána's investigation.'

'It's early days.' She straightened her skirt. 'I spoke with DS Wilson yesterday and he was still looking into Lennon's background to find a motive for the attack.'

'The investigation is proceeding.'

'I expect a briefing this evening.'

'The CC and I are most anxious that you join us here in Castlereagh as soon as possible.'

Davis didn't respond.

'You have a great future ahead of you in the PSNI,' Jennings continued. 'I have no doubt that someday you'll move into this office and probably sooner rather than later. I've been giving some thought to retiring.'

'You're being too kind.'

'Nonsense, we've all been most impressed with your performance to date. The problem with a career like yours is what's known as the Icarus Effect. You are aware of the story of Icarus?'

She nodded.

'The closer you get to your objective the greater the risk you run of falling all the way back. One mistake is all it takes to lose everything. I've had some representations from Chief Superintendent Rodgers concerning Sergeant Jackson. I understand that Wilson has launched a European Arrest Warrant for him.'

'Yes, in relation to the attempted murder of DC Davidson.'

'We have no idea of the validity of that warrant in the context of Brexit. We may have to cancel it.'

'What would you like me to do?'

'I would like to see what evidence we have against Jackson. What physical evidence do we have of wrongdoing? Why did Jackson try to kill Davidson, if that was what he did? I wouldn't want us to make fools of ourselves in this pursuit of Jackson.'

'I'm sure DS Wilson would not have launched the arrest warrant without sufficient evidence.'

'I need to see physical evidence, chief superintendent.'

'I'll see what I can do.'

'Do better than that.'

'Is that all, sir?'

'You can go.' He watched her leave the room. She would relay every word to Wilson. Damn McCann for putting him in this position.


DAVIS STRODE TOWARDS THE LIFT. Why did she always feel like taking a shower when she left Jennings' office? Did she really want to occupy that same office some day? She had nearly blurted out that the real reason they wanted to drag Jackson back was to link him to the Carlisle murder and through him get at the real culprit, Helen McCann. She suspected Jennings had already made that link and his need to see the evidence had more to do with protecting McCann than with the integrity of the PSNI over a European Arrest Warrant. But he was right on one count. One slip by her and he would pounce. She was in a precarious position and it was plain that she could provide a significant service for him by letting him see the phone that linked Jackson and McCann to the murder of Jackie Carlisle.

'WHERE ARE we on McCluskey and Coleman?' Wilson had arrived back in Belfast in mid-afternoon and gone straight to the station.

O'Neill looked away from her computer. 'The difficult I can do straight away, the impossible takes a bit longer.'

'Message received. Check out the guy who owns Feeney's Builders Providers in Crossmaglen as well. Get me everything you can on them and put them on a whiteboard.' He felt a surge of energy. Since he'd joined Duane's investigation, he had the impression that everyone was holding something back. Now he was sure. McCluskey had been following them, which meant that someone was interested in who they met and spoke to. Whoever it was would eventually serve up McCluskey but not until he had a damn good reason for him being on their tail for the best part of the afternoon. The one positive effect of the search for McCluskey is that whoever wanted to know about their movements wouldn't try that again.

Wilson noticed that Moira was looking a little sheepish. He motioned her to follow him into his office.

'Out with it,' he said as soon as the door was closed.

'I may have made an error of judgement,' she said as she sat in the visitor's chair.

'Tell me.'

'I went to Best's club this morning.' She watched Wilson's eyebrows rise. 'I know. I know it was stupid. But I'd never met them, and I wanted to have the experience. I needed to see Hills in the flesh.'

'So far, it's not too stupid. Tell me the rest.'

'They gave me all this smart talk about auditioning for a job as a stripper and I felt I had to shoot something back. I told them that we had footage from a drone over Helen's Bay at the time that the BMW was torched. And that Hills appeared in the footage.'

'That was incredibly stupid. I can see that you might want to cast an eye over Hills but letting them get under your skin to the extent that you expose a possible piece of evidence, that's just not Moira McElvaney. You're supposed to be the intelligent one.'

'I've been kicking my own arse all afternoon.'

'What's done is done. How did Best and Hills receive the news?'

'I think Hills would have killed me on the spot, but Best was coolness itself.'

'That means they're going to try to establish whether or not you were bullshitting first.'

'And how will they do that?'

'You're not so naive as to think they don't have contacts in the PSNI. Best's main line of business is drugs. The money he makes on the streets is being laundered through his club and you can bet there's plenty over to keep bent coppers on his payroll. He has dozens, and one or two of them are in this station. He'll know soon enough that we have a handful of nothing.'

'I'm sorry, boss.'

'Best and Hills are very bad men. They ruin people's lives and they kill without conscience. They make the Rices and Gerry McGreary look like schoolboys.'

'Can't we take them off the streets?'

'Our Drugs colleagues bust the lower echelons of their organisation, but Best and Hills stay well out of sight. Look at Hills' army record, he likes killing people. Maybe he got a taste for it in Afghanistan, or maybe he was always a psychopath. Sooner or later he's going to leave a trail, and when he does, we'll have him.' Wilson would like to have believed his own words, but the truth was solving murders was a damn sight easier than putting the bastards behind bars. His phone rang. He was wanted upstairs.

DAVIS LOOKED MORE HARRIED than usual. She'd had a rocky start as the station chief, but she'd worked through that and seemed to have found her comfort zone. Lately, he'd noticed a return of the black marks under her eyes.

'Ma'am,' he said, slipping into her visitor's chair.

She closed a file and moved it aside. 'Does it ever stop?'

'Not as long as they keep cutting numbers and asking us to do more.' He put up his hand. 'Don't worry, I'm not going to ask you about DS Browne's replacement. I can see that you're harassed enough.'

'You don't know the half of it. At the last meeting with the counsellor, my former husband produced a list of twenty-eight things that are wrong with me. Twenty-eight! I was totally blindsided. I went there to discuss our relationship and he went to pour shit on me. I know I'm going to regret saying this, but I'm seriously contemplating killing the bastard.'

'I didn't hear that. You looked better when you weren't trying to get back with him. Sometimes a clean break is the best.'

'So says Mr Single with zero children. I care about my family. I don't give a damn about the character who used to snore in the bed next to me. Anyway, I didn't bring you here to listen to my tales of woe. I was called to HQ this afternoon for a conference with the DCC. He's worried about the validity of our European Arrest Warrant against Jackson in the context of Brexit.'

'How very noble of him.'

'He wants to see the evidence we have against Jackson. In particular, the physical evidence.'

'That man is as transparent as a pane of glass. I'm ninety per cent sure he was responsible for the disappearance of the file on the murder of Bridget Kelly. And I would be very surprised if that was the only case where he undermined the investigation. We've never officially logged McCann's phone as evidence, yet he knows about it.'

'That shouldn't surprise you, his network is extensive.'

'He'll disappear the phone if he gets his hands on it.'

'Then there's only one solution. We have to make the Carlisle investigation official.'

Wilson knew she was right. He was sure that the chief constable would agree when the evidence was put before him. Mind you, Baird wouldn't be so happy with the fact that a serving member of the PSNI Special Branch gave Carlisle the lethal hotshot. That was not going to sit well with the public. Neither would the fact that the investigation would be concentrated on the good and the great of the province. But the moment they announced the investigation, the cover-up would begin. The suicide verdict would be dead in the water, but a feasible alternative narrative would be developed. 'Maybe you're right. It's about time we stepped out into the open. As long as we all realise the risk that we're taking.'

Neither of them spoke.

Davis broke the silence. 'Twenty-four hours.'

'Aye, twenty-four hours.'

'What's happening with Lennon?'

'It's slow and we're not getting much help locally. We're still banging away on a motive.'

'Keep me informed.'

'It'll work out,' he said but didn't believe it. He stood and went to the door. 'Have you decided yet whether it's worth it?'

'Yes, but I'm not telling you.'

## CHAPTER TWENTY-FOUR

Wilson was alone in a snug at the Crown. He could have invited Moira along, but he'd had enough PSNI talk for one day. Despite all his protestations about how the job ultimately ruined the lives of everyone who committed to it, he knew he was one of those already on the road to ruin. He was happy to pit his wits against the likes of Best and Hills. They were a known quantity. Their motivation was money, pure and simple. They had no aspirations beyond filling their bank accounts and dreaming of a life of ease when their work was done. The only cloud on their horizon was that some other gang would come along and out-vicious them. Death at the hands of a rival was an occupational hazard. They had no fear of the law. They would simply use their ill-gotten gains to employ the finest legal brains. If that failed, they would serve their time and then take up where they left off. He sipped his Guinness. He didn't like drinking alone. And he didn't enjoy pitting himself against the likes of Helen McCann. He reminded himself of that wise saying: never take a knife to a gunfight. McCann was in a totally different league to Best and Hills. She wasn't in it for the money; she already had enough of that. She was in it for the power. There was an ideology behind what she was doing, and she would pursue that ideology to the end, even if it meant corrupting the body politic of the province and undermining the institutions of law and order. He didn't want her and her friends to win, but he wasn't sure that he could stop them. Jock McDevitt had tried to rile him by showing him the article in the *Chronicle* about Kate McCann becoming the next attorney general. When that became a reality, her mother might well be untouchable. He remembered Carlisle's story: the Judge, the Queen, the Lord, the Mogul, the Politician and the Policeman. All the bases were covered.

The door of the snug opened and Reid bounced in with a big smile on her face that faded when she saw Wilson's frown. 'Oh, oh, trouble at mill.'

He forced a smile. 'I should never drink alone. The dark thoughts take over.'

Reid ordered them both a drink and snuggled up close. 'I think I've been neglecting you lately.'

'Not true, you've been busy.' He took a deep breath. That damn elephant was padding around the snug using up all the air and smelling like hell.

'I'm going to dedicate myself to lifting your foul humour. What shall we do tonight?'

He knew what he wanted to do. He was sorry he had refused Jack's offer to take part in the raid on the diesel plant and the vodka distillery. What did that say about him? He was sitting beside a beautiful woman, who for some reason he couldn't fathom wanted to be with him, and he was thinking about sitting in the rear of a police van with six sweaty men stinking of testosterone. He thought himself pathetic. The elephant turned and looked at him, then disappeared. 'I think it's one of those evenings for a takeaway, a good bottle of red and something on Netflix.'

'That sounds a bit sedate. I was thinking of something a little wilder.'

Their drinks arrived and Reid paid for them.

'What's happened?' she asked after they had toasted.

'Long day.' He started on his second pint. It tasted better.

'There have been lots of long days, what is different about this one?'

He told her about his conversation with Davis.

'Only twenty-eight?' she said. 'My list might run to fifty.' She saw the look on his face. 'I'm only joking.'

'They've been married for thirty years and that's the way it ends.'

'You're worried we'll end up writing lists of each other's faults.'

'It's a possibility.'

'One thing I learned in the Congo: don't make plans. We're alive today and that's all that counts. We have no idea what's in the future so there's no point worrying about it.'

'I hope you're happy.'

'In as much as I can be.' She downed her drink. 'Finish up. The takeaway and the bottle of red are okay. We'll put Netflix on hold though. I think I need to show you how happy I am.'


IT WAS pitch-dark when the white garda van containing the raiding party turned onto a small road north of Lough Mucknoo in County Monaghan. Duane looked at the five officers dressed in combat gear seated along the side of the van. He considered the number excessive, but his boss, Chief Superintendent William Nolan, had insisted. Excessive was good. The people they were dealing with had bad reputations and nobody was to be hurt. A large red enforcer lay along the centre of the van. The diesel washing plant was in a former barn and had been under observation for several days. Two tankers had arrived and were ready to take the clean fuel. That meant that sixty thousand litres of fuel were about to be washed and put on the market. It showed a high level of confidence by the criminals.

The driver stopped at a prearranged spot and the back of the van opened. The remaining four hundred metres would be covered on foot. The men's nervous banter ceased, and Duane led the way into a nearby field. The men had already been briefed on their approach to the barn. They put their night-vision glasses on and struck off in the direction of the barn. Duane raised his hand to indicate a stop thirty metres from the barn. The building was built from concrete blocks and a large steel double door was the only entry and exit point. The fuel tankers were parked close to the door. There was no guard in sight. Duane motioned the officer carrying the enforcer forward. 'Hit the door and get out of the way.' He waved the rest of the men forward.

The officer swung the enforcer and the steel door parted with a loud crash, Duane and the raiding party poured through the gap screaming as they went. 'Police, on the floor, now, now.' The shouts filled the barn.

There were four men in the barn. Two were busy filtering the dye from the red diesel while the other two were drinking beer. Duane watched as they flung themselves onto the ground. Thankfully there was neither a sign of weapons nor resistance. It was obvious that they had been taken unawares. Duane approached the leader of the officers. 'Call the van up and deposit these boys in Dundalk. They speak to no one until I get there.'

Duane looked at the filters that had been set up. In the past, people had used cat litter, disposable nappies and tampons crammed into traffic cones as the filters to remove the red dye. This plant used proper filters that would process the fuel in eight or so hours. Some of the dye would still be present, but it would be invisible to the naked eye. The four men were handcuffed and led away. A clean-up crew would arrive within the hour to take control of the diesel and the vehicles. It was going to be an expensive night for the criminals. Job done, the team relaxed and Duane waited to hear the result of the raid on the vodka distillery.

# CHAPTER TWENTY-FIVE

Wilson woke and disentangled himself from Reid's arms. The Carlisle investigation was getting to him. He desperately wanted to put Jackson and McCann away but had to face the reality that it was going to be far from easy. He'd already put in twenty years on the force and that was as much as many could take. He was meeting more and more colleagues at every level who couldn't stand the pressures of police work. Loved ones often suffered as much as the officers themselves. Davis was struggling again, and he didn't have the capacity to help her. Moira had disappeared into herself since she'd taken on the Carlisle file. O'Neill was so self-contained he wondered whether anything touched her. Graham was so bound up with raising his girls that the job had become simply a means to an end. That might change further down the road. He turned and kissed Reid. She snuggled closer. Last night, he had needed to be held and she had been there. It was like she always knew what he needed. He slipped out of bed and put on his running gear.

REID HAD BEEN CLIMBING out of the shower when he'd

returned from his run. He'd pushed himself hard and felt energised by the exercise. He had grabbed her, kissed her passionately and pulled her back into the shower. This day is off to a good start, he thought as he sat down for breakfast. It could only go downhill.

'Thank God you've ditched that dark humour of last night.' She put a plate of scrambled egg in front of him.

'Dark humour goes with my job. I don't suppose you ever feel futility.'

'Oh God no, cutting up dead bodies is a barrel of monkeys. Going to the hospital every morning is as exciting as visiting Disneyland. If you look at the mental breakdown statistics, I think you might find that pathologists rank higher than police officers. That aside, what's on your mind?'

'We're going to have to go public on the Carlisle investigation.'

'What's so bad about that?'

'Forewarned is forearmed, and they have a lot of resources to arm themselves with. They appear to know that we have the phone that McCann received the message from Jackson on. Davis had a conference with Jennings yesterday, and while he didn't mention the phone specifically, he asked for all the physical evidence against Jackson. He used the validity of the European Arrest Warrant in the context of Brexit as an excuse. I think he means to disappear the phone. He has a history of being about the place when vital evidence has disappeared. The only way I can block him is to have Baird make the investigation official.' He forked some scrambled egg into his mouth.

'Then you'll have additional resources.'

'I'll need them. As soon as we announce we're looking into Carlisle's death, the shredding machines will be running hot. We have nowhere near enough evidence.'

'It'll be a race between you. The black mood means you don't think you can win.' She finished her coffee and put her plate and cup in the dishwasher. 'I've met a lot of people who saw you play rugby. They all mention that you gave a hundred per cent in every game, but I doubt you ever won any one game on your own. You had fourteen other players that you could depend on. And even then, you didn't win every game.' She stood behind him, put her arms around his neck and kissed the top of his head. 'Give it your best shot. If that means making the investigation official go for it.'

He turned and kissed her.

'And no more dark moods.' She picked up her coat and walked to the door.

'No promises,' he said after the door closed.

DARAGH FLYNN WAS NURSING the mother of all hangovers as he drove to work. He'd spent half the night playing online poker while drinking whiskey. He contemplated calling in sick but that might be risky with Duane in town. He had made enquiries about Duane but nobody seemed to know much detail about him. What they did know was that he wasn't someone to mess with.

Flynn was surprised to find a sign pointing him away from the parking spaces directly in front of the station. As a DI he had a reserved spot. He cursed and made his way to a parking spot around the side of the station before walking back. Two white police vans with Dublin licence plates were parked across the reserved parking spaces. Someone was going to get a rocket up their arse for taking his spot.

As soon as he entered the station, he noticed there was a lot more activity than usual. 'What's up?' he asked the duty sergeant.

'Crowd down from Dublin, sir. The cafeteria is full of them having breakfast.'

'What are they doing here?'

'They raided a red diesel plant and a vodka distillery last

night. We have six men in the cells and a mountain of confiscated material all over the place.'

Flynn's heart had already gone into overdrive. 'Why didn't I know about these raids?'

'No idea, sir. Maybe you should ask the chief super.'

'Where's Duane?'

'He was out with the raid on the diesel plant. He'll be in later.'

The room began to spin, and Flynn had difficulty staying on his feet.

'You don't look too good, sir,' the duty sergeant said.

'No, I'm a bit banjaxed. It's just a dose of something.' He should have expected this, but he hadn't. Feeney would be hopping mad about the raids. The closing of a diesel plant and a vodka operation in one fell swoop was going to hurt. Six men in the cells would be nothing. The most they would get would be a couple of months if even that. Feeney would feel the main pain and it would be in his pocket. The duty sergeant was still staring at him. Flynn looked in the direction of the Lennon incident room, then turned and left the station. He needed time to think.

He'd cost Feeney a lot and knew there would be a brutal response. Would Feeney dare to murder a serving garda officer? Who was he kidding? Feeney would kill his grandmother for the price of a pint. Another worry was that the raids had been carried out without the knowledge or under the direction of the Dundalk station. That meant Dundalk wasn't to be trusted and the success of the operations proved it. There would be a witch-hunt and sooner or later that would shine a light in his direction. He reached his car, jumped in and drove away quickly. He had no idea where he was going or indeed whether there was anywhere he could go. The hunt would soon be on for him. Who would find him first? Gambling had got him into this mess, but his betting debts paled into insignificance against the possibility of being skewered by Feeney or of being handed a stiff jail sentence. The priority was to evade both sides for a while so that he could think.

By a quirk of fate, it was payday, which meant three and a half thousand euro had just been lodged into his account. The amount would give him some breathing space. He drove to his bank and withdrew all his cash. He wouldn't be able to use his debit or credit cards if he didn't want to be found. He drove towards his house in Mount Street but parked around the corner when he arrived. The raids had happened eight hours ago, which meant that Feeney already knew. As soon as he turned the corner, he saw the car with two men inside parked fifty metres from his front gate. They hadn't been there when he'd left; otherwise he would have been picked up already. Collecting his passport and packing a bag were now out of the question. So far, he'd been lucky. They probably just missed him at the station as well. Feeney would already have the word out on him and Feeney's connection with dissident republicans covered the whole island.

Flynn retraced his steps to the car. He needed to get out of Dundalk and as far away from Feeney as possible. Under normal circumstances, he could hide out with his in-laws in Tipperary, but he wouldn't be welcome there. He'd go west, Mayo or Sligo, lie low and make a plan. He had something to trade.

# CHAPTER TWENTY-SIX

Everyone was at their desk when Wilson entered the squad room. O'Neill motioned to him.

'Morning, boss,' she said as he stood beside her desk. She handed him two buff-coloured folders. 'Sheets on McCluskey and Coleman.'

Wilson took the folders. 'Give me the highlights.'

Graham left his desk and joined them.

'Both were members of the South Armagh Battalion of the IRA. They were in Long Kesh together and were released following the Good Friday Agreement. We have plenty of intel on them, but it all dates from the 1990s. Since their release, they appear to have kept their noses clean.'

Wilson flicked through the files. The Lennon investigation was getting interesting. 'Good work, Siobhan.' He turned to Graham. 'We're off to Dundalk as soon as I've had a word with Moira. I'll be ready in a half-hour.'

Wilson motioned Moira to the visitor's chair in his office. He briefed her on the meeting between Davis and Jennings. 'I've been given twenty-four hours to hand over the evidence against Jackson.'

'So, he'll have all the statements and the phone. He'll

destroy that evidence. What if he's the police officer in Carlisle's story?'

Wilson had wondered the same thing. In effect it could be anyone, even the CC, but his money was on Jennings. The connection with McCann and her friends would explain Jennings' meteoric career. 'He'd be a suspect, but there are others.'

'I know you've decided something. What is it?'

'I'm going to Baird with what we've got. It's about time we went public on this.'

'It's a risky strategy.'

'I know. As soon as the story breaks, evidence will start disappearing like it's an endangered species. But it also means that the investigation will be properly resourced and funded.'

'That might not help if there's no evidence to find.'

'There's another problem. The investigation into Carlisle's death could be wider than the murder. There are some very powerful people involved and they are not going to sit on their hands while we investigate them.'

'It'll be dangerous.'

'That it will. They murdered a major political figure and we're still in the dark over Grant and Malone. They won't hesitate to increase the body count. And nobody on the investigation will be safe.'

'I've already accepted that. Don't let Baird take it away from us.'

'I'll try, but no promises. There's a fifty-fifty chance he won't approve an investigation. Carlisle's death has already been ruled a suicide. It'll take balls to reverse the coroner's verdict.'

'It's been done before.'

'Under different circumstances.' Wilson stood. 'I wish we didn't have to go this road.'

.  .  .

DUNDALK GARDA STATION was a hive of activity when Wilson and Graham arrived. There was no sign of either Duane or Flynn when they entered the Lennon incident room. Wilson located a sergeant and approached him. 'Are you in charge today?'

'Looks like it. I'm DS James Guiney.'

'Where's DCI Duane?'

'He's away to Dublin,' Guiney said. 'Giving a briefing to the higher-ups on the raids last night.'

'How did the operation go?'

'They closed down a fuel laundry and a vodka distillery, and they bagged two fuel transporters and six men. We've to wait for DCI Duane to return before we start the interrogations. There are two solicitors in the waiting room ready to assist their clients.'

Wilson had been there before. Whoever ran the operation would have provided the solicitors to ensure that the minions didn't talk and simply accepted the blame. There would be no mention of someone at the top. 'When do you expect him back?'

'Sure the man is a law unto himself. We have no idea when we'll be seeing him.'

'Where's DI Flynn?'

'The duty sergeant says he turned up earlier, looking like something the cat dragged in. Then he walked back out and disappeared off home. Well, that's what the sergeant thinks away.'

'He didn't set up a command before he left?'

'No, sir. He came and went in the same breath.'

'Great. I guess we'll have a cuppa and decide how we can usefully spend our day.'

'You'll have to fight the gang from Dublin for whatever's left in the cafeteria. Them fellas would eat a cow if you gave them the chance.'

. . .

GRAHAM PLACED two coffees and a piece of lemon cake on the table. 'It's the last piece of cake,' he said as he sat down.

'You're welcome to it,' Wilson sipped the coffee. The tactical teams had recently departed having done their impression of a pack of ravenous wolves. He had tried to call both Duane and Flynn, but neither was picking up. It was a hell of a way to run a murder investigation but since the Garda Síochána was in the driving seat there wasn't much he could do.

'What do we do now, boss?' Graham asked, stuffing half the cake into his mouth.

'We start where we left off yesterday. McCluskey hasn't bothered to telephone us so we're obliged to visit his workplace a second time. This time we don't do nice cop.' Wilson's coat was on the chair behind him and he could feel something sticking into his back. He put his hand back and pulled out the calendar he had taken from Lennon's house. It was a cheap book-sized calendar with the logo of St Patrick's Church, Parish of Upper Creggan on the front cover. Inside the cover, Brian Lennon had added his name and address. The calendar contained a page for each month and each was headed by an appropriate passage from the Holy Book. It had been well used. Some days had been labelled 'shopping' or 'mart day'. Others had had names and times or telephone numbers jotted under them. The days of the month of August were particularly annotated and Wilson knew why when he noticed 'Dad's funeral' written diagonally under the twenty-first. As soon as Duane returned, he would give him the calendar and get his team to run down the dates, times and names that could be relevant to the investigation. He heard a cough and looked up to see that Graham had finished while he had been engrossed in the minutia of Lennon's life. Wilson gulped his coffee, which was cold, then stood and took his overcoat from the chair. 'Okay, Harry. Time to head north again and see what was on McCluskey's mind when he was following us around.'

• • •

THEY WERE BACK in Crossmaglen and parked in front of Feeney's Builders Providers. Wilson led the way in and went straight to the counter, where there was the usual clientele of boiler-suited men. A counterman ran upstairs as soon as he saw Wilson enter. He knocked at a door and as he opened it Wilson could hear an ongoing heated argument. The door closed but the raised voices were still partly audible. Wilson waited. The voices trailed off and eventually Con Coleman exited the office with the counterman and made his way to where Wilson and Graham stood.

'Good afternoon, Mr Coleman,' Wilson said. 'I'm afraid we didn't make ourselves clear on our last visit. Our desire to speak to Mr McCluskey was non-negotiable. We expected a call at the latest this morning; however, it seems we were overly optimistic. I want to speak to Michael McCluskey now. Go get him.'

'I'm afraid I can't.'

'Then Mr McCluskey had better be completely inca-pacitated.'

The door of Coleman's office opened, and a large middle-aged man looked down at the two police officers. When Wilson looked up, the man retreated into the office.

'Michael is not available.'

'Not good enough,' Wilson said. 'Where is he?'

'In Dundalk Garda Station,' Coleman said. 'He was arrested last night.'

'On what charge?' Wilson asked.

'I'm not sure. We're waiting to hear from his solicitor.'

'He wasn't arrested on a police raid by any chance?'

'That appears to be the situation.'

'That gentleman who just left your office and looked down on us, who is he?'

'I didn't see him.'

'Middle-aged, broad. You were possibly just speaking with him.'

'That would be Mr Feeney, the owner.'

'Mr Feeney didn't sound too pleased.'

Coleman didn't comment.

'We'll talk again, Mr Coleman. I'm pretty certain of that.'

'WHERE TO, BOSS?' Graham asked when they were back in their car.

'Back across that bloody border, Harry. Now that McCluskey is in custody, it's the perfect time to have a word with him.'

DUANE HADN'T SLEPT in thirty hours. After the successful raids, he'd travelled to Dublin to brief CS Nolan, and then the minister. It was congratulations all round for him and the tactical teams. For Duane it was a pyrrhic victory. They'd damaged the organised crime group that operated on both sides of the border, but they hadn't finished them off. The distillery would be up and running within two weeks and the fuel laundering would continue as long as the price differential between red and clear diesel persisted. He'd managed a quick breakfast after his conference with the minister before heading north to Dundalk to begin the interrogation of the six men arrested during the raids. He hadn't been surprised to find the two solicitors sitting patiently in the reception area. There was a good chance that none of the arrested men would comment on their activities and that they would be released on bail before the day was out. The interrogations had to go ahead as a matter of course and Duane started straight away. He was exiting one of the interview rooms when Wilson entered the reception area.

Duane looked at his watch. 'This is a fine time to arrive.'

'We were here a few hours ago but neither you nor Flynn was anywhere to be seen. Anyway, you look like death warmed over so I'm not going to argue with you.'

'Let's go to my office.'

They passed through the incident room and settled into Duane's office.

'I'm buggered,' Duane yawned. 'I'm not as young as I used to be.'

'None of us are,' Wilson said. 'This business with the raids is a bit of a sideshow. We need to get on with finding Lennon's murderer.'

'Tell me about it. I have people in Dublin trying to pull me in four different directions. They all think I work exclusively for them.'

'In the meantime, we're going nowhere on the investigation.'

'I wouldn't say that. Have your forensic boys finished with the Lennon house?'

Wilson looked at Graham.

Graham's face fell. 'The report is due today, but early indications are that they found nothing useful.'

'Maybe I did though.' Wilson pulled the calendar from his pocket. 'Lennon may not have had a diary, but he marked events directly on this calendar.' He passed it to Duane. 'Get your lads to make a copy for me and have them run down the names and numbers annotated on the dates.'

Duane flipped through the calendar. 'This is going to take a while.'

'Do they have something else to do?'

'No, you're right. We must follow up every possible lead. I'll get them on it straight away.'

'What about Flynn? Someone should be in charge here if you're going to be gallivanting all over the place.'

'We appear to have a missing DI. Nobody has seen him

since this morning. If he doesn't show up soon, we'll have to canvas the hospitals.'

'What about calling his wife?'

'It appears that Mrs Flynn is on an extended visit to her parents in Tipperary. I must get busy on processing the men we arrested last night. I don't think we're going to get much from them, but you never know, and there are people in Dublin who are getting anxious about the level of organised crime in this area.'

'You have a guy called Michael McCluskey in the cells. When you're finished with him, I'd like to have a chat with him.'

'Is he connected to Lennon?'

'I don't know, but he's the guy who was dogging us a couple of days ago.'

'Then McCluskey will be next on the list.' Duane motioned DS Guiney to join them. 'Get the lads to put a link into the interview room. Detective Superintendent Wilson wants to view the first interview. And tell the duty sergeant to bring McCluskey up from the cells and install him.' He turned towards Wilson. 'That suit you, Ian?'

Wilson nodded.

# CHAPTER TWENTY-SEVEN

Most police interview rooms look like they were designed by an IKEA architect and Dundalk's were no different: white walls, a wooden table with four metallic chairs set around it. The CCTV camera was set high in the corner of the room facing the person to be interviewed and an audio recording device was on the table. McCluskey looked fresh for a man who had spent much of the night and a morning in the cells. Wilson knew that this wasn't McCluskey's first dance, but the man's relaxed manner showed that he had no fear of the police or probably of any other institution representing the law. If it is true that the face you end with is the face that your life has earned, then McCluskey had had a hard life. He had been there, wherever that was, and he had survived. His head was shaven, his jaw was strong and his eyes flicked occasionally to the camera. Sitting beside him, Michael Coyle looked pale and soft against the strength of his client.

Duane entered the room along with a young female officer. He tossed a folder on the table and sat facing McCluskey. He nodded at his companion and she started the recording.

'Detective Chief Inspector Jack Duane and Detective Garda Meg Hearney,' she said.

The solicitor said his name. McCluskey remained silent.

'Let's not piss about, Michael,' Duane said. 'We need to get on with this. You know the procedure.'

McCluskey continued to look straight ahead.

Duane looked at the solicitor, who whispered in McCluskey's ear.

'Michael McCluskey.'

'That's a good boy, Michael,' Duane said. 'You were arrested last night while in the process of distilling illegal liquor. A series of labels were found which indicate that you intended to furnish fake vodka. Would you like to tell us about your operation?'

'No comment.'

Duane opened the file. 'You have a chequered history. I have a copy of your PSNI file here and you've been a very bad boy. Arrested twice for GBH and three times for ABH. Some prison time in Long Kesh.'

'Those cases were dropped,' the solicitor said and wrote a note on his pad. 'And Mr McCluskey was for a period a polit-ical prisoner.'

Duane closed the file. 'The stuff you're putting into bottles with branded labels on them can do people harm.'

'No comment.'

'I wish to apply for police bail for my client,' the solicitor said. 'His offence is relatively minor.'

Duane sighed and nodded at Hearney, who stood.

'Would you please stand, Mr McCluskey,' she said.

McCluskey remained sitting.

'You don't stand,' Duane said. 'You stay here until you do.'

McCluskey looked at his solicitor, who nodded. He rose in slow motion.

'Michael McCluskey, I am arresting you for offences under the Trademarks Act 1996 relating to the sale and supply of counterfeit items. You do not have to say anything, but what you do say will be recorded and may be used in evidence against you.'

The solicitor closed his notebook. 'I'll arrange for Mr McCluskey's bail.'

'Not so fast,' Duane said. 'Mr McCluskey is the resident of another jurisdiction. I think the issue of bail should be referred to a judge. In the meantime, he can stay here with us.'

'I think your reaction is a little excessive,' the solicitor said. 'I would expect that Mr McCluskey is looking at a non-custodial sentence, and therefore holding him is inappropriate.'

Duane stood. 'You might explain to your client what constitutes appropriate behaviour.'

McCluskey rose.

Duane nodded at Hearney, who switched off the recording equipment. 'Stay where you are, Michael. A couple of officers from the PSNI want a word with you before you head back to the cells.'

When Duane re-entered the incident room, Wilson gave him a silent clap. 'You handled that pretty well. You're not quite over the hill.'

'I think McCluskey is the toughest of the bunch,' Duane said. 'If you're not tough when you're sent to Long Kesh, you're tough when you get out. None of the others will say a word. They've been well drilled. They know that, despite the custodial sentences available, the judges generally give suspended sentences in relation to the Trademarks Act. It's only the Americans who have custodial sentences up to ten years and millions of dollars in fines. I'm going to rush through the others now and then get back to Dublin for a good night's rest. In the meantime, McCluskey is all yours.'

McCluskey was wearing a sullen expression when

Wilson and Graham entered the interview room. The solicitor was still at his client's side.

Graham introduced Wilson and himself. 'This is a preliminary interview,' Graham said. 'And as such will not be recorded.'

'Is this interview in relation to the charges brought against my client by An Garda Síochána?'

'No, it's related to another matter entirely,' Wilson said.

The solicitor frowned. 'I don't understand. My client is here on charges relating to a breach of the Trademarks Act. That breach took place outside the PSNI's jurisdiction.'

'Absolutely,' Wilson said. 'And if Mr McCluskey doesn't want to talk to us, we'll be outside when he's bailed and delighted to accompany him back across the border. Once there, we'll take him to Newry PSNI Station where we'll continue this interview.'

'Most unusual,' the solicitor said.

'We attempted to speak with Mr McCluskey at his place of employment yesterday, but unfortunately he was out on a delivery. DC Graham left his card with a request for Mr McCluskey to call in order to arrange a time for an interview. We happened to be in this station at the same time as Mr McCluskey, so it seemed opportune to have a few words.'

'I reserve the right to terminate this interview at any point,' the solicitor said.

'Mr McCluskey,' Wilson leaned forward. 'Two days ago, DC Graham and I were conducting a series of interviews in Crossmaglen concerning the murder of a resident called Brian Lennon.'

McCluskey remained immobile.

'In the course of our enquiries, we noticed that a blue Hyundai was tailing us. I took the registration and established that your wife is the owner. We spoke to her yesterday and she told us that you were driving her car on the day in question. We'd like to know why you were following us.'

'I wasn't following you,' McCluskey said. 'Crossmaglen is a small place. It's not unusual to run into people more than once in the course of a day.'

'So your wife says. But several times I noticed you sitting in your car as though you were on surveillance. I'm asking myself why you should be so interested in our movements, particularly when we were conducting a murder enquiry.'

'You've got it wrong. I was out on deliveries. The van had broken down and I was forced to use the wife's car. My manager, Con Coleman, will be able to show you the delivery dockets.'

'I'm sure he will.' Wilson looked at the solicitor. 'I think that your legal adviser will advise of the serious nature of a charge of impeding the police in the course of an investigation. If I find that I'm right, you won't be looking at a suspended sentence.'

The solicitor put away his notebook. 'I will not accept you threatening my client. We're finished here. Mr McCluskey answered all your questions openly and honestly. All you've done is to threaten him in return for his cooperation.' He stood up and motioned McCluskey to do the same.

'It's okay, we know where to find you,' Wilson said.

'And we know where to find you,' McCluskey said before his solicitor could stop him.

WILSON AND GRAHAM went back to the incident room.

Duane was sitting at a computer screen showing the empty interview room. 'Interesting,' he said.

'I thought you were interviewing the other men,' Wilson said.

'I left them to Guiney. They're foot soldiers. They'll clam up and reply, 'No comment' to all the questions and then we'll bail them like they expect.'

'Can we concentrate on the Lennon murder?'

Duane nodded at two young detectives beavering away in the corner. 'They're working on your calendar. It's the best chance of a breakthrough.' He picked up the original calendar from the table in front of him and tossed it to Wilson. 'We'll work on the copies.'

Wilson caught the calendar and put it in his inside pocket. 'You always knew that McCluskey was in Long Kesh.'

'I know everything about Michael McCluskey. The question is: do you like him for the Lennon murder?'

'I wouldn't make him my prime suspect, but he's certainly a person of interest.'

'We're also very interested in McCluskey.'

Duane's eyes were tired but there was a glint there that bothered Wilson. 'I asked you this before, Jack. Are you telling me everything you know about Lennon's murder?'

Duane repeated the cross-on-the-heart procedure. 'You know everything I know about the murder.'

'But I don't know everything you know.'

'You're a smart man, Ian.' Duane stood. 'We'll keep McCluskey as long as we can, but I'll bet his solicitor is already working to get him out without appearing before a judge. I've got to get back to Dublin and sleep, otherwise I'll fall down.'

# CHAPTER TWENTY-EIGHT

Con Coleman had managed to move the argument that had raged in his office to Feeney's house, an imposing Texan-style residence on the edge of town. Mrs Feeney had made herself scarce on a hastily planned shopping trip to Belfast. She had experienced Storm Feeney enough times to know it was safest to get herself out of its path.

'I want that fucker's head on a pole.' Feeney had been drinking since he learned about the raids, and he was slurring his words. 'Find the bastard.'

'He's not at Dundalk Garda Station and I have two men posted outside his house,' Coleman said. 'Sooner or later he'll appear, and we'll pick him up.'

Feeney downed his whiskey and poured himself another. Coleman knew from experience that his boss was dangerous in this mood. 'Calm down, Tommy, and for God's sake give the whiskey bottle a rest. We have to think our way out of this.'

Feeney slugged back half a glass of whiskey. 'Never trust a bent copper. I should have known better. I want that fucker in the bog by tonight.'

'Think about it from their angle. Every raid on our operations has been a screw-up. Duane is a smart bastard and it didn't take him long to figure out that someone in Dundalk Garda Station was talking. They probably don't even know that it's Flynn.'

'He's a gambling addict, his wife has left him and the bank is about to foreclose on his house. He'd sell his children for a sound tip on the three o'clock at Kempton. He'll sell us down the river without batting an eyelid. Whether they know about him or not, he has to go.'

'He owes us more than a hundred grand.'

'Don't talk to me about chicken feed. Flynn knows too much. Last night emphasises that his luck has run out. Get the fuck out there and find him. Put the word out to our friends in Belfast and Dublin.'

Coleman knew that arguing was useless. Once Tommy Feeney made his mind up, nothing could change it.

FLYNN HAD DRIVEN south and skirted round Dublin before heading west on the M4. For once, gambling was not the first thing on his mind. His survival trumped gambling every time. Feeney was a hothead and would be going apeshit and blaming Flynn for the raids on his business. He needed to find a place to lie low and hope that Feeney's anger would eventually blow itself out. He'd ring the station tomorrow and say that one of his children was ill in Tipperary and he'd be back shortly. In a few days, he'd contact Coleman and see how the land was lying.

He reached Galway in mid-afternoon. He stopped at a large shopping centre and bought himself some underwear, a pair of black cotton pants, three T-shirts and a sweater. He loaded up with enough provisions for several days. He would have to steer clear of big cities like Galway for a while as Feeney's tentacles stretched throughout the country.

He continued west without a plan. Outside the small village of Barna, he saw a group of deserted holiday cottages on a side road leading to the sea. He stopped at a local shop and enquired about renting a cottage. The shopkeeper, who also managed the letting of the cottages, was delighted to rent one off-season. Flynn stowed his car out of sight and checked out his new digs before pouring himself a large whiskey. He'd spent six hours alone in his car thinking about his future. Whatever way he looked at it, he was fucked.

WILSON SPENT the short trip back to Belfast in silence. There was something nibbling away at the back of his mind and he couldn't put his finger on it. It had something to do with why he'd had to ask Duane whether he had all the information on the Lennon murder. There had to be a concrete reason why someone wanted to kill Brian Lennon. He hadn't had time to examine the pathologist's report, the garda CSI report on the murder scene and the FSNI report on Lennon's home in detail. Given his cursory examination, he could not discern any possible motive for murdering Brian Lennon. There was no point in moving on to consider means and opportunity until they had the motive. He had an uneasy feeling about McCluskey. He wouldn't be surprised if he had played some part in the murder. But then again what motive did McCluskey have? Despite his protestations, he had been following Wilson and Graham as they went about their business in Crossmaglen. Why? Someone wanted to know who they met and talked with. Did one of the six men involved in the murder have the motive or was everyone in Crossmaglen mad with a man universally described as harmless? It didn't make sense. Mind you, Wilson had seen plenty during his career that didn't make sense. The Good Friday Agreement that led to McCluskey and Coleman being released in 2001 along with all the other political prisoners was an act that only made sense in the context of an end to conflict. But he had been responsible for putting a number of those freed men in jail and he wasn't happy that they were out and walking the streets. He leaned back and closed his eyes. He hated his inability to turn off.

He took a couple of deep breaths to clear his mind but found it quickly filled back up with the Judge, the Queen, the Mogul, the Lord, the Politician and the Policeman. They could all be a figment of Carlisle's imagination or they could be the reason Carlisle had to be silenced. It boggled his mind that there might have been an elite group orchestrating criminal activities during his entire career as a policeman. He couldn't really believe it, but three young men had been murdered because they were about to expose corrupt practices at the heart of government. On the face of it, Sammy Rice was responsible for their deaths. Rice was now missing presumed dead. There was no presumed about it as Richie Simpson had admitted to putting a bullet into Rice's head. Rice wasn't capable of setting up a sophisticated system of bleeding money from government contracts. But Helen McCann had the financial acumen and ability to establish such a scheme. Where was the evidence though? McCann would laugh in his face if he proposed such a theory. She was a well-respected figure, a major business leader. Her husband had been a pillar of the judicial system. Her daughter was about to become the highest law officer in the province. Where was his head? The phone was evidence, but it wasn't nearly enough to put her in the dock. Carlisle and probably Rice had been cleaned up. There were no loose ends that he could see. If he were chief constable, and some idiot blundered into his office with such a phantasmagorical tale, he'd send for the psychiatrist.

Wilson opened his eyes and saw that they were close to the station. He wished the Carlisle investigation and the pursuit of Helen McCann were just parts of a bad dream.

# CHAPTER TWENTY-NINE

Wilson stood at the top of the squad room with his small team facing him. 'What am I missing?' He tapped the photo of Brian Lennon on the whiteboard and looked at O'Neill. 'Siobhan, you've been through his life from birth to death. Why did someone want him dead?'

'Search me, boss. He was a regular guy. He worked on the farm during the week and had a few drinks at the weekend. He never applied for a passport, so he never travelled abroad. He may have gone to England or Scotland, but I can find no record of it. He played a bit of football and socialised with the team.'

'Have you got his bank statements?' Wilson asked.

'Yes, and I don't think anyone murdered him for the contents of his current account. There's a farm account that shows an excess of four thousand, six hundred and fifty pounds. That's mainly because they managed to sell some hay at the end of the year. I've spoken with their accountant and he told me they were just scraping by.'

'What's the value of the land?'

'I've had a look at that.' She shuffled some papers. 'The farm is forty-eight acres and has very little road frontage.

There's a small cottage and a stone barn on the property. An estate agent in the area estimated something around two hundred and fifty thousand pounds.'

'Not a fortune,' Graham said. 'And anyway, that sum will be divided among a number of inheritors.'

'Unless a will appears,' Moira said.

'It's unlikely,' Wilson said. 'But if one did appear, at least it would give us a suspect. One last thing.' He removed the calendar from his pocket and handed it to O'Neill. 'Duane's team in Dundalk are examining the annotations on the calendar. I want you to do the same.'

'Isn't that covering the same ground twice?' Moira asked.

'It is, but it's all we have to go on. Anyone got any other suggestions of where we go from here?'

'Home,' Graham said hopefully.

'Right you are, Harry. There's no point standing here flogging a dead horse. Think about a motive in your off-duty hours.'

'Do we have off-duty hours?' Moira said.

'Off home with you.' He ambled towards his office and almost closed the door in Moira's face. 'Don't you have a home to go to?'

She went inside and sat down. 'Do you still have the bottle in the bottom drawer?'

He bent and came up with a bottle of Jameson and two glasses. He put a generous measure into each glass. They toasted and drank. 'You look tired.'

'Have you looked at Siobhan and Harry? We all look tired, including you.'

'How can I be tired when I'm just back from a holiday? I'm joking, sleeping has been an issue.'

'Tell me about it. I generally nod off at around two in the morning.'

'You've caught the Helen McCann bug.'

'That woman is dirty and dangerous. She's also smart and

if Carlisle's fairy story is right, she's the central string in this province's DNA. I checked with Belfast International by the way and although the plane left, neither McCann nor Jackson was on board.'

'They're still in Belfast?'

'McCann left the Merchant and gave a forwarding address of Coleville House in Ballymoney.'

'Home of the Lattimers. I assume wedding planning is on the agenda.'

'So, you're not over Kate yet?'

'Totally, but you'll have to permit me a little pique now and then.'

She drained her glass and presented it for a refill. 'Only a small one, it'll help me sleep.'

Wilson gave them both a small measure. 'It's never worked with me. How are things at home?'

'My mother is in the process of forgiving me for ruining my life. I've promised to go home for a weekend soon. Dad is all right with it.'

'Where is the transcript that Gowan prepared from Carlisle's notebook?'

'In my desk.'

'Let me have it.'

She went to her desk and returned with Gowan's folder. 'Not exactly bedtime reading.' She handed the folder over. 'If I were an editor in a publishing house, I'd entitle it Ramblings of a Fevered Mind.'

'You never know where you might find the key that opens the treasure chest.' He downed his drink and motioned her to do the same. 'Off home with you, I have to prune our budget still further.'

He switched on his computer and had just logged on when he saw CS Davis brush past the departing Moira and head for his office.

'Do you have time for a night cap?' she asked, dropping into his visitor's chair.

The bottle was still on his desk. 'As long as it's just the one.' He produced a fresh glass and poured her a measure.

'Just the one is perfect.'

'It's all getting to you.' He toasted her.

'I'm emotionally drained.' She sipped her drink. 'I envy these women who claim they have it all, the high-flying job and the perfect family. You don't know how lucky you are.'

'I'm sure you wouldn't give them up.'

'I'm not. When I thought I was finished with Richard, I didn't feel sad. In fact, I was elated. It felt like a little bubble of pressure in my brain had broken. The bubble is back. And I think I rather hate him now.'

'I wish I could help.'

'The DCC's office called and asked when they could expect to receive what they called the Jackson file. We both know what they really mean. Have you made up your mind?'

He swirled the whiskey in his glass. 'No.'

'I'm taking two days' leave on family grounds. That gives you a bit more time. Use it well because as soon as I return, there's bound to be half a dozen messages from the DCC.'

'I don't like adding to the pressure on you.' He wanted to advise her to keep her weapon locked up for both her own sake and her husband's. More than one spouse had been shot with an official weapon. 'I'll have a decision by the time you get back.'

She finished her drink, put the glass on his desk and pushed herself out of the chair. 'I'm away home, or whatever it is.'

'Keep the faith,' he said to her retreating back.

'Aye.'


McDEVITT HAD SPENT the day trying to get something out of

the gardaí in Dundalk. He'd learned that there had been a couple of successful raids the previous night on a fuel laundering operation and an illegal distillery. That was not the kind of news that would put him on the front page. Neither would a story about how young Keating had got beaten up outside a well-known nightspot. The only story with legs was the murder of Brian Lennon, but the investigation seemed to be proceeding very slowly. He was not inclined to visit Crossmaglen on his own. He'd been down the beaten-up route before and he had no desire to go there again. He hadn't managed to run into Wilson in Dundalk, and it didn't look like he was Wilson's best friend. Not for the first time, he felt like he'd just wasted a day. He had been about to return to Belfast when he passed by Louth County Hospital and decided to see how Keating was getting on.

'How are you doing?' McDevitt sat in the chair beside Keating's bed. Keating looked like he'd gone three rounds with Conor McGregor. The bruises on his face were blue-yellow and his eyes were reduced to slits.

He turned his head away from McDevitt and slurred, 'Fuck off.'

'I'm sorry, genuinely. I didn't think it would end like this. The guards think it might have been about a woman.'

Keating turned back to McDevitt. 'It was about you.'

McDevitt thought as much. 'Did you recognise them?'

'Balaclavas.'

'Accents?'

'South Armagh.'

'Message?'

'Next time, worse.'

'Do you think it has something to do with Lennon?'

Keating nodded.

McDevitt stood. Maybe there was a story here after all. 'When you get out, contact me. I owe you one.'

'Fuck you.'

. . .

FEENEY WAS in conference with Coleman and McCluskey, his most trusted lieutenants. The two men he'd stationed at Flynn's house had reported back that there was no sign of him and that his car was missing. Feeney had called a contact at Dundalk Garda Station, who told him that there was a major fuss at the station regarding the disappearance of Flynn.

'The bastard has done a flit,' Feeney said.

'Do you blame him?' Coleman said. 'He'd have heard that the latest raids produced a result. That fucker Duane was sent to flush out our contact and he's managed it. Flynn feared what you might do, rightly, and he scarpered. That's your problem, Tommy: the red mist is always your first reaction. He knew that if you found him, he would end up with his head flattened under a concrete block.'

'Never trust an addict,' Feeney said. 'I've dealt with drunks, junkies and gambling addicts and they're the greatest bunch of gits you could ever meet.'

'What do you want us to do, boss?' McCluskey said.

'Let's see if any of our friends turn up a line on the snivelling hoor. Tell our contacts in the guards that I want to be the first to know if they get information on where he can be found. If they get to him first, he'll blab. When we find him, no matter what he says, we put a bullet in his head.'

# CHAPTER THIRTY

'I'm not too happy about this.' Duane was in CS Nolan's office in Dublin. In front of him on the conference table were the remains of a takeaway Chinese meal.

'I'm not here to make you happy.' Nolan was wrinkling his nose at the smell of the food Duane was wolfing down. 'How can you eat that foreign muck?'

'We're not all meat-potatoes-and-two-veg men.' Duane rubbed his mouth with a serviette.

'More's the pity.'

'Wilson's asked me more than once if we're giving him all the information on the Lennon business.' Duane pushed away the cardboard boxes in which the meal arrived and picked his teeth. 'He's a clever boy is Ian Wilson. He feels he's being played and I'm not going to lie to him again. I think it's time we brought him into our confidence.'

'I've never fully trusted the nordies.'

'Is that because you're from Kerry and the Black and Tans shoved a bayonet up your grandfather's arse?'

'Leave my grandfather's arse out of this. In a couple of months, the cooperation we've enjoyed over the past forty years might be in the toilet. And whose fault is that?'

'I think it might be the gobshites in Westminster who are to blame. The nordies, as you call them, voted to remain.'

'We'll have soldiers on the border again, mark my words.'

'Put it upstairs. I want Wilson to know everything and I want an answer by tomorrow morning.'

'There's more at stake here than your friendship with Wilson. You and I have political considerations.'

Duane stood up. 'Tomorrow morning.'

'You'll threaten me once too often, Jack. There are some people in government who'd like to see the back of you. And more than a couple in HQ as well. The days of putting up with cowboys are on the way out. Careful as you go.'


WILSON WAS home by eight-thirty and Reid turned up ten minutes later.

'If you expect me to cook something,' she said. 'You are going to be sorely disappointed. I want a hot bath, a glass of Chardonnay and some takeaway in that order.'

'Tough day?'

'Two post-mortems, a lecture and a management meeting followed by report writing.' She had already dumped her clothes and was on her way to the bathroom. 'You can join me if you like but only after you bring me my glass of wine and organise the food.'

It took him ten minutes to open a bottle of Chardonnay, order an Indian takeaway and dispense with his clothes. 'The takeaway will be here in forty-five minutes.' He eased himself into the hot water. He'd already placed two glasses and the wine bottle on a small table beside the bath. He passed a glass to Reid and they drank.

'Is this bath getting smaller or are we getting bigger?' Reid asked as water sloshed over the edge. 'I can feel your toes in places they shouldn't be.'

Wilson laughed. He was aware that he'd put on a few

pounds. Reid, on the other hand, was as svelte as ever. 'For a pathologist you have a decent sense of humour. But you're right about the bath.'

'We'll go looking at Jacuzzi baths at the weekend.'

'I have something to run by you.'

'Nothing about death and destruction please.'

He told her about Carlisle's notebook and Gowan's version of the coded contents. By the time he finished, the water in the bath was getting cool and the bottle of Chardonnay was empty.

'I'd like to read it.' She climbed out of the bath and water ran down her body. She looked down at him. 'Down periscope, I'm ravenous.' She wrapped herself in a terrycloth bathrobe. 'Maybe Carlisle had a literary bent and fancied himself as a children's author.'

Wilson took the bathrobe she proffered. 'I don't think a story about murder and corruption is a good entry into the genre.'

There was a ring at the door.

'The takeaway has arrived,' Reid said.

They ate their meal still dressed in their bathrobes.

'Sometimes you open a door that you should leave closed.' Wilson had opened a second bottle of wine. It was going to be one of those nights.

'I have an idea you've done that more than once. What's on your mind?'

'According to Carlisle's fairy story, this group have been operational for some time. I only fell across them during the investigation into the death of David Grant. And the contact was the most fleeting. You brush against them and they flit away. The men who murdered Grant and Malone were mechanics. They were brought in by Sammy Rice who, as you know, is no longer with us. I never thought of it until Carlisle's early demise, but perhaps he was the link in the chain just above Sammy.'

'You really think a prominent politician like Carlisle would be a participant in several murders?'

'I think Minister Noel Armstrong murdered two prostitutes at the very least. If Carlisle is the politician in the fairy story, then I think it is very possible he used his link with Rice to arrange several deaths. It all goes back to a financial company called Carson Nominees, which turned out to be a dead end.'

'So many dead ends.' She collected the dishes and started putting them into the dishwasher. 'I think you might be obsessed with Helen McCann.'

Maybe she was right. He was tantalisingly close to having enough evidence on McCann, but he knew there was huge potential to end up with egg on his face. He didn't want to talk about McCann anymore. 'You and I are all right, aren't we?' The words were out of his mouth before he could stop them.

She turned and faced him. 'Where did that come from?'

'I suppose I've been a bit unsettled lately and I'm thinking about where we might be heading.'

'Do we have to head somewhere? Are you not happy with where we are?' She sat beside him.

'I'm not sure I know what you want.'

'My mother left when I was still in my teens. My parents' marriage was a sham and maybe I've generalised that into a conclusion that all marriages are a sham. In any event, I don't need it.'

'And children?'

'I'm not at all sure I want to bring children into this world. Some bad things happened to me in the Congo.' She lapsed into silence.

'Want to talk about it?'

'Maybe when I have less drink taken.'

He knew better than to push her.

'There are a lot of people out there who think we're already down the road to extinction,' she said. 'I find myself in agreement with them. I may change my mind, but I don't think so. If children are an issue for you, I need to know.'

'I don't want to lose you.'

'You won't. But we need to be honest with each other. A damn sight more honest than my parents were.'

'Children are not an issue for me.'

She leaned forward and kissed him. 'I'm tired and emotional. Why don't you pick me up in those strong arms of yours and carry me to the bedroom?'


MOIRA HAD JUST ENDED a long telephone conversation with her mother. Ostensibly it was about a coffee morning her mother had with some friends and how well their daughters were doing. They all had fine husbands in good jobs and were procreating at a goodly rate in order to fill the empty bedrooms in their new semi-detached houses. Her mother hadn't been able to say a word about her wayward daughter who had thrown away the chance of a lifetime to net a Harvard professor, and him from a rich Irish American family. Moira had listened and had finally agreed that she had failed her parents. Mrs McElvaney had responded with a wish that Moira would get sense someday.

Afterwards Moira had taken a few deep breaths and then turned to the wall of her living room. It was covered with paraphernalia related to the death of Jackie Carlisle. Photos of Helen McCann and Simon Jackson stared back at her. How could she explain to her mother that she didn't need the fine husband, the brood and the semi-detached? Maybe someday she would change her mind, but right now all she wanted was to help her boss put a gang of murderers away.


FLYNN'S BOTTLE of whiskey was almost empty. He poured the dregs into a glass and downed it. Alcohol was never the answer, but it dulled the senses. He lay back on the bed. His life was in the shit. He thought about calling Angela and asking to speak to the kids. He loved them but gambling had control of his mind. If he spoke to them, he would probably cry and that might be the last memory they'd have of him. Duane would have worked out by now what his disappearance meant and would use all available resources to locate him. At the same time, Feeney would be using all his republican mates to locate him first. He was about to be squeezed from two sides. He flung the empty whiskey bottle against the wall and it shattered. 'Eeny, meeny, miny, moe. Catch an eejit by his toe. If he squeals, don't let him go. Eeny, meeny, miny, moe.' He laughed hysterically. It was so funny to be a dead man and still able to breathe.

# CHAPTER THIRTY-ONE

Wilson ignored the cheery 'good mornings' from his team and went straight to his office. He'd picked up a cup of what passed for tea from the duty sergeant. It was by way of a cure since he wasn't feeling on top of the world. He had developed his capacity for drink as a young man. Alcohol was always a part of his rugby life: the spectators drank and so did the players, some to excess. But that was then, and this was now. He stared at the steaming cup and asked himself whether he really wanted to do this. The devil on his left shoulder screamed no, while the one on his right told him to get on with it. Beyond the glass partition the others were beavering away. He switched on his computer and brought up his emails. As he started reading, his phone rang.

'Morning, Ian.'

'Morning, Jack. Where are you?'

'Dundalk. We have a problem, or should I say we have an additional problem. Daragh Flynn is nowhere to be found. I sent some officers to check his house and he's not there. The lads gained entry and his bed hasn't been slept in and his car is missing.'

'You've checked with his wife?'

'She's left him and taken the kids. Hasn't spoken to him in weeks.'

'Does this have something to do with the Lennon enquiry?'

'Maybe. I'm keeping an open mind. You have anything on today?'

Wilson looked at the mass of unread emails, several of which were marked urgent. 'Nothing that can't be put off. But I have an appointment out of the office this morning that I can't cancel.'

'I'd like you to come down to Dundalk as soon as you can.'

'I don't think I'm going to be much use in the search for Flynn.'

'I'd like you to come down to Dundalk.'

'I get the message. We'll be down as soon as I can get away. But it will be this afternoon.'


It took Wilson just over an hour to drive from Tennent Street to Portaferry. It was a foul day and the streets of the small town were empty. All the retirees were probably tucked up at home watching box sets of *Game of Thrones*, or more likely *Gunsmoke*. He'd phoned ahead and was surprised when Miriam Spence had tried to deflect him from visiting. On the way down, he castigated himself for not keeping up the contact with his former boss and mentor, Donald Spence.

Miriam answered the door. 'Ian, darling, it's good to see you.' She motioned him in and dropped her voice. 'I'm afraid that Donald isn't the best. He was taken to the hospital last week and they're going to do some investigations on his heart.'

'I'm sorry to be a bother, Miriam. I won't keep him long.'

'He'll be thrilled to see you. He misses the old days so much. Retirement hasn't been kind to him. I think he would have preferred to die in uniform. He's in the living room. Go ahead and I'll bring the tea in.'

Spence was in his favourite chair wrapped up in a Welsh blanket. The sight made Wilson smile.

Spence made to get up, but Wilson pushed him back and held his hand. 'The next time you're in hospital, I'm to know about it.'

'It's only a bout of flu but that silly woman has me at death's door. She has me wrapped up here like a child.'

Wilson sat facing him. 'I need your advice. I promised Miriam I wouldn't stay long so just let me talk.'

Wilson went back over the Carlisle investigation and outlined the evidence Davidson had found. Then he gave a short briefing on Carlisle's notebook and the fairy story. Miriam served tea and Spence listened intently but didn't speak. 'We've reached a crunch-point,' Wilson concluded. 'If we hand over the evidence to Jennings, we may never see it again. The only solution I can think of is to go to Baird and ask him to make the investigation into Carlisle's death official. But if Carlisle's story is to be believed, there is a senior policeman in the group. I want to believe that it might be Jennings, but equally it might be Baird.'

'I suppose it never crossed your mind that it could be me,' Spence said.

'No, it didn't.'

'You can relax, it's not me, and I don't think it's Norman Baird. But you never know. One thing I do know is that this province is bedevilled by conspiracy theories.'

'Carson Nominees was real enough. The murders of Rice and Carlisle are real enough.'

'I've heard rumours about a secret society running things in Ulster. I'm not talking about the Masons, the Orange Order or Opus Dei. But every country has rumours of a "deep state". In America there's the Skull and Bones Society at Yale, in England it's the Oxbridge gang in government and finance.'

'So you think Carlisle's notebook is just bullshit?'

'I didn't say that.' He rubbed his chin in thought. 'I

remember one time I was approached by a colleague whom I thought was a fantasist. He asked me to join a group of like-minded officers who were dedicated to preserving the Union and who were willing to go to any lengths to do so. I told him I was a member of just such an organisation, the Royal Ulster Constabulary, and I really didn't like the use of the phrase "any lengths". I thought he had his head up his arse but perhaps I was wrong.'

'And Baird?'

'Aside from you, he's the only other man I'd trust with my life. But let me warn you, Ian. You're putting your feet into very deep water. Stick to dragging in the villains. It's the surest route to picking up your pension. Helen McCann is a dangerous opponent. She's rich and powerful in her own right and her daughter will, sooner or later, be the attorney general. You go against them, and they'll break you, if you're lucky. If you're not, it may be the last case you handle. Let it lie, Ian, you have too many good years left in you.'

Wilson stood and approached Spence's chair. He bent and hugged his old boss.

'Say you'll take my advice,' Spence's voice was weak.

'I can't. It must play out. People can't get away with murder just because they're rich and powerful,' Wilson said as he left the room.

Miriam was waiting for him at the door. 'What did he tell you about his health?'

'A bout of flu.'

'A bout of flu be damned. The man is ill.'

'The next time he's in hospital, the first phone call is to me. Reid will keep us informed on the hospital's opinion.'

She opened the door. 'You're a good lad, Ian, take care of yourself.'

'I'll be on to you.'

Miriam watched him go and then returned to the living room.

'You heard?' Spence said.

'Yes.'

'He's going to get himself killed.' Tears ran down Spence's cheek. 'Would you look at me, crying like a child. I'm a shadow of myself. Be a good woman and bring me some writing paper and a pen.'

'Don't do it.'

'He has to know.'

'No, he doesn't.'

'Only when I'm dead. Writing paper and pen.'

Miriam went to the desk and brought him the pen and paper. She thought about entreating him one last time but realised he had made up his mind. He was writing as she left the room.

# CHAPTER THIRTY-TWO

Moira spent the morning rereading the file on the burned-out BMW. Once it was all put together it certainly looked like Eddie Hills was their man. The question was whether she could collect enough evidence to pull him in. Although it could not be confirmed, the working hypothesis was that Mickey Duff was the victim. Why did Hills want to murder Duff, a mere foot soldier in the Best organisation? What had he done to deserve being torched? That's where she would have to go next. She'd forget Hills for the moment and concentrate on Duff. The case was going cold at a rate of knots. Her phone rang.

'Hi, may I speak with Moira McElvaney.'

Her heart jumped at the American accent, and for a moment she thought it was either Brendan Guilfoyle or Frank Shea. 'Speaking.'

'Hi, it's Joel Feinstein.'

The name meant nothing to her.

'Don't you remember?' Feinstein said. 'I'm a colleague of Brendan's at Harvard. You contacted me some time back in relation to a company you were interested in, Carson Nominees.'

She dragged the recollection from her memory bank. 'Yes, Joel, of course I remember you. I hope I thanked you for your help at the time.'

'You sure did. Look, I'm attending a conference in Belfast at the moment and I thought we might have dinner together. I've never been here before and I need someone to point me in the right direction.'

She hesitated. Across the room, O'Neill was listening in.

'And I've got some good stuff for you,' Feinstein continued.

'Like what?'

'You'll see, but you have to agree to have dinner with me first and show me around.'

'Where are you staying?'

'The conference organisers booked me into the Merchant. It's very swish.'

'So I hear.'

'They told me to book Holohan's on the Barge for dinner. Is that all right with you?'

'Sounds good.'

'You can choose where we go afterwards.'

'Okay.'

'Eight o'clock good for you?'

'Yes.'

'I'll make the arrangements. You won't be sorry. I'll meet you there.'

'Eight o'clock at Holohan's.' Moira replaced the handset and googled Joel Feinstein. There were several pages of references to him. She clicked on his Harvard Business School profile. Judging by his photo, Feinstein doesn't look half-bad with his dark wavy hair and brown eyes. His curriculum vitae gave his age as thirty-six, which was young for a full professor. He was the author of seven books on finance and had lectured at Oxford and in France. He seemed an attractive prospect. What the hell was she thinking? This wasn't a date. He had some information for her, and she had agreed to have dinner with him. He was in town for a couple of days, which made him a perfect dinner companion in her eyes. Despite her rationalisations, she was a little excited at the prospect of going out to dinner with a man.

FLYNN HAD WOKEN up with the mother of all hangovers. The booze wasn't going to help him out of his predicament. After a breakfast of boiled eggs and tea, he sat down and tried to plan. He took all the money he had from his pocket and laid it on the kitchen table. It came to two thousand, five hundred pounds and seven hundred and twenty-six euro. He'd heard that criminals on the run would consider a thousand pounds a day as appropriate run money, and that assumed that some fellow criminal was hiding them. Nevertheless, he was sure he could last for a month on the money sitting in front of him. But then what? Maybe he'd been hasty in running? There was no evidence linking him with Feeney. He could always say that he needed some time with his wife and children but doubted Duane would buy that. Dundalk hadn't been advised of the raids because they weren't to be trusted. That meant Dublin already knew that someone in the station was leaking. It didn't mean that they had already identified him. But even if he could tough it out at work, he'd still have to deal with Feeney. The men stationed outside his house were proof enough that his goose was cooked. He put his head in his hands. Whatever way you diced it; he was in trouble. He needed a way out.

THE INCIDENT ROOM at Dundalk Garda Station was sombre when Wilson entered. He hadn't bothered to return to Belfast to pick up Graham. Instead he'd taken the ferry across the mouth of Strangford Lough and driven via Downpatrick and Newry to Dundalk.

Duane was stomping around the room shouting at

whomever he was closest to. As soon as he saw Wilson, he approached him. 'We need to talk.'

He led Wilson away towards the interview rooms and entered the first free one. 'Flynn is in the wind.'

'What does that mean?'

'Remember I told you we had a problem with Dundalk?'

'Your raids were coming up empty and you thought there might be an inside man. Do you think it was Flynn?'

'I have someone in the incident room looking into Flynn. What he's come up with isn't encouraging. I also had a long talk with Mrs Flynn this morning. She's back with her parents because her husband has a gambling problem. And not just a small gambling problem, he's about to lose their house.'

'Criminals always have an eye for the weak ones or the ones who have a weakness. But can't you leave Flynn up to whatever your equivalent is of our Professional Services? Or do you think he had something to do with Lennon's murder?'

'No, I think maybe he's just a corrupt copper. He needed money to fuel his addiction and the gang supplied it.'

'Then hand finding him over to others.'

'The lads I sent to his house saw two guys in a car staking the place out. As soon as my guys arrived, the car left. It had a Northern Ireland registration.'

'Did they take it down?'

Duane took a page from his pocket and handed it to Wilson.

'I'll have O'Neill run it down.'

'His bookie is probably on your side of the border too.'

'We're treading water on the Lennon case. We need some forward momentum.'

Duane was silent. He took out his phone and looked at Nolan's message, which simply stated: *The answer is no.*

'There's something I'm missing,' Wilson said. 'Don't play games with me, Jack. You may be made that way but I'm not.'

'Dublin thinks that Lennon's murder may be linked to an organised crime group in the north.'

'I don't believe it. I'm not saying that I wasn't fed a heap of bullshit in Crossmaglen, but I examined Lennon's house and more importantly his bank statements and if he's linked to organised crime, I'm a monkey's uncle. Maybe you're the one feeding me the bullshit, Jack.'

'National security is involved.'

'Whose national security: yours or ours?'

'Maybe both.' Duane's phone rang. He looked at the ID. 'I need to take this.'

He walked away from Wilson, who noted that for a change Duane was doing none of the talking.

After a few minutes, Duane re-joined him. 'I hope you have no plans for this evening.'

'Why?'

'Your boss is on her way here and, when she arrives, we're all off to Dublin.'

# CHAPTER THIRTY-THREE

McDevitt was frustrated. There had been a murder on his patch, well not exactly on his patch but close enough, and he hadn't been able to get it on the front page. Lennon's murder had made page three and then been dropped. The editor of the *Chronicle* wasn't interested in the death of a yokel at the hands of some other yokels. McDevitt was asked whether sex was involved and when he answered 'no' he saw the editor's eyes glaze over. Where had all the old grizzled newshounds who could smell a story a mile off gone? McDevitt imagined that his own nose for a story was as infallible as the Pope speaking ex cathedra. He'd checked up on the post-mortem and there was no way six men beating another man to death with axe handles wouldn't lead to a big story. But it wasn't opportune to call the editor a half-blind arsehole who should be running a free paper for the ex-pat residents of Benidorm. The latest round of cuts had been announced and might aptly be described as swingeing. There would be more empty desks in the newsroom, and he would have to shell out for the leave party and the inevitable farewell presents. Up to now, McDevitt had gotten away with presenting a signed copy of his book on the Cummerford case as his contribution to the farewell gift. But now he was running out of author copies.

Earlier in the day, an intern had dumped a weighty dossier on his desk. He picked it up and saw it was the result of an extensive search he had commissioned into Helen McCann. Moira McElvaney had piqued his interest. Often people's chance remarks struck a chord with him and sent him off on the trail of a story. It didn't always work out, but that was life. There were several hundred pages in the dossier before him. McCann was a legend in financial circles and had connection across Ulster and Great Britain. The impending nuptials would join the McCann family and the Lattimer family to create a mighty powerbroker. He would have to be careful with his research. Lattimer was not only a board member of the *Chronicle*, he was also on the boards of half the companies that took out advertisements in the paper. He picked up his phone.

'DS McElvaney.'

He noted her lovely soft voice. 'Jock McDevitt here, I was just thinking of you.'

'I'd really like it if you'd forget about me.'

'We still have our little arrangement.'

'I paid you back on that.'

'Tut tut, we can still be friends. I'd like to meet to discuss your interest in Helen McCann.' He heard the intake of breath down the line.

'Do I have an interest in Helen McCann? My interest in those photos lay elsewhere.'

'Let's meet this evening for a drink.'

'I can't.'

'I suppose you have a date.'

'I do actually.'

'I've compiled a dossier on McCann. Maybe we could exchange notes.'

The line went dead.

Well, well, McDevitt sat back in his chair. His nose for a story hadn't let him down.

Wilson had been examining the whiteboard on the Lennon murder in the Dundalk incident room when DS Guiney informed him that CS Davis had arrived and was speaking with the boss of the station. She would meet him at the car outside as soon as she was free. Wilson only had time to take his seat in Davis's car when she flounced out of the station and sat in beside him. The car started off immediately.

'What's this about?' she asked.

'No idea.'

'Bullshit, this is something you and DCI Duane cooked up.'

He noted the use of Jack's full title. 'It's got to be something to do with the Lennon enquiry. But I have no idea why we've been summoned to Dublin.' He could tell that she didn't believe him.

Davis took up her briefcase, removed a file and started reading.

Wilson took the hint and they spent the remainder of the trip in silence. It was well over an hour later when they reached the five-storey, red-brick Garda Síochána building in Harcourt Street. A sign outside describing it as the centre of the Garda Bureau of Community Diversity and Integration caused them both to raise their eyebrows and eased the tension between them.

The driver dropped them at the door and they were directed to take the lift to the top floor, where they would find the office of Chief Superintendent Nolan.

'Yvonne.' Nolan rose from his desk and came to greet his PSNI colleague. 'Sorry we had to drag you down here.'

'Good to see you, Bill.' Davis and Nolan air-kissed. 'We're always happy to pay a visit.'

'Detective Superintendent Wilson,' Nolan extended his hand.

'Sir.' Wilson shook. There was no sign of Duane.

'We have to move to the conference room down the hall.' Nolan led the way and held the door open for his visitors. He ushered Davis to a seat at the top of the table.

Wilson saw that Duane had been talking to a small group of people at the front of the room. The group dispersed and took seats at the table. Nolan sat at the top of the table with Davis on his right. Wilson sat in the empty seat beside her. Duane nodded to Wilson before taking his seat beside Nolan.

'I'd like to welcome our visitors from the PSNI, Chief Superintendent Yvonne Davis and Detective Superintendent Ian Wilson. On our side, you already know DCI Duane, and I'd like to introduce Nuala O'Brien, programme manager for the Minister of Justice; Chief Superintendent Michael Moran, Head of Intelligence Branch; and Anne Walsh from the Department of the Taoiseach. The objective here is to review our operations against an organised crime group operating on the border. Yvonne, would you like to say a few words?'

'We're always happy to cooperate with our garda colleagues, but I'm wondering why we're having this meeting in such an ad hoc manner.'

'Our operations against this gang have been ongoing for some time without much success,' Nolan began. 'The fact that they operate on both sides of the border means we've lacked coordination. We're aware that the uncertainty concerning our relationship after the UK leaves the EU might lead them to believe that they are entering a new golden era. The uncertainty means we need to break them sooner rather than later.'

'And how does this affect us?' Davis asked.

'Their centre is in your jurisdiction.'

Davis looked at Wilson, who shrugged.

'We believe the leader of the gang is a former high-ranking officer of a terrorist organisation,' Nolan continued. 'He believes himself to be immune because of his political connections.'

'The last two raids we made on installations operated by the gang were successful,' Duane said. 'They were hurt but not fatally. Most of the gang members are tough former terrorists and they're extremely loyal to their leader.'

'And can I take it that the Lennon murder is the first time they have put their heads above the barricades?' Wilson asked. He noted that the meeting was effectively between Nolan, Duane, Davis and himself. The other participants were busy taking notes so they could brief their bosses.

'That's our reading of it,' Nolan said.

'You know who ordered Lennon's murder,' Wilson said.

'We have a good idea,' Nolan said.

'For God's sake,' Wilson said. 'My team and I have been faffing around for the past few days and you could have pointed me in the right direction. That's the very definition of wasting police time, and I, for one, don't appreciate it.'

'We understand your feelings,' Duane said. 'And I wasn't happy with our policy of keeping you in the dark on this. The instruction came from upstairs and we need to follow the chain of command. Also, this isn't an episode of *Columbo* where we simply establish who did it and then fit the evidence around him. If we want to break this gang, we need solid evidence. That's where you come in, Ian. We had nothing at the crime scene. We're shaking the tree on our side and we need you to do the same on yours. Their boy is smart; our boy has to be smarter.'

'We've suspected for some time that there's been a leak from our Dundalk station,' Nolan said. 'The success of our latest Dublin-led operation against this gang indicates that we were correct.'

'Does Flynn's disappearance figure in your deliberations?' Wilson asked.

'We're examining the possibility that DI Flynn may have been in contact with this organised crime group,' Duane said. 'We have no idea where he is, but we are actively searching for him.'

'There's a possibility that this OCG has already eliminated him,' Wilson said.

'We know that,' Nolan said.

'Do you have the name of the leader?' Wilson asked.

'We do,' Nolan said.

'It's Feeney,' Wilson said.

'I knew you were already there.' Duane smiled. 'Yes, it's Tommy Feeney, but we don't know why, and we don't have any evidence against him.'

'We were supposed to be working together on this, but you've kept me in the dark.' Wilson stared at Duane.

'Don't blame Jack,' Nolan said. 'I'm sorry Yvonne. Our minister has spoken to yours and our commissioner has spoken with your chief constable. Everyone is behind the strategy of bringing this organised crime group down. They're not the only OCG operating on the border, but if we bring one of them down the others will take note.'

'We all work under these types of constraints,' Davis said.

'Where do we go from here?' Wilson asked.

Moran, the Intelligence man, pushed a dossier across the table. 'We're working up a dossier on the gang. We're adding the latest intelligence and we'll let you have a full briefing shortly. Your people must have something similar. This gang is ruthless and could cause havoc if our ability to cooperate across the border is restricted.'

Davis took the dossier and put it in her briefcase. 'I can assure you that DS Wilson will do everything he can to bring the killers of Brian Lennon to justice. We understand the political sensitivity, but a murderer is a murderer.'

'Thank you, Yvonne,' Nolan said. 'And I hope that DS Wilson will accept my apology for keeping him in the dark.'

Wilson nodded.

'Good.' Nolan looked around the table. 'Thank you all for taking time from your busy schedules to join us.'

There was a general nodding by the participants and a collecting of papers. Finally, Nolan, Davis, Duane and Wilson found themselves alone in the conference room. 'Would you like to join us for a small libation?' Nolan asked.

Davis looked at her watch. 'Not this time, thanks. I think we should head home.'

Nolan hugged Davis. 'Then I'll wish you *bon voyage* and hope that we'll see each other again soon.'

'Well be in touch,' Davis said.

Duane led them back to the lift. 'Sorry about all this, Ian. I had to push Nolan for this meeting. The top brass fear the repercussions of not bringing this gang down.'

They entered the lift together.

'I suppose I'll get over it,' Wilson said.

As the lift doors opened on the ground floor, Duane said. 'Ian, do you mind if I have a private word with Yvonne?'

Davis nodded at Wilson and he walked ahead into the reception area. Five minutes later Davis joined him, and they went outside to the car.

'What a mess!' Davis said as Wilson opened the door for her.

'It'll work out,' he said.

'I hope so, because it seldom does.'

# CHAPTER THIRTY-FOUR

D espite herself, Moira was a little excited. Beneath all the baggy shirts and pullovers she usually wore to work, she had a good figure that she maintained with three visits a week to the PSNI gym. On arriving at her flat, she had pulled out from under her bed a case that she hadn't opened since returning from Boston. It contained the only clothes she had that were suitable for an evening out. She was shocked to realise that this would be her first date since she came back. Then she was equally shocked to note that she was thinking of the meeting as a date. She had a bath and selected her outfit. She chose a dress Frank Shea had bought her, so it was expensive. She wondered what Frank was up to now. She was pleased to see that the dress still fitted her perfectly. Her hair was naturally curly so all it needed was a comb. Not half-bad, she thought as she inspected herself in the mirror. She had half an hour to spare so she decided to stop into the Cave on Oxford Street for a drink. She wouldn't look out of place there and it was a two-minute walk from Holohan's.

JOEL FEINSTEIN WAS STANDING close to the gangplank with

a bunch of flowers in his hand when she arrived at Holohan's. He came forward to meet her. 'Hi, Moira.' He held out the flowers. 'Your picture doesn't do you justice.'

She took the flowers from him and forced a smile. He looked older than the photo she'd seen earlier on the Harvard website. His black hair was tinged with grey at the temples. He was dressed casually in a blue button-down collar shirt open at the neck, a navy blazer, blue jeans and tan boat shoes. The look was cool and expensive. 'Thank you, Joel.' She smelled the flowers. 'They're lovely.'

They were seated at the first table on the right side of the barge with a view across the Lagan. The waitress gave them menus and took Moira's flowers for safekeeping.

'What do you recommend?' Feinstein asked.

'I'm afraid I haven't been here in years. But back then everything was good.'

'I'm only in Ireland for a couple of days, what should I try?'

'Anything with the name boxty, it's a traditional dish.'

They ordered a drink and their meal.

'What made you think of me?' Moira asked.

'Brendan showed me your photo once and it made an impression. I vowed that if I were ever in Belfast, I'd look you up. Also, I've been doing some research lately and I thought of our previous contact. But hey, let's leave the business talk until later.'

'Have you seen Brendan lately?'

'Sure, we see each other all the time. It's a pity things didn't work out for you guys. I suppose you know he's seeing someone.'

'I didn't know, but I'm happy for him.' She decided to change the subject. 'What are your plans for your visit?'

'I'm speaking at a conference tomorrow and the day after I'm on the *Game of Thrones* tour. I can't wait to see some of the locations.'

Their meals arrived and they continued to chat about *Game of Thrones*, Boston, Harvard and Belfast. He was, like most academics, a good talker and a couple of hours passed easily and quickly. By the time dessert was consumed, Moira was beginning to wonder whether Feinstein had conned his way to a dinner date.

'That was a great meal,' Moira said as she put her dessert spoon down. 'Now, what's this piece of information you have for me?'

Feinstein called for the bill. 'First let's have some music and a few drinks. Then we'll go back to the Merchant for a nightcap and business. I hear the music in Kelly's Cellars is good.'

It was after midnight when they finally got to the bar of the Merchant. Feinstein had tried to cajole Moira into discussing business in his room, but she had demurred. The bar was quiet with only a few residents enjoying a nightcap. Feinstein put a large folder he had fetched from his room on the table. 'Okay.' His speech was slurred. 'You've heard about the Panama and Paradise Papers, right?'

Moira shook her head. She'd ordered water as her nightcap.

Feinstein looked disappointed. 'The Panama Papers consist of eleven and a half million leaked documents that detail financial and attorney–client information for more than two hundred thousand offshore companies. The documents, some dating back to the 1970s, were created by, and taken from, the Panamanian law firm and corporate service provider Mossack Fonseca. They were leaked in 2015 by an anonymous source. The documents contain personal and financial information about wealthy individuals and public officials that had previously been kept private. While offshore entities are legal, reporters found that some of the Mossack Fonseca shell companies were used for illegal purposes, including fraud, tax evasion and evading international sanctions. Are you with me so far?'

'Sort of.'

'The Paradise Papers are over thirteen million confidential electronic documents relating to offshore investments. They were leaked to a couple of German reporters, who handed them over to an international consortium of investigative journalists. There are so many papers most of them haven't yet been examined. The documents originate from a legal firm called Appleby as well as two corporate service providers and business registries in nineteen tax jurisdictions. They contain the names of more than one hundred and twenty thousand people and companies.'

Moira remembered lecturers like Feinstein from her time at university. Once they got into their subject, there was no stopping them. 'Thanks for the lesson, Joel. But how does that relate to me?'

'I've been examining these documents for the past three years as part of a group of researchers in ten universities. We're interested in movements that involve fraud and arms dealing. And guess what name came up in the course of our research?'

'Tell me.'

'Your old friend Carson Nominees.'

Moira was stunned. The name hit her like a bolt of lightning. The last she'd heard about Carson Nominees was that it had been liquidated and its funds had disappeared into the ether.

'Yeah, I thought that would hit home.' Feinstein lifted the dossier from the table. 'I've put together all the documents we found relating to the operations of Carson.' He smiled. 'There are over four hundred pages.'

'What do they contain?'

'Every shady deal that Carson was involved in up to the dissolution of the company.'

She took the file from Feinstein and skimmed through it. It could have been written in double-Dutch for all she knew. 'Have you broken it down?'

Feinstein's smile faded. 'No. Carson is a minnow in our research. We've concentrated on international terror groups like al-Qaeda.'

'How the hell am I going to decipher all this stuff?'

'Find your local Joel Feinstein. This is my gift to you.'

'Thanks heaps.'

Feinstein downed his drink. 'Now that business is out of the way, are we going to sleep together? I always wanted to make it with a redhead.'

She hesitated more than she would have liked to. She hadn't had sex since Boston and she wasn't totally against the idea. Feinstein would be gone in two days so he wouldn't be a complication. 'You're a sweet man, Joel, but you'll have to look elsewhere to realise that fantasy. Thanks for dinner and thanks for this file.' She stood up. 'Anyway, what would Mrs Feinstein think?'

'Probably nothing. She's shacked up with some surfer dude down in Cabo. What about a sympathy fuck?'

'It's not your lucky night.' She kissed him lightly on the cheek. 'Goodnight and good luck with the speech tomorrow.'

She was almost at the door of the bar when she turned and walked back. 'I suppose a girl can change her mind.'

# CHAPTER THIRTY-FIVE

Wilson stood at the whiteboard and gathered his depleted team around him. He'd already written 'Tommy Feeney – Prime Suspect' beside the photo of Brian Lennon. Graham and O'Neill seemed chipper and alert, but Moira looked the worse for wear. She was obviously still burning the midnight oil in her pursuit of Helen McCann. He resolved to have a word with her. He couldn't afford to lose another member of the team. He briefed them on his meeting in Dublin. 'Siobhan, I need you to gather everything we have on this Feeney character. I also want a list of all his known associates.'

'I'm working on it, boss. By the way, I finished with the calendar you gave me. It wasn't much of a task as Lennon didn't have an extensive social life. I can tell you that there were references to meetings and Feeney featured once. They had a meeting several months before his death. He also met with his bank manager, Richard King, and with a local councillor called Dáithí Ó Brádaigh, which is the Gaelic for David Brady.'

'Harry and I will follow up on that,' Wilson said. 'While I have the greatest respect for our colleagues in the Garda

Síochána, we don't have a shred of evidence linking Feeney to Lennon's murder and we shouldn't presume that we're going to find any.'

'We don't have a shred of evidence linking anyone to Lennon's murder,' Graham said.

'What about the tape of the call to the police?' Wilson asked.

'It's still with the boffins at FSNI,' O'Neill said. 'There's a backlog over there. Maybe you could chivvy them along.'

'I'll add it to my list of things to do,' Wilson said. 'Harry, call Feeney, King and Ó Brádaigh and tell them we'd like to speak with them today in relation to the meetings they held with Lennon. We'll leave for Crossmaglen in an hour, so choose times that will coincide with our arrival. Okay, hop to it. Moira, come with me.'

'I'm getting worried about you,' Wilson said when they were in the office alone. 'You look like you've been up most of the night.'

'Insomnia,' Moira said. She was holding the ring binder containing the dossier on Carson Nominees in her hand.

'You've got to pull back from the Carlisle inquiry. You're spending too much free time on it.'

She put the binder on the desk. 'Remember I had contact with one of Brendan's friends in Harvard when we were investigating David Grant's death.'

'Remotely.'

'Well, he's attending a conference in Belfast and I met him last night for dinner. Did you ever hear of the Panama Papers or the Paradise Papers?'

'In passing. They're a bit like WikiLeaks. Someone dumped a load of information about rich people and their money onto the Internet and caused a stir for a while.'

'Millions of pages of information. Brendan's friend, Joel Feinstein, is an expert on finance. He's working with a group of researchers on those millions of pages and he's come up with this dossier on Carson Nominees.' She tapped the ring binder. 'I've skimmed it and I don't understand a word. Feinstein thinks there may be some juicy morsels in there, but he's too busy with other work to find them. Carson is a minnow according to him. He's after bigger fish, like al-Qaeda.'

Wilson picked up the binder and flicked through the pages. They were crammed with figures and names of companies. 'So we need to find someone who can decipher this stuff.'

'Are you seeing Baird about making the Carlisle investigation official?'

'Davis is on two days' leave, which gives me some breathing space.' He closed the binder. 'This gives us more ammunition for Baird.'

'That depends what's in it. Maybe we'll find no link to McCann.'

'And maybe we can tie what's in it to Carlisle's fairy story.'

'Like my mother used to say, if ifs and buts were pots and pans there'd be no work for tinker's hands.'

'This is what we do for a living, Moira. It doesn't always work out. That's why we have thousands of cold cases. We may discover who killed Mickey Duff tomorrow or we may never get justice for the poor man. And don't get too caught up in your pursuit of McCann. We're looking for justice not vengeance.'

'I'll try to remember that. But if McCann, Carlisle and their friends have been polluting this province for years and we don't put them away, I don't think I could take it.'

'The good don't always win.'

She picked up the binder. 'I'll add this to the evidence we already have.'

He watched her leave the room. He loved the job, but he was aware of its shortcomings. On balance, he wanted to continue, but it was a decision he had to make again each day. The more they dug into McCann and Carson Nominees the more he saw the danger to their lives. The figures on the pages

Moira had shown him ran into millions. Their lives meant nothing against money like that. He'd faced up to hardened criminals in his life. The Rices and McGreary hadn't managed to throw a scare into him, but he feared the fallout from investigating Carlisle's death. The recent attempt on his life couldn't be laughed off. If Duane hadn't been in his corner, he might not have prevailed. It was a sobering thought. Maybe it would be more prudent to leave McCann alone. Pity prudence wasn't one of his virtues.

FLYNN HAD BOUGHT a mobile phone in Galway and put ten-euro credit on it. He needed to know how things stood with Feeney and Duane. He placed the first call to the source of greatest risk: Feeney.

'Yes.'

'It's Daragh Flynn.' He had already slewed off the DI.

'Where the fuck are you, you rotten bastard?'

'I've taken a few days off.'

'You cost me a fucking fortune and you fuck off on holiday. You've got some balls.'

'I needed to get away. Duane was getting close.'

'I'd like to see you when you get back to Dundalk.' Feeney's voice lost its harshness. 'There's no hard feelings about the raids. I know it was all down to that bastard Duane.'

'Is that why you had two men stationed outside my house?'

'I was anxious to speak to you.'

'I have a feeling you intended something more than a civilised chat.'

'I was royally pissed and I over-reacted in the heat of the moment, but I've passed that stage now. Come back to Dundalk and come to me first. Duane will have worked out that you're the inside man at the station. If you go back to him, you're going to jail. And there isn't a jail in Ireland where you'll be safe from me.'

'It's good to hear that you've calmed down. I'll be in touch.' Flynn's hand holding the phone was shaking. It might have been the hangover, but it was more likely the fear of what might happen to him if he went to jail. Handing himself over to Feeney would be the road to a quick death. He thought of his wife and children and he didn't want to die. He had sacrificed them to his gambling addiction.

He took Duane's business card out of his wallet and composed the mobile number.

'Duane.'

'It's Daragh Flynn.'

'We've been looking for you these past two days. Are you okay?'

'Yes, I just needed a break.'

'I hear the wife and kids have left.'

'Yes.'

'When are you coming back?'

'I don't know.'

'You need help, Daragh. You're not the first police officer to have marital problems. Take it from one who knows. Come back and we'll get you help.'

'You're a devious bastard, Duane.'

'How so?'

'You're all concern for my welfare when really you just want me back to jail me.'

'No, I don't. We've known for some time that information was leaking from Dundalk. What did they have on you?'

'They bought up my gambling debts. I owe them more than a hundred grand.'

'Did you steal any money?'

'No, just borrowed it.'

'Who did you deal with?'

'A guy wearing a balaclava.'

'How much do you know about their operation?'

'Not much, I wasn't part of the crew. I just passed along

the information about upcoming raids. They cleared out the factories so no one was around when the hammer fell.'

'We can clear this up. The boys at the top won't want to expose a bent copper.'

'So, I'll just walk away. Yeah, that seems plausible. They'll haul me over the coals.'

'The alternative is a hole in a bog and you better believe that.'

Flynn cut the call. Maybe there was a way out after all. If he could just believe that Duane was on the level.

DUANE HANDED his phone to a young detective in the incident room. 'Find out where that call came from and put out an APB for Flynn and his car.'

Flynn's flight confirmed Duane's suspicions. The DI was the inside man. He didn't believe that Flynn was totally ignorant of the gang's operations either, which meant that they would be searching for him as well. He hoped for Flynn's sake that he found him first. Feeney was not noted for taking prisoners or leaving loose ends.

# CHAPTER THIRTY-SIX

The Ulster Bank was in a non-descript converted two-storey house in the centre of Crossmaglen. Wilson and Graham entered, showed their warrant cards and asked for the manager. Richard King's office was at the rear of the building.

'Good afternoon,' King stuck out a hand. He was a short, rotund, balding, middle-aged banker in a worn pinstriped suit.

Wilson shook his hand and he and Graham sat in the chairs King indicated.

'Coffee or tea?' King asked.

'Neither,' Wilson replied for both. 'You may have heard that we've been looking into the death of Brian Lennon.'

'Crossmaglen is a small town. Horrible business, Brian was such a nice young man.'

'That's what everyone says,' Wilson said. 'We've been looking through his bank account and we know that you had a meeting with him two weeks before his death. Would you like to tell us what you discussed?'

'The Lennons have been clients of this bank for longer than I can remember. The farming business is anti-cyclical, by which I mean that expenditures and receipts are out of step with each other. The farmer invests in crops and/or livestock but doesn't see the return for months or maybe even years. We provided loans to the Lennons over the years.'

'So Brian Lennon was asking for a loan?' Wilson asked.

'In a nutshell, yes. A rather large loan.'

'The business was not going well.'

'You could say that. If you already have the bank statements, and possibly the annual tax returns, you'll know that the Lennon farm was rarely in profit.'

'Were you receptive to his request?'

'No. He didn't have much in the way of collateral.'

'What about the farm?'

'His family has owned that land for generations and he didn't want to be the one to lose it. And lose it he probably would have. Half the farmers in this county survive on EU subsidies and guaranteed prices from the Common Agricultural Policy. If those subsidies disappear with Brexit, so will they.'

'Do you have any idea why someone would want to murder Brian Lennon?'

King shook his head. 'It certainly had nothing to do with his bank balance.'

Wilson and King shook hands and the police officers left.


OUTSIDE, Wilson looked around the area.

'What's up, boss?' Graham asked.

'I still feel like someone is dogging my tracks. It's nothing as obvious as McCluskey and his blue Kona, but it's there all the same.' He looked around again. There was nothing out of place. 'Must be my imagination. Let's go see Mr Feeney.'


THE GATE to Feeney's house was down a long drive off the Coolaville Road. The house was set in a copse of trees and looked like it had been transported from the set of *Dallas*. JR and the rest of the Ewings would have been right at home in the sprawling hacienda-style house. The lawn to the right of the driveway was perfectly manicured and there was a BMW 7 series parked in front of a double garage. Graham pulled up outside the house and they stood surveying the residence before knocking on the door.

Wilson half-expected a Mexican maid to open the door, but instead it was a stocky man with a grizzled lived-in face. Tommy Feeney looked like he had lived an eventful life.

'Mr Feeney?' Wilson said.

'Detective Superintendent Wilson,' Feeney tried a smile that didn't quite make it. 'I've been expecting you.' He looked at Graham. 'And this would be Detective Constable Graham, all the way from Belfast to visit us all in bogland once again. Come in.'

Wilson got the message. Feeney already knew who they were and why they were there. He had his finger on the pulse of Crossmaglen.

'Impressive,' Wilson said as they entered a huge living room. The whole of his apartment would fit into half of the room.

'The wife designed it.' Feeney nodded towards a couch. He sat in a handcrafted rocking chair. 'How can I help you?'

'We're looking into the death of Brian Lennon,' Wilson said.

'Aye, poor man. I thought he was killed on the other side of the border. Shouldn't the guards be the ones doing the investigating?'

'They are, but they have no jurisdiction on this side of the border. The chief constable has agreed that we should help with the inquiry.'

'What have I got to do with Brian Lennon's death?'

'We're just speaking with everyone who had dealings with Mr Lennon during the last few months of his life. We found a note that you met with him a month before he died.'

'I met the lad about the town several times.'

'But this was a meeting that he had marked down specifically on his calendar. Something he didn't want to forget. Can you remember what you talked about?'

'I own a builders providers and he wanted to set up a line of credit. He told me he was thinking of making some improvements to the house. His father died only six months before him.'

'That sounds pretty innocuous,' Wilson said. 'I would have thought he would arrange something like that with the manager of the shop, not the owner. Any reason he'd have marked it down as important on his calendar?'

'None that I know of.'

Wilson stood. 'Thanks for agreeing to see us. Do you have any idea why someone would have wanted to see Brian Lennon dead?'

Feeney ushered the two police officers towards the front door. 'Not an idea in the world. I didn't really know him, but he seemed a pleasant enough bloke. I've heard that it was a punishment beating.'

'That's what some folk would like us to believe.' At the door, Wilson produced a business card and handed it to Feeney. 'If you think of anything else.'

Feeney took the card and looked at it. 'Now I know where to find you.'

'Oh, I think you've always known where to find me. I'll be seeing you.'

Graham took his place behind the wheel. 'I wouldn't like to be tangling with that fella.'

'I don't think Mr Feeney is a model citizen. But we have no evidence that he's a murderer.'

'He didn't get that house by sitting on his arse.'

'Do I detect a note of envy?'

'No, boss, I'm happy with my lot.'

'However, like everyone else we've interviewed, he fed us a

line of bullshit. Let's move on. We don't want to keep Cllr Ó Brádaigh waiting.'

Graham drove to Newry Street and parked outside a two-storey house with a large poster displaying Ó Brádaigh's smiling face in the front window.

When they knocked, a young lady opened the door.

'I'm Detective Constable Graham and this is Detective Superintendent Wilson, we have a meeting with Mr Ó Brádaigh.'

'You're expected.'

·   Inside the house, the ground floor had been turned into an open-plan office. It was presently empty except for a man seated behind a desk at the rear. There was a large poster on the wall behind him with a picture of a dilapidated former customs office on the border and the legend 'NO BREXIT – NO BORDER'. Wilson and Graham walked towards the desk.

Ó Brádaigh stood as they approached. 'Detective Superintendent Wilson and Detective Constable Graham, welcome to our little office. Please take a seat.'

Wilson and Graham did as requested. The young man facing them was more grim-faced than the picture on the poster in the window. He was in his mid-thirties with thinning fair hair and a pale, freckled face. The look was more bureaucrat than charismatic leader.

'We're a bit busy right now,' Ó Brádaigh said. 'Every politician and his friend want to visit us here. Except, of course, the ones who keep insisting that the border issue is a fiction. They all want to see what's causing such a great fuss in Westminster. But that's got nothing to do with you. How can I help you?'

'We're investigating the death of a constituent of yours, Brian Lennon,' Wilson said.

'A sad business. I didn't know Mr Lennon personally, but I've already expressed my condolences to the family and, of course, I'll be attending the funeral. I don't know how I can help, but fire away.'

'We're looking into Mr Lennon's movements prior to his death. He wrote down important meetings on a calendar. One of those meetings was with you.'

'I meet so many people in the course of my work.' He picked up a desk diary and flicked through it. 'What date was this meeting?'

Wilson gave him the date.

Ó Brádaigh flicked through the diary and found the page. 'You're right we did have a meeting scheduled for that date.'

'He didn't turn up? I'm surprised.'

'No, he did turn up. I remember it now. We only spoke for a couple of minutes.'

'Do you remember the subject of your discussion?'

'I'd like to keep that confidential.'

'I don't think the concept of confidentiality extends to councillors.'

Ó Brádaigh hesitated. 'He wanted to have part of his land zoned for building. I told him it was impossible and that I couldn't help.'

'That was it?'

'Like I said, we're up to our eyes with this Brexit business and the border. That's it as far as I can remember.'

'That's disappointing. We were hoping for something more substantial. Everyone we talk to says that Brian Lennon was a nice young man who wouldn't hurt a fly. Yet someone had motive enough to beat him to death in a most vicious manner.'

Ó Brádaigh coughed and reached for a glass of water on his desk. He took a large swallow. 'I'd really like to help, detective superintendent, but I've told you all I know.'

Wilson continued to stare into Ó Brádaigh's face. The councillor seemed nervous. 'DC Graham and I have been interviewing the relevant individuals here in Crossmaglen. We are both experienced police officers and murder detectives. We are certain that in some cases we are being deliberately lied to. Should we find proof of someone knowingly making a false statement, they will be charged with wasting police time, which carries a penalty of six months in jail and/or a fine.' Wilson stood and tossed a business card on the desk. 'If you change your mind about the content of what you've told us, contact me. Thank you for your time.' He turned and started to walk away.

'YOU THINK HE WAS LYING?' Graham said when they were outside.

'Through his teeth. Like the rest of them. I'm pissed off with the lies and deception. It was time to put the shits up someone, and Ó Brádaigh is as good a candidate as any.'

Wilson's mobile phone rang as he was about to take his seat in the car. 'Jack.' He looked around him and felt a pair of eyes on him. The street was empty, but he couldn't shake the feeling.

'Where are you?' Duane asked.

'Crossmaglen.'

'I'll meet you in Magee's Bar on Merchants Quay in Newry in half an hour. It's on your way home.'

SIMON JACKSON WATCHED Wilson and Graham come out of the house on Newry Street and get into their car. He'd been following Wilson for the past three days, changing cars every day. Although he'd seen Wilson look around several times, he was sure that Wilson hadn't noticed the tail. With the red wig and the horn-rimmed glasses, his own mother wouldn't recognise him. He was sitting in his car one hundred metres from the PSNI men. McCann was sure that Jennings would succeed in destroying the evidence that Davidson had collected regarding the murder of Carlisle. Jackson wasn't so sure. And he was the one who would go down for the murder. The witness evidence from the neighbour wasn't worth the paper it was printed on. Rodgers had already arranged a watertight alibi and any half-decent brief would tear the identification to pieces. The phone was another matter. Jackson had spent twenty years living on his nerves and his instincts were telling him that he was in some deep shit. If he went down, he wouldn't be alone. He'd told McCann about the video and what would happen to it if he had some sort of accident. He knew that without it he would already be in the ground. Graham moved off in the direction of Newry. Jackson smiled. Wilson was fully occupied with this murder case. He could safely drop his surveillance.

Duane was sitting in the snug inside the front door of Magee's when Wilson and Graham entered. Both men opted for a soft drink when the barman came to their table.

'What have you been up to?' Duane asked.

'There were three meetings marked on Lennon's calendar,' Wilson said. 'King, the bank manager, plus Feeney and a local councillor called Ó Brádaigh. I thought we should interview them concerning the nature of the meetings.'

'And?'

'And nothing. Nobody has any idea why someone should want Lennon dead.'

'What did you make of Feeney?' Duane asked.

'I wouldn't like to cross him.'

Duane took an envelope out of his inside pocket and handed it to Wilson. 'This is what our Intelligence Branch has on him.'

Wilson took the envelope and withdrew three sheets of A4 from it. 'O'Neill is preparing a dossier for me in Belfast. I'll pass it along.' He was speed-reading the documents. 'Our friend Feeney has been busy. Lots of allegations but no prison time aside from his stay in Long Kesh.'

'He's still high up in the organisation,' Duane said. 'And he has friends in high places, north and south.'

'Why would he want to kill Lennon? We haven't yet identified any connection between them aside from one meeting a couple of months ago.'

'That, as the Yanks say, is the sixty-four-thousand-dollar question. But everything that happens in this neck of the woods is down to him.'

'Sounds like you're paranoid, Jack.'

'Maybe I am. I've been trying to nail that bastard for longer than I care to remember. I wouldn't like to leave the force before seeing him in jail. I know he didn't swing an axe handle, but he gave the order.'

'Don't tell me that you're thinking of retiring.' Wilson saw that Jack's jaw was tense. He knew how he felt. There was more than one unsolved case in Wilson's locker that he'd dearly like to put to bed before he handed in his warrant card. It was a frustration that all coppers suffered.

'Don't tell me that you're not.'

Wilson was taken aback. 'I wasn't, until you put the idea in my head.'

'I'm sick being the dogsbody for the guys at the top. They've played me like a puppet for so long that I wonder will I be able to operate without the strings.'

'You'll get Feeney before you quit.'

'This is the first mistake he's made, the first chink in his armour. I'm not going to let him walk away this time. I don't care what the people upstairs say.'

'It's just the politics getting to you.'

'Fuck the politics. This job stinks.'

'What about Flynn?'

'He called today. Said he needed some time, which is bullshit. He split because he was afraid of Feeney's reaction to the raids. We've established that he was feeding information to Feeney's gang, but he's probably not the only one. Garda salaries are not great and the odd brown envelope doesn't go amiss. In any event, we need to get to Flynn first. Feeney had two men stationed outside Flynn's house and they weren't there to wish him a happy birthday.'

'Did you ever run across this Cllr Ó Brádaigh guy?' Wilson asked.

'I've heard of him but not met him.'

'Lennon met him two weeks before he was murdered. Ó Brádaigh gave us some bullshit about Lennon looking to rezone some of his land as residential. I didn't buy it. Unlike most of the other people we've interviewed, Ó Brádaigh isn't a consummate liar. I could almost see the wheels in his mind making up what he thought was a convincing story. Is there any contact between Feeney and Ó Brádaigh?'

'Are you kidding? They sing from the same hymn sheet.'

'Then I don't think that I'm finished with either Feeney or Ó Brádaigh.'

Duane's mobile phone rang and he took the call. 'They've traced Flynn's phone to a tower in a place called Furbo outside Galway. I'll get on to our guys there and get them to ask around.'

'You've got a head start on Feeney.'

'I wouldn't be so sure.'

FEENEY PUT down the phone and looked at Con Coleman. 'He's in Galway. His phone pinged off a tower in Furbo. Get a hold of the local boys there and get them on his trail. I don't want him damaged. If they get to him first, I want him brought up here to me.'

'Don't act hastily, Tommy,' Coleman said. 'We've been doing okay by keeping our heads down. Killing a garda could bring the combined weight of Dublin and Belfast down on us. Flynn is a flea on the arsehole of the world.'

'He knows too much.'

'He can shoot his mouth off, but he doesn't have any hard evidence. He can't tell them much more than they already know. Leave him be and let the guards deal with him.'

'We didn't come this far to let a loser like Flynn bring us down. Pass the word to the lads in Galway, find him, take him and bring him to me.'

FLYNN SPENT the afternoon in a pub overlooking Furbo beach. He was drinking and running through his options. None of them were good. If he went to Duane, the price of staying out of jail would be shopping Feeney. That was the equivalent of signing his own death warrant. What good was freedom if you had to look over your shoulder every day? He could just return to Dundalk and brazen it out. He could say that the departure of his wife and children had pushed him over the edge. He'd been depressed and needed time to reflect on his life. The powers that be wouldn't like it known that a major criminal had paid off a DI. He would have to resign, but he wouldn't have to shop Feeney. That was his best option. But would it satisfy Feeney? There was the possibility that he would flip and start talking and he doubted that Feeney would take that chance. He might get to resign and move away, but in time he would be the victim of a hit-and-run driver. He signalled to the barman for another pint of lager. There had to be another option.

# CHAPTER THIRTY-EIGHT

Wilson and Graham arrived back in Belfast just before the end of the shift. Moira and O'Neill were still at their desks. Wilson gathered the troops at the whiteboard and briefed them on the interviews with King, Feeney and Ó Brádaigh. He handed over the garda intel on Feeney to O'Neill.

'I've contacted PSNI Intelligence about Feeney,' O'Neill said. 'They got a bit snotty with a simple DC, but I mentioned your name and they suddenly became more cooperative. We'll have everything they have on him by tomorrow morning.'

'Get me what we have on Ó Brádaigh as well and put it all up on the whiteboard.'

'FSNI got back about the 999 call. The caller was using a simple voice changer app. They were able to decipher it.' Her fingers sped over the keyboard and the voice of a man came over the speakers: 'There's a dead man in a deserted barn just outside Inniskeen.'

'He's a man of few words,' Wilson said. 'And obviously has a bit of a conscience. We need to find him.'

'Will I send it to DCI Duane?' O'Neill said.

'Not at the minute.' The paranoia was catching.

'What's next, boss?' Graham said.

'Write up today's interviews and we'll go over everything again from the beginning. Feeney is the prime suspect but he's only that. We need to find evidence.'

Wilson moved to his office, turned on his computer and brought up his emails. There were more than a hundred unread and half of them were marked urgent. His first reaction was to trash the lot, but then he remembered he was a superintendent and he had bureaucratic obligations. He messaged Reid to meet him later in the Crown and started on the emails, beginning with the oldest.

THE CHAUFFEURED POLICE car pulled up in front of the Lattimers' mansion in Ballymoney. DCC Jennings descended from the car and cast an eye over the Lattimer family pile. Their home was a five-bay, three-storey detached house, built about 1800. To the southwest there was an early eighteenth-century wing. To the north, a modern conservatory and to the southwest, a range of late nineteenth-century outbuildings. The panelled front door was flanked by three-quarter Ionic pilasters and plain sidelights; these supported a projecting stone cornice and an elliptical-headed radial fanlight. Jennings had been born on a housing estate in Portadown. As a boy, he had aspired to live in a house such as Coleville House. Ulster had been kind to the Lattimers. He had no idea who had bestowed the original house on the family or what they had done to deserve it. He assumed the reason involved chicanery and was buried beneath the sands of time. But he had no reason to begrudge them their good fortune. Without the assistance of the Circle, he would never have risen to the second highest office in the PSNI. But the Circle wasn't altruistic. They hadn't promoted his cause because they liked him or appreciated his acumen. They needed someone like him at the top to do their dirty work. And he had done it. If evidence needed to disappear, he was their man. If an individual needed to be fitted up and then blackmailed, he was their man. The Circle had claimed their pound of flesh for assisting him. Lattimer's factotum took his cap and pointed him at the great hall.

When Jennings entered, he found himself directly facing the staring eyes of Sir Philip Lattimer. Jennings strode towards the empty chair across from him. It reminded him of being hauled before the headmaster during his days at Portadown Independent.

'Thanks for coming, Roy,' Lattimer said.

Jennings sat. He had assumed he was to attend a meeting of the top echelon of the Circle, but there was no Helen McCann or Lord Glenconnor. And the smell of a coup was in the air. He knew from Jackson that it had been tried before and McCann had meted out a severe punishment to Lattimer. Perhaps that had been forgotten. But maybe it hadn't been forgiven. 'Why am I here?'

'I want to pick your brain.'

'If I can be of assistance.'

'I understand that Helen asked you to procure the mobile phone they used in the Carlisle business.'

'She did.' Jennings was still a police officer who had been trained in interview techniques, so he wasn't about to say something that could be used to hang him later.

'Have you managed to get your hands on it?'

'Not yet, but I'm hopeful.'

'Does Wilson have enough to arrest Helen?'

'Good God no, he's not even close.'

'So, she's in no danger?'

'I don't think so.'

'Some of us think that she's overstepped it a bit lately, particularly in relation to the decision to terminate Carlisle and the failed attempt on Wilson's life. She appears to have an obsession about that man.'

Jennings didn't speak. There was no need to mention his own obsession in that direction.

'It would be particularly worrying if a senior member of the Circle were to be arrested and tried. And that relates more to Helen than anyone else. She knows where all the bodies are buried.'

And where all the money is stashed away, Jennings thought. 'I'm there to make sure that never happens.'

'Are you so sure you can guarantee that?'

'I've never failed before. The mobile phone is a piece of evidence, but on its own it's meaningless. Wilson is still stumbling around in the dark. He doesn't know that you exist.'

'That's good, of course, but we live in strange times. The Circle has evolved over the years. Helen still lives in a past where we must defend the Union at all costs. It is my view that our primary objective is to preserve our assets in the judiciary, the government and the security apparatus.'

Jennings thought that, in the end, it's all about the money. And the power. We mustn't forget the power. 'I'll keep a weather eye on Wilson and his team.'

'And let us know if there's any danger to our beloved chairlady.'

'Who is soon to be related to you by marriage.'

'I'm very fond of Kate. I'd hate it if something happened to her mother.'

Jennings looked at the gold Rolex on Lattimer's wrist and had a mental vision of him in his underpants. No, Helen McCann hadn't been forgiven for belittling him.


WILSON STUCK it out until Reid messaged that she was about to come to Tennent Street to drag him out of the station. She was on her second drink and in earnest conversation with McDevitt when Wilson flopped down on the seat beside her in the snug.

'Pint,' Wilson said.

McDevitt pushed the bell summoning the barman. 'How's our man in bandit country?'

'Struggling.'

McDevitt ordered the drinks. 'That makes three of us.' He nodded at Reid. 'I'm glad I don't have Steph's job.'

'I've been sounding off,' Reid laughed. 'Let's all tell each other what shitty jobs we have. But we'll all still turn up tomorrow morning for a replay.'

'It's the human condition.' Wilson took the pint of Guinness from the barman and drank half of it in one gulp. 'How's young Keating getting along?'

'He'll mend,' McDevitt said. 'But I don't think he'll be so keen on investigative journalism when he does.'

'Duane has some CCTV footage of the attack.'

'Two guys in balaclavas and black clothes beating the shit out of a young man,' McDevitt said. 'He can stick it on a shelf with all the other pieces of CCTV footage of punishment beatings in that part of the country.'

'We haven't seen Jack around much lately,' Reid said.

Wilson finished his drink and pushed the bell.

'Leave me out,' Reid said. 'Two is enough. Probably like you two, I haven't eaten since breakfast.'

Wilson ordered for him and McDevitt. 'Have you given up on Lennon?' Wilson asked.

'The editor has. My nose tells me there's a story down there, but nobody at the *Chronicle* is interested. There's a rumour around that some shower of investors wants to take the paper over. We're all quaking in our boots. Jobs are scarce out there.'

'Did I tell you that I read an interesting article today?' Reid said.

The two men looked at her.

'Three hundred to four hundred doctors die by suicide every year,' Reid said. 'Female doctors are at higher risk than men and show rates of two hundred and fifty per cent higher than the general population.'

Wilson and McDevitt looked at each other.

'And if my partner doesn't invite me to dinner, I'm going to bloody well consider suicide myself.'

Wilson downed his pint, as did McDevitt.

'Dinner's on me,' Wilson said.

Reid smiled. 'Thank you and no shop talk during the meal.'

# CHAPTER THIRTY-NINE

Detective Sergeant Donal Flatherty and Detective Garda Noleen Joyce had been given the unenviable task of locating some rogue garda inspector and returning him to his mammy. Flatherty was an old hand and would have made a perfunctory attempt to find the man, except the request had come directly from HQ in Dublin, which meant someone's arse was going to be kicked if they didn't find him. And Flatherty had a wide arse that didn't like being kicked. He and Joyce had been given the job because they were both natives of the area where the head buck-cats had the last contact with the missing man. They knew the area around Furbo well and everyone in it. They had spent the evening moving among the locals and asking about recently arrived strangers. Furbo was in Connemara, an area that welcomes tourists year-round so every place they stopped they heard stories of someone renting a caravan or cottage in the locality. What alarmed Flatherty was hearing from some of his contacts that he and his companion weren't the only ones looking for a new arrival. Two local men known to have connections with a terrorist organisation were also combing the area. That piece of information spurred him forward at a faster pace.

They eventually arrived at the pub that stood on the edge of Furbo beach. Flatherty put the photo he'd received from Dundalk of DI Daragh Flynn on the bar. 'Have you seen this man?'

The barman examined the photo. 'He was in here drinking all afternoon.'

'Did you speak to him?'

'We talked a bit about sport. The snooker was on the TV and we spoke about that for a while.'

'Did he have a northern accent?'

'That's him.'

'Any idea where he might be staying?'

'He said something about renting a cottage. The only place I know that's open at this time of year is Peadar Tom's. By the way, you're not the first to make the enquiry.'

'I know two heavy types were here already. How long ago?'

'A good half-hour.'

He thanked the barman and went outside.

'We have a problem,' Flatherty said as he climbed back into the car. 'It looks like we've been beaten to the punch. I don't know what this fella's done but half the country seems to be looking for him. If there's trouble, you stay out of the way.'

'If there's trouble,' Joyce said. 'We'll call it in and get an armed response unit out.'

'That'll be your job. Now let's get up to Peadar Tom's.'

HAVING SPENT most of the day in the pub watching sport on TV and drinking pints of Guinness, Flynn had left about six o'clock to return to his cottage. He'd drank more than he was used to and his head didn't feel the best. The cottage was situated on a small road, which led up a hill with a fine view over Galway Bay. The evening was still bright and he'd decided to walk to the top of the hill, where he could look down at the

Atlantic Ocean and the beach below. There was a steady stream of traffic coming out from Galway and the pub car park was filling up with patrons seeking a sneaky pint before heading home. He sat down on a large boulder. The scene was so normal. It would be wonderful if he could just stay like this. But he had screwed up and there was a price to pay. He became aware of the light fading and started back down the hill.

Beneath him he could see the lights of a car coming in his direction. It stopped a hundred metres beneath the cottage and the lights went out. His cottage was the last house on the road up the hill. It made sense that its final destination must be his cottage. He left the road and climbed over a stone wall into a field where gorse was growing wild and reached almost to his shoulder. Two men exited the car and made their way slowly towards the cottage. Flynn had excellent night vision and he followed their progress as they skirted his cottage. They didn't look like policemen, which meant Feeney had found him.

His first inclination was to turn and run. His second was to stand up and hand himself over. He'd been running for two days and he was already tired of it. This couldn't be his future. If he gave himself up, he'd been taken to Feeney and it would be over. He'd be dead and his children would grow up without a father. He crouched down behind the gorse and watched the men's stealthy approach. When they arrived at the cottage, they checked his car and nodded at each other. The door of the cottage was locked. The larger of the men kicked the door at the location of the lock and it splintered. They rushed inside.


FLATHERTY SAW the car parked at the side of the road and concluded that the opposition was still around. He was tempted to put on the siren but preferred the element of surprise. Joyce stopped the car close to the cottage and the two police officers exited. Flatherty looked at the door hanging off its hinges. He turned to Joyce. 'Time to send for the cavalry.'

She made the call on her radio.

He was almost at the door when two men emerged. Flatherty was six foot three, weighed two hundred and forty pounds and was a former garda boxing champion.

'What have we here, DG Joyce?' he said as the men stopped dead in their tracks. 'Right now, lads. I have you for breaking and entering. If you've clean records, you might get off with probation. If not, you're looking at time. If it goes any further, you could be looking at a lot of time. We have a record of your car's registration. If it's not stolen, we have you. We have already radioed for assistance. So, let's all relax until the heavy mob arrive.'

The two men were ashen faced.

'DG Joyce, take their particulars. And be careful now to arrest them properly and advise them of their rights.' He waited while Joyce took out her notebook and started writing. Flatherty moved forward and examined the car parked in front of the cottage. It was the one that Dublin was looking for. Flynn was somewhere about. Joyce was taking names and addresses and getting on with the arrest. In the distance, he could hear sirens. He entered the cottage and moved quickly though the rooms. Peadar Tom wouldn't be happy at the condition of his door. One of the bedrooms was in use and there was a shattered bottle in one of the corners. There was no sign of Flynn, but he wasn't far away.

FLYNN WATCHED the drama being played out in front of the cottage. The heavy-set garda had handled the situation perfectly. However, his own situation was greatly changed and for the worse. His means of transport was gone, and night was falling. He heard the sirens in the distance. The place would soon be swarming with gardaí and it was only a matter of time before they found him. He had no place to stay and spending the night in the open would not help. Two squad cars sped up the road and stopped at the cottage. Armed officers climbed out of the second car. The gig was up. He climbed back over the stone wall and made his way down the road.

'DI Flynn I suppose.' The heavy-set guard came forward to meet him. 'DS Donal Flatherty, it looks like we arrived just in time. I think those two gentlemen had evil intentions towards you, but they'll deny it with their last breath. You can ride along with my colleague and I back to Galway, and one of the lads will drive your car. We can inform Dublin and Dundalk of the good news.'

Flynn was only half-listening. He was busy working on his cover story. It was out of the question to implicate Feeney. He was guilty of leaking information but not directly to the top man. 'Thanks, sergeant.' Flynn sat into the rear seat of Flatherty's squad car.

# CHAPTER FORTY

When Wilson reached the station there was a flashing urgent message on his phone. It was from Duane. He was to proceed to Dundalk immediately. Flynn had been located and was in the cells. This meant another trip south but hopefully not a fruitless one. He contemplated heading off on his own but decided to collect Graham first. A half an hour here or there wouldn't change anything. This was the last day of his stay of execution from Davis. If he was going to bring the Carlisle case to Baird, he would have to do it soon. He walked to the squad room and O'Neill beckoned him over.

'Morning, boss. Feeney's file from Intelligence arrived. It makes interesting reading.'

'Let's have it.'

'His sheet is extensive, so I'll stick to the highlights. He was born in 1947. He joined the IRA early and was allegedly a member of the South Armagh Battalion. He's suspected of planning and taking part in several gun attacks and bombings. His involvement was never proven. After the signing of the peace accord, he concentrated on establishing an organised crime group involving some of his former comrades. His prominence is such that his name appears on the BBC's

Underworld Rich List. The OCG makes money principally from smuggling oil, grain, cigarettes and pigs. He also owns several legitimate businesses. Our Intelligence people are aware that the Garda Síochána is planning a major operation to take him down. Those are the highlights, but there's a lot more.'

'The conclusion is that we're dealing with a bad man. Put it on the board.'

'It's already there.' She held out a USB stick. 'This is the unscrambled 999 call. You can give it to Duane, if you like.'

Wilson took the USB and put it in his pocket. 'When the time is right.'

She handed him the file on Feeney. 'Only problem is the caller's voice is not too clear.'

'Good work.' He turned to Graham, who was sitting at his desk. 'Harry, put your coat back on, we're heading south again.'

Wilson flipped through Feeney's rap sheet. The gang leader might not be in the Premier League of Criminals, but he was up there. Why the hell would he involve himself with a man like Brian Lennon? There was no sense to it.


DUANE PULLED BACK the viewing slide of Flynn's cell in the basement of Dundalk Garda Station and saw Flynn lying on the bed with his back to the door. He stood aside and Wilson took his place. Duane had insisted that Flynn was not under arrest but simply in protective custody.

'The sleep of the just.' Wilson closed the slide.

'At least we got to him in time,' Duane said as they climbed the stairs to the ground floor. 'We have two guys in the cells in Galway. They'll be interviewed this morning under caution. I doubt we'll get anything out of them. Officially they've been arrested for breaking and entering, but a search of their car produced a gun. They're known to us and both have a connection with a terrorist organisation. They'll go down for possession of the gun.'

'It looks like Flynn had a lucky escape.' Wilson followed Duane into the incident room.

'It would appear so. But did it scare him enough to make him tell us all he knows about Feeney? I don't believe a word about his contact always wearing a balaclava. Feeney would have dealt with a DI directly.'

'Threaten to throw him out on the street.'

'That mightn't be much of a threat. Feeney will know eventually that he didn't talk, which will probably be enough to take him off the kill list. We need to muddy the waters a bit.'

'What do have in mind?'

'Just play along.'

'What does this all mean for the Lennon investigation?'

'Precious little is my guess.'

Wilson took out Feeney's PSNI Intelligence file from his jacket pocket. 'This is what we have on Feeney. It's the mirror image of what your Intelligence people have. There's no doubt that he's a bad dude as you might say, but I'm stumped for a motive for killing Lennon. It makes no sense.'

'Where does sense come into what these guys do?'

Wilson fished out the USB from his pocket. 'FSNI cleaned up the 999 call. This is the guy's actual voice.'

Duane took the USB and handed it to one of the detectives sitting at a computer. 'Play it.'

A soft voice came out of the speakers. The message was short and to the point.

'Play it again,' Duane said.

The detective did as he was told.

'Damned if I haven't heard that voice,' Duane said.

It sounded like every voice Wilson had heard in Crossmaglen. 'It's no good unless we have something to compare it to.'

'And voice-printing every male in south Armagh is probably out of the question.'

'Budget restrictions,' Wilson said.

'Most definitely.'

DS Guiney approached them. 'When do you intend inter-viewing Flynn?'

'Tell the duty sergeant to wake him and give him breakfast, then we'll take a run at him.'

'What about McCluskey? He's in the interview room with his solicitor.'

Duane turned to Wilson. 'One of the guys on the CCTV footage of the attack on Keating has the same build as McCluskey. Your guys picked him up for us and handed him over. We want to keep the pressure on him. And I want him to see Flynn being brought into the interview room.' He turned back to Guiney. 'You handle the interview. We'll watch.'


McCLUSKEY STARED at the camera in the corner of the inter-view room. Michael Coyle sat at his side.

Guiney entered the room accompanied by Meg Hearney. He sat across from McCluskey while Hearney started the recording equipment. 'DG Hearney, caution him.'

Hearney cautioned McCluskey.

'Mr McCluskey, a young man was assaulted by two men outside DJ Dave's nightclub three nights ago.' Guiney put a still photo from the CCTV footage on the table. 'We've shown the victim your photo and he suspects that you were one of the men.'

McCluskey ignored the photo. 'No comment.'

'The men in this photo are wearing balaclavas,' the solic-itor said. 'How could the victim recognise my client?'

'Your client has the same build as one of the men in the photo,' Guiney said.

'Half the men in the county have the same build as my client.'

Guiney looked at McCluskey. 'So, you're not one of these men?'

'No comment.'

'Were you in Dundalk three nights ago?' Guiney asked.

'No comment.'

Guiney put another photo on the table. 'This is a still from a CCTV camera in Tom Bellew Avenue ten minutes after the assault. It shows two men with the exact same physique as the attackers.' He put a photo showing a blow-up of the faces of the men. 'I don't think that there's any doubt about who the man on the right is.' He looked at the solicitor, who was examining the photo.

'No comment.'

'He didn't ask you anything, thickhead,' Hearney said.

McCluskey shot her a glance.

'This photo was taken within ten minutes of the assault and two hundred metres from where it took place. Would you show me your hands please?'

McCluskey kept his hands in his jacket pocket.

Guiney looked at the solicitor. 'Would you tell your client to show me his hands. Otherwise I'll arrest him and take his fingerprints and a photo of his knuckles.'

'I need to confer with my client,' the solicitor said.

Guiney nodded and Hearney stopped the recording. They left the room.

'GOOD MAN,' Duane said when Guiney met them in the viewing room. 'Get ready to bring McCluskey out and we're having Flynn brought up from the cells. They have to pass each other in the corridor as naturally as possible.' He turned to Wilson. 'Ian, you and I are big pals with Flynn, got it?'

'I get it.'

'Right then. Let's go to reception and collect Flynn.'

· · ·

'YOU LOOK RESTED, DARAGH,' Duane said. 'Let's go to an interview room, it'll be more private.'

Flynn looked at Wilson. 'Why is he here? I had nothing to do with Lennon.'

'We know,' Wilson said.

'You're a sound man, Daragh,' Duane had his arm around Flynn's shoulder.

'The best,' Wilson added.

They were walking along the corridor leading to the interview rooms when a door opened and Guiney ushered McCluskey and his solicitor into the corridor.

Duane opened the nearest door and bundled Flynn inside. Wilson followed up and closed the door.

'You fucker Duane,' Flynn said when they were inside. 'You set that up. You wanted McCluskey to see me. That's why you were doing the pals act. Are you trying to get me killed?'

'Sit down, Flynn,' Duane said. 'I hate bent coppers. So watch your mouth.'

'Fuck you,' Flynn said. 'Everybody knows you're the fixer for the big boys in Dublin. You're more bent than me.'

Duane bunched up his fist and Wilson put a hand on his shoulder.

'I'm tempted to toss you out of here right now and let you take your chances,' Duane said. 'But I'm hoping you remember the oath you took when you passed out of Templemore.'

'I'm saying nothing,' Flynn said.

'We saved your bacon last night,' Duane said. 'We won't do it again.'

'Go ahead,' Flynn said. 'Toss me out and live with the consequences.'

'We have you on corruption in public office. I'll be handing you over to Professional Services and I've no doubt that the Director of Public Prosecutions will be involved. But in the meantime, let's go by the book. Stand up.'

Flynn stood.

'Daragh Flynn, I'm arresting you on a charge of corruption in public office under the Criminal Justice Corruption Offences Act 2018. You do not have to say anything, but anything you do say will be taken down and used in evidence.'

Flynn fell back into the chair and put his hands to his head.

'You betrayed your colleagues for money,' Duane said. 'We're going to keep you here in the cells. If you were half a man, you'd tell us everything you know about Lennon.'

'I know nothing and that's the God's truth. I was only leaking information about the raids.'

'THAT DIDN'T GO TO PLAN,' Wilson said when he and Duane were alone again.

'It was worth a shot.'

'It's nice to know you have a heart in there somewhere.'

'There but for the grace of God, go I. If we asked for his colleagues without sin to cast the first stone, there'd be precious few stones cast.'

'But none of our questions about Lennon have been answered.'

'I'd like to visit Feeney, but you'll have to come along as he's in your jurisdiction.'

'Butch Cassidy and the Sundance Kid.'

'Always.'

# CHAPTER FORTY-ONE

'Would you sit down, Tommy,' Coleman said. 'You're wearing a hole in the carpet with all that pacing.'

'One fucking hour.' Feeney continued pacing. 'If they'd arrived an hour earlier or if the guards had arrived an hour later, we'd have had him.'

'He won't talk.'

'I have it on good authority that he already has.'

'But he won't name names. It looks like he's going to take the fall himself.'

'Maybe he will and maybe he won't. I'll only know for certain when Flynn is in a hole in the ground.'

Feeney's phone rang and he answered. He listened but didn't speak.

'That was Coyle.' He terminated the call. 'Flynn is in Dundalk. McCluskey saw him all pally with Wilson and that bollocks Duane. I told you, we'll only be safe when Flynn has been planted.'

'A lot of our friends are getting nervous. There are two decent men banged up in Galway because of us. They're probably going to spend a couple of years inside.'

'Well any friends who are wavering should remember what I've done for them.'

'People's memories are short. I think we should lie low for a while.'

'Have you lost your balls? We didn't build this organisation by lying low.'

Coleman looked around. 'I'm still living in the same house I was in twenty years ago. I work as a manager in your builders providers. I'm the kind of employee you'll throw under the bus when it's required.'

Feeney stopped pacing and put his arm around Coleman's shoulder. 'We've both done well out of our little business.'

Coleman didn't respond.

The doorbell sounded and Feeney nodded at Coleman, who strolled towards the front of the house. He returned with Dáithí Ó Brádaigh in tow.

'What the fuck do you want?' Feeney said.

'I had the peelers around to see me yesterday,' Ó Brádaigh said. 'Asking questions about Brian Lennon.'

'So, what's new?' Feeney said. 'Don't get your knickers in a twist.'

'They wanted to know what Lennon and I spoke about.'

'I can well imagine. And what did you tell them?'

'He wanted part of his land zoned residential.'

'Did they swallow it?'

'I don't know. That Wilson character doesn't give away much.'

'And you're not such a great liar,' Feeney said. 'I can just picture you spluttering away, trying to think on the hoof. You'll never make it in politics unless you learn how to lie with a straight face.'

'Belfast and Dublin are worried about you,' Ó Brádaigh said. 'They've supported you in the past because of your commitment to the cause, but their patience is growing thin.

This Lennon business put the tin hat on it for some. You lost the rest of them with last night's fiasco in Galway.'

Feeney grabbed Ó Brádaigh by the throat. 'I'm surrounded by a bunch of eunuchs. Tell the ballless fuckers in Belfast and Dublin that they don't tell me what to do.'

Coleman prised Feeney's hands free. 'Dáithí is only doing what he's been told.'

'Go back and tell your pals that they owe me, big time. Nobody welshes on Tommy Feeney. Now get the fuck out of here and be happy that you're leaving in one piece.' Feeney shoved Ó Brádaigh towards the door.

'I'll pass along the message.' Ó Brádaigh rushed out of the room, rubbing his neck as he went.

Coleman heard the front door open and slam shut. 'We can't operate without friends, Tommy. You can't go around shitting on people who have supported us.'

Feeney moved his face close to Coleman's. 'I can do anything I fucking well want. I think they need you at the shop.'

Coleman turned and left. There was no talking to Tommy when he was in this mood.

WILSON AND DUANE had almost reached the entrance to the driveway leading to Feeney's house when a car shot out without looking and almost hit them. Wilson recognised the driver. 'That was our friend Dáithí Ó Brádaigh, the local councillor. Now I wonder what he was doing here.'

'I could hazard a guess,' Duane said. 'My superiors are keeping the business in Galway quiet. The two men arrested in Galway are known former members of the IRA. We know that Feeney uses his links with the organisation to cover his ass and spread his influence. My guess is that Feeney is rapidly pissing people off.'

'Do you have something else I should know?'

'No, other than that there's a commitment to bring Feeney down.'

Wilson pulled up outside the Texan-style house. 'Let's poke the bear in the eye.'

They were approaching the front door when it opened, and Coleman exited. He stopped dead in his tracks.

'Tommy's inside,' he said and moved off in the direction of a white van parked at the side of the house.

'Not a happy fella,' Duane said.

Wilson knocked on the door and pushed it open wider at the same time. He saw Feeney exit the living room and cross the hallway.

'Ah hell, if it isn't Tweedle Dum and Tweedle Dee,' Feeney said. 'I get rid of one bunch of fuckers and another bunch arrives. What do you want?'

'We need to speak to you about some matters that have come to our attention.'

'Fuck off.' He moved to close the door.

Duane put his body against the door.

'We can do it here or in Newry PSNI Station,' Wilson said.

Feeney stared at Duane. 'You've been living on borrowed time. Maybe it's about to run out.'

'Drop the macho bullshit,' Duane said. 'Anytime you're in the humour, you know where to find me.'

Feeney released his grip on the door. 'That we do.' He turned and walked back into the house.

Wilson and Duane followed Feeney into the living room.

'State your business and get on your way,' Feeney said.

'We have DI Flynn in custody in Dundalk,' Wilson said.

Feeney pointed at Duane. 'That clown has no jurisdiction here. I want him out.'

'DCI Duane is leading the investigation into the death of

Brian Lennon,' Wilson said. 'He's here in that capacity and I cover any jurisdictional issues that might arise.'

'I already told you that I had nothing to do with Lennon's death. If that's what you're here to question me about, you can leave now.'

'Or we can continue at Newry PSNI Station,' Wilson said.

'Get on with it then. But I'm not answering questions from him.' Feeney pointed at Duane.

'DI Flynn has admitted providing information to an organised crime group operating across the border.'

'What's that got to do with me?'

'We're convinced that sooner or later Flynn will name you as the person he provided the information to.'

'You have your head up your arse. I don't even know this character Flynn. Anyway, what has providing information to some gang or other got to do with Lennon's death?'

'We believe there is a connection between the two.' Wilson was watching Feeney's face carefully. The movement of the lips was slight, but it was there. It was the quarter-smile that said Feeney knew there was no connection between the two crimes, and he was happy that's the way the investigation was going.

'This is no concern of mine. I'm a legitimate businessman.'

'You're a piece of shit who has infected this area,' Duane said. 'You've been protected much too long and everybody has had enough of you.'

Feeney made to grab Duane, who evaded the attempt. 'Who the fuck do you fellas think you are? You think you're the law here. Well you're not. I'm the fucking law here. Now get the hell out of my house before I do something I might regret.'

'You're getting old, Tommy,' Duane smiled. 'Ten years ago, you would have had me by the throat.' He tapped Wilson on the shoulder, and they walked to the front door. 'Be seeing you.' Duane called over his shoulder.

'I think you might have poked the bear a little hard in the eye,' Wilson said as he and Duane sat back into the car.

'Feeney has a short fuse. We need him good and mad.'

'Oh, I think he's good and mad all right.'

# CHAPTER FORTY-TWO

Moira found McDevitt sitting at the same table in McHugh's he'd occupied on their previous meeting there.

'How did your date go?'

'What date?' Moira said.

'The one you were on when you couldn't meet me two nights ago.'

'Yeah, one of my ex-boyfriend's colleagues was in town and he asked me to dinner. Why the hell am I telling you this?'

'Because I'm a journalist and my gift is getting people to tell me things they should keep to themselves.'

The waitress came and they ordered lunch.

'I'm paying for my own lunch this time,' Moira said. 'You got me the photos and I gave you the heads-up for the arrest of Vincent Timoney and the action at his house. We're even.'

'I have an eye for talent, Moira. And I think you're going to be the big boss in the Murder Squad one day. I can help you get there. I'm the one who made your boss one of the most recognisable names in the province.'

'Get away with it. Ian Wilson was one of the most recognisable names in the province long before he met you.'

'Only among the small percentage of people interested in rugby. I made him famous with the working class.'

Their lunch arrived but neither started eating.

'What exactly are you up to?' Moira asked.

'I need to know why you're interested in Helen McCann.'

'I never said I was interested in her.'

'You never said you weren't.'

'It was the man in those photos that I'm interested in.'

'Who is he?'

'The man who assaulted DC Peter Davidson.'

'What's his name?'

'I can't tell you.'

'Then what's the man who assaulted Davidson doing in a photograph taken at McCann's house?'

'I don't know.'

McDevitt removed a tome from his messenger bag. 'This is everything that's available publicly that an intern could find on Helen McCann.' He handed the folder across.

Moira flicked through the pages. She recognised many of the articles she had downloaded herself but there were also some new ones. She handed the folder back.

'She's an interesting woman,' McDevitt said.

'If you say so.'

'I saw the way your eyes lit up when you flicked through those papers. You're like a dog that's picked up the scent. You have an alertness about you when you hear her name. Tell me why and I'll help you as much as I can.'

Moira started on her salad. She wasn't hungry. She could feel McDevitt's eyes boring into her. 'I'm only interested in the man in the photo.'

'The man whose name you can't divulge.'

'There are reasons.'

'I've been around this city a long time. You need a strong stomach to be a crime reporter here. And to be a Murder Squad detective. We both get to deal with some of the lowest life forms. McCann is a very dangerous woman. If you and Ian are attempting to take her on, you're going to need to accept whatever help is on the table. I don't expect you to tell Ian about our little arrangement but remember what I said.'

Moira tossed a ten-pound note onto the table. 'I've got to get back to the station.'

'Come on, you've hardly touched your lunch. Don't make me eat alone. Stay and we'll be Irish and talk about the weather. Anything except Helen McCann.'

She hesitated. Perhaps she was over-reacting.

McDevitt was smiling at her. 'Relax and I'll tell what it's like to pitch a book to the lads in Hollywood.'

She sat down. It was the second time in a few days that she'd changed her mind.


WILSON AND DUANE returned to Dundalk Garda Station and had a sandwich and tea in the cafeteria while Flynn was brought up from the cells and installed in an interview room. Wilson and Duane entered soon after.

'You're still under caution,' Duane said before starting the tape.

'Detective Superintendent Wilson and I visited Tommy Feeney this morning after we spoke to you. He was very agitated. I'd go so far as to say that he's very bloody angry. And I suppose you know what Tommy does when he's angry.' Duane opened a folder in front of him and took out an autopsy photo of Brian Lennon. 'I think that Tommy was pretty angry with Lennon.'

Flynn remained silent.

'McCluskey has reported back that he saw you here in the station. You like a gamble. What do you bet that there's a car outside somewhere with a couple of heavies in it waiting for your friendly face to walk out the door?'

'I was lifted at seven o'clock,' Flynn said. 'That gives you another five hours to question me. I need a solicitor.'

'Remember who you're playing with,' Duane said. 'If you saw a black mamba in your cell, would you try to talk it out of killing you or would you run for your life? Tommy lost a lot of business goods in those raids, he's in the frame for murdering Lennon, and you're a loose end he liked to tie up. Do the maths.'

Flynn slammed his hands onto the table. 'You fuckers are trying to get me killed.'

Duane put a new photo of the bloody and battered body of Lennon on the table in front of Flynn. 'Tommy was mad with Lennon. Now he's mad with you. The last thing we want is to be examining photos of your body.'

'We're done here,' Flynn said. 'Solicitor.'

Duane picked up the photos and put them back in his file. 'I said this before but now I really mean it, it's your funeral Daragh. You've already proved that you're stupid, but this is downright crazy.'


Wilson and Duane walked back to the incident room.

'You're not really going to cut him loose are you?' Wilson asked.

'Only when I have to.'

'You'll never see him again. Look at Feeney's sheet. He'd kill his own family if they threatened his operation.'

'I'll apply for an extension to the time I can keep him. I might get it and I might not. But sooner or later he's going to be on the street. Other than his admission, we have no concrete evidence that he was leaking information on the raids to Feeney. If he withdraws his statement then we have nothing. I have a couple of lads working on gathering what evidence is out there. We've got his bank statements and his phone logs. It's only a matter of time before we get enough evidence to satisfy the DPP. In the meantime, his solicitor will apply for police bail and we'll be hard put to refuse.'

It was mid-afternoon by the time Wilson arrived back in Belfast. He went straight to the station and his office. Davis would be returning tomorrow so his time was up. He used his mobile phone to call Chief Constable Norman Baird on his private mobile number. The phone rang but wasn't immediately answered. Then the ring was cut off. Wilson put his phone in front of him on the table and waited. Ten minutes elapsed before his phone rang.

'This had better be important,' Baird said.

'We need to meet.'

'Outside the office?'

'I'm afraid so.'

'Why do I have a pain in the pit of my stomach all of a sudden?'

'Because you know I wouldn't call unless I had to.'

'How long will it take?'

'It's a long story.'

'I'll get back.'

The runes were cast. If the chief constable was bent, it was the end of Wilson's career.

# CHAPTER FORTY-THREE

DCC Jennings could feel the walls closing in on him. He tried to put his finger on what was bothering him. The Circle was at the zenith of its power. The organisation had a hand in every corner of the province, wielding more power than the Masons and the Orange Order put together, and yet hardly anyone knew it existed. The whole question of secret networks and the existence of the dark state was the realm of the conspiracy theorists, but this conspiracy was real. The state had proved itself incapable of functioning, and still the Circle had held things together. Its grip on the police, the justice system, the civil service and business life had been instrumental in keeping the province operating normally and maintaining the status quo. If ever there was a justification for the deep state, then the Circle was it. It had also proved its capacity to cream off its share of the monies that flowed into the province after the signing of the peace accord. Like the paramilitaries, the Circle had morphed from a bulwark against change into a criminal enterprise par excellence. Jennings was proud to be part of an organisation so powerful and yet so unknown. He recognised that such organisations were organic and need to grow and change with the times. But, like

Lattimer, Jennings had identified a shift back towards the fanaticism of the past. The ghost of Judge McCann hung over the Circle like a malignant presence. He had always respected Helen McCann. She had a brilliant mind and she deserved the lifestyle she enjoyed because of it. But lately her decision-making was out of kilter. The murder of Carlisle and the attempt to kill Wilson were rash and unnecessary. He, more than anyone, would have welcomed Wilson's death, but as the dead bodies multiplied so did the chances of exposure. He had so far failed to retrieve the evidence that McCann had demanded. And a psychopath like Simon Jackson was now close to the centre of power. McCann should know that power is only useful if it's used sparingly. For the first time since he had been inducted into the Circle, Jennings felt doubt.

WILSON DROPPED into the station when he got back to Belfast. He'd examined his phone a half-dozen times to see if he had missed a message from Baird but there was nothing. He wondered whether was a reason for the delay in responding. The chief constable was a busy man, of course. There was also a possibility that he would run a potential meeting by one of his assistants first. Wilson hoped not. The fewer people in the loop the better. The team was in the squad room when he entered. He went straight to the whiteboard and looked at the additions O'Neill had made. Feeney had been installed as the prime suspect in the murder of Brian Lennon.

'What's new, boss?' Moira asked.

'Nothing much in Dundalk,' Wilson said. 'Flynn is in custody but isn't talking. The poor fool thinks that if he keeps his mouth shut, Feeney will allow him to fade away into the sunset. That's not the MO of the man whose CV is on this whiteboard. Duane is trying to convince him that his best chance is to come clean.'

'Is Feeney definitely our boy?' Graham asked.

Wilson nodded. 'I still don't know why he did it, but I'm certain he's behind the murder.' He turned to O'Neill. 'Anything on the phone records?'

'I put in the request, but you know what the suppliers are like. I'll get on to them again.'

'Keep at it. Moira, come into my office for a minute.'

Moira closed the office door after them and sat in Wilson's visitor's chair. 'Why the deep frown, boss?'

'I called Baird.'

'And?'

'He said he'd call me back, but I haven't heard from him. I have no idea what that means.'

'If Baird doesn't come through, we'll need some outside help.'

'If Baird doesn't come through, we've shot our bolt. If there's any evidence out there against Helen McCann, it's about to vanish. Baird could close this whole unit down. Even if he does meet with us, there's no guarantee he'll believe our crazy story.'

'There's got to be something in the papers that Feinstein gathered. We just need someone with the expertise to find it.'

'We are where we are. I'll let you know when the meeting with Baird is on.'

'What about Davis?'

'She'll shit a brick. All our careers are on the line. I've gone all in on this one.'

'Jackson is the key. If we could just lay our hands on him.'

'Yes. I wonder where the elusive Mr Jackson is these days.'

DUANE LAY back in his chair, put his feet on the desk and closed his eyes. CS Nolan wanted him back in Dublin where the powers that be were discussing an all-out war against the organised crime groups operating on both sides of the border. He was stalling and using the fact that Flynn was still in the cells as an excuse. He'd been charged with bringing back the head of Tommy Feeney, metaphorically speaking, which was an objective he was failing to achieve. Although it wasn't for the want of trying. But Jack Duane was seldom associated with failure. He'd pinned all his hopes on Flynn finally getting the little bit of sense God granted him by spilling all he knew about Feeney's operation and the death of Brian Lennon. He'd applied for, and got, an extension of twelve hours to keep Flynn on remand. Given that most of the extension would be overnight, it meant he had one last chance before he would be forced to allow Flynn out on bail. The charge of malfeasance in public office wasn't grave enough to hold him indefinitely. He could feel his eyes burning in his sockets. He imagined Wilson in the snug at the Crown cradling a pint of Guinness. He took a deep breath and opened his eyes. He picked up a file and left the incident room.

'GOD BUT YOU LOOK GLUM.' Reid dropped her attaché case and sat beside Wilson. 'Be a good man and order me a drink and make it a big one.'

Wilson pressed the bell and made the order.

'As the man said to the horse, why the long face?' Reid kissed him.

'I think I might have screwed up.'

'What's new?'

The barman appeared with a gin and tonic for Reid and a refill for Wilson.

'No, I mean it. I let my emotions run away with me. There's no real evidence that Helen McCann is responsible for murdering Carlisle. We have a PSNI Special Branch officer called Jackson down for giving Carlisle a fatal hotshot, but we have no idea why. Maybe my initial hypothesis was wrong. Sticking my nose into the Carlisle affair could have got poor old Peter Davidson killed. Now, I've involved Moira and she's as obsessed with nailing McCann as I am. And Davis's stellar career will be ruined because they'll say she didn't control me. It looks like I've done it this time.'

'Does this have anything to do with you and Kate?'

'Absolutely not, that relationship was dead before we ever made the connection between Carlisle, Jackson and McCann. Helen McCann received a phone call from the man we believe murdered Carlisle a few minutes after the murder took place. That could be the most coincidental piece of evidence ever. Any prosecutor would laugh it off if I presented that as a reason to pursue McCann.'

'What's brought this on?'

'I called Baird. We can't keep treading water. I want him to make the investigation official and give us the resources we need to complete it. I thought we could inch our way towards nailing her, but I was wrong. We need to piss or get up off the pot.'

'If it has nothing to do with you and Kate, why did you say you've allowed your emotions to get the better of you?'

'Because I allowed Helen to get under my skin. Maybe I recognised that she was dirty from the get-go.'

'You're claiming second sight?'

'No, it's just that when Peter turned up the mobile phone and the connection with Jackson it seemed to fit.'

'Where is Jackson now?'

'He's working for Helen McCann.'

'That's more than coincidental.'

'I know.'

'So, what's the problem?'

'McCann is a powerful woman. Her daughter is slated to become the next attorney general. In going to Baird, I was aware that I was putting my career on the line. But then it came home to me that I've also put Davis's and Moira's careers on the line. Davis has known about the unofficial investigation for some time. That might be enough to finish her. The same goes for Moira.'

'I see.'

'And Baird hasn't responded.'

'Everything happens for a reason. Remember that you can only control those events within your control. There's nothing you can do about Baird, and there may be nothing you can do about Helen McCann.'

'I have a feeling that Carlisle is going to be "my case". You know, the one that I'll still be thinking of when I'm sitting in a chair in the care home. Every detective has one.' He picked up his glass and drank half the contents.

'What about your case with Jack?'

'We know who was behind the murder, but we may not be able to prove it.'

'Will that be another of your "cases"?'

'Brian Lennon depends on Jack and me to get him justice. I would be royally pissed off if we failed.'

Wilson's phone indicated the receipt of a message: *Tomorrow. 7 a.m. Benedict's Hotel. Room 205.* He showed it to Reid. 'The point of no return.'

DUANE AND DS GUINEY entered the interview room. Flynn immediately stopped speaking with his solicitor. Duane sat heavily on the chair facing Flynn, looked at Guiney and nodded. The DS started the recording equipment. 'Well Daragh, we've reached a sorry state. Your career is in the toilet. I've been in contact with the DPP and they've decided to rip you a new arsehole. That's something you may not appreciate when you're inside.'

'DCI Duane,' the solicitor said. 'May I ask you to refrain from threatening my client.'

'Okay,' Duane said. 'Nobody likes a bent copper, not even the lags. We've offered you as much assistance as we can for your cooperation, but you have declined.' He removed a photo from his file. 'This is a photo of a young man named Keating who was severely beaten for assisting a journalist in his enquiries regarding Lennon's murder.' He put a second photo on the table. 'This is a photo of two men stationed outside your home.' He put a third photo on the table. 'This is a photo of two men waiting outside this station for you to leave. Now, in the name of God do not put yourself at the mercy of someone like Tommy Feeney.'

# CHAPTER FORTY-FOUR

W ilson woke at three o'clock and quickly realised that he wasn't going back to sleep. The dream involving his death was still vivid in his mind. He could feel Reid's body snuggled into his back and he had no desire to wake her. She wouldn't rouse until seven, so he had four hours in which to mull over the Lennon murder and the folly of investigating Carlisle's death. Both cases posed substantial problems. He had two prime suspects but not a shred of evidence to implicate either of them. He had no idea of the motive for either crime. And there were two crime scenes that had yielded no concrete evidence.

He focused on Brian Lennon. The pathologist had concluded that at least six men had been involved in beating Lennon to death. Where are they? Assuming Feeney is behind the murder, who owes allegiance to him? Why are two of the best detectives in Ireland floundering about? Either Feeney is a criminal genius, or he and Duane are incompetent coppers. The veil of silence that hangs over Crossmaglen was going to be difficult, if not impossible, to penetrate. Feeney is rich and has powerful political backing. Lennon had no connection with criminality and was poor and vulnerable into the bargain.

What possible connection could there be between the two men? He let his mind go back to when he first saw the body. There didn't seem to be any significance in the location. Duane had established that the house and barn had been derelict for some time. The owner of the property had no apparent connection to Feeney but was a well-known republican sympathiser. There was no CCTV in the area. There were tracks of a minibus but no sign of the vehicle itself. The tyre tracks would fit any minibus and would lead nowhere. The autopsy had revealed that an otherwise healthy young man had been beaten to death. There would have been substantial amounts of blood spatter. That might count if they ever found the clothes the murderers had worn. Otherwise the autopsy had yielded no additional evidence that might point to the attackers. There was the 999 call. They had the voice of the caller but nothing to match it against. It was another dead end. The case was getting cold and would soon get colder. The investigation would be wound up and the file would be stored in some underground bunker. Is Feeney going to get away with the perfect murder? Perhaps. Unless he and Duane put their skates on and cracked the motive.

Wilson's mind flipped to Carlisle. His optimism about putting Helen McCann in the dock for Carlisle's demise might have been misplaced. Reid was right. They need to find Jackson. They could place him at the house at the time of Carlisle's death, but they couldn't put the syringe with the hotshot into his hand. There were no witnesses to what happened in the conservatory. Davidson had done a great job of picking up pieces of circumstantial evidence, but the DPP would laugh him out of the office if he put what he had on the table. Given that he couldn't even get an arrest warrant for Jackson on what he had, what chance did he have of proving that McCann had given the order. Carlisle's death was worthy of investigation, but it was headed down the same road as the Lennon case. There were holes in the suicide theory and there were holes in his hypothesis. Perhaps his call to Baird had been premature. He'd discovered a long time ago that he was not capable of solving every crime. Sometimes the deck is stacked against the police. The requirement to find credible evidence where none exists or it is well hidden is a major stumbling block. The days when a suspect could be badgered into signing his life away were long gone. Feeney and McCann might be worlds apart in some respects, but they both think they're smarter than the police and so far, maybe they are. Wilson was about to reveal to the chief constable that he had been running an unofficial murder investigation and that his prime suspect was one of the province's most prominent citizens. The CC would be justified in considering him crazy and demanding his warrant card.

Morning light was filtering into the room and he could feel Reid stirring against him. He wondered how many more sleepless nights he would endure.

BENEDICT's HOTEL is in Bradbury Place between the city centre and Queen's University. Wilson arrived five minutes early and saw Moira already sitting in the reception area. He was feeling a lot less confident about the pitch he was preparing to make than he had been when he placed the call to Baird. 'Let's go,' he said as he passed her. She joined him and they took the stairs to the second floor. Wilson rapped on the door of Room 205.

Baird opened the door. He was an imposing figure in full uniform. 'Come in and grab a coffee.'

'Sir,' Wilson said. 'This is my colleague DS Moira McElvaney.'

Baird stuck out his hand. 'Pleased to meet you, Moira.'

'Sir.' Moira shook.

Wilson looked around. The early morning news was playing on the television and the lead story was Brexit, once again. There was a flask and two clean cups on a sideboard beside Baird's cap and the CC had sat in the only chair in the room. Wilson poured a coffee for Moira and himself and sat on the end of the double bed.

'Fire away,' Baird said.

'I believe that Jackie Carlisle was murdered,' Wilson began.

'Good God, are you out of your mind?' Baird was half out of his chair. 'His death has already been ruled as a suicide. He was terminally ill. He had six months to live at the most and he was in extreme pain. Why in God's name would someone murder a dying man?'

'I don't know the answer to that question.'

Baird eased himself back into his chair. 'Lay it out for me.'

'Carlisle wasn't the type to take his own life. His son was due home from the US the week after his death. He wouldn't have killed himself without saying goodbye to his son.'

'Pain and a death sentence can do strange things to people. How was he murdered?'

'He was given a massive shot of morphine. His medication was being supervised by the local hospice. They have very strict control on their medicines, and they swear he didn't get the drug from them. He was due an injection on the day of his death, but someone rang and cancelled the visit. However, a man dressed in a nurse's white jacket was seen outside Carlisle's house.'

'Maybe someone called to reinstate the visit.'

'A neighbour has identified the male nurse as Sergeant Simon Jackson of the PSNI Special Branch.'

Baird put down his cup. 'Identified how?'

'DC Peter Davidson was carrying out a preliminary investigation. He showed the neighbour a selection of photographs and the neighbour picked out Jackson. We have proof that Jackson made a single phone call from the scene and Davidson traced the call to a mobile phone found at Belfast International

Airport. The phone had been dumped in the VIP lounge and was recovered by Davidson from lost property. He sourced the phone's point of sale and examined the CCTV from the shop. A porter from the Merchant Hotel purchased the phone. The instruction to buy it was issued by Helen McCann.'

'You had no approval for any of this investigation,' Baird said.

'None, it was a preliminary investigation. I just wanted to see whether there were grounds to launch a proper investigation.'

'Let me summarise. You are telling me that Helen McCann received a call from the man who had just murdered Jackie Carlisle. By this, you are implying that McCann was the person who suborned the murder. And you are saying that the murderer is a serving PSNI officer.'

'Yes, I think that might be the situation.'

'Then I hope that you are out of your mind, because if you're not, you are going to have to prove that one of the richest and most prominent women in the province murdered a dying man for some reason that you can't explain. Do I get it right?'

'That's pretty much it.'

'And what do you want from me?'

'To make the investigation into Carlisle's death official.'

'You want me to go in front of the media with the story you've just told me?'

'There's more.'

'Let me have it then.'

'During the investigation into the Grant and Malone murders, we uncovered possible corruption in the Housing Executive. It involved Sammy Rice and a financial group called Carson Nominees.'

'You got someone for those murders.'

'We didn't get them, but we know who committed the murders. Two mechanics from Glasgow, one of them was killed in Spain and the other's whereabouts is unknown. We know that Grant and Malone were about to reveal the corruption and they would have named names. Except they're all dead. Rice is also missing, presumed dead, and Carson Nominees disappeared into the ether at the same time. Then Carlisle was murdered. I believe all these events are linked.'

'What evidence do you have?'

Wilson looked at Moira.

'We have one of Carlisle's journals. He has some wild story about a group involving a Judge, a Queen, a Lord, a Mogul, a Politician and a Policeman. It's written in story form, but the group's objective is to protect the realm by controlling the judiciary, the police and the economy.'

'So, Carlisle had literary aspirations,' Baird said.

'Perhaps,' Wilson said. 'Or the group could actually exist. And Carson Nominees could be part of it. Maybe it's the reason Carlisle had to die.'

'Recently there have been two leaks of the financial dealings of the great and the good,' Moira said. 'The Panama Papers and the Paradise Papers.'

'I'm aware of them,' Baird said.

'A Harvard professor friend has gathered together all the papers relating to Carson Nominees,' Moira continued. 'It's a four-hundred-page tome of detailed financial dealings.'

'Let me get this straight. There's some shadowy group made up of six or so people who are involved in corruption. And to cover it up they murdered Grant, Malone, O'Reilly, Rice and Carlisle. And Helen McCann is one of this group.'

'She would be the Queen,' Moira said.

'Yes. That's pretty much it,' Wilson said.

'Have you both lost your marbles?' Baird asked.

'No, sir,' Wilson said. 'We've been behaving like PSNI detectives. Jackson found out somehow that we were on his tail and he almost murdered Davidson. Someone hired a professional assassin to take me out. We must be getting too close. If we dismiss the idea that Carlisle's story is a fantasy, then we're left with the hypothesis that the group actually exists.'

'This is a conspiracy theory,' Baird said. 'There is no way in heaven or hell that I would go public with such a fantastic story.'

'Maybe it is a fantastic story,' Wilson said. 'But we need you to give us the resources to prove you right, and in the meantime, to protect our integrity.'

'Why now?' Baird said.

'What do you mean?'

'Why have you come to me now?'

'The DCC has told CS Davis that he wants to examine the physical evidence against Jackson, which includes the phone that links McCann to the murder of Carlisle.'

Baird stared at Wilson. 'What are you trying to suggest?'

'I've worked on cases before where evidence has gone missing.'

'I refuse to believe that the DCC would destroy evidence. I know that you and him have a history, but you're going too far.'

'One of the characters in Carlisle's fairy tale is the Policeman.'

The room fell silent.

After a few moments, Baird looked at his watch. 'I have to think about this. If you're correct, and that's a mighty big if, this will have far-reaching consequences. We're not going public, but I'm not trashing your request for a further investigation either.' He stood, picked up his hat and looked at Wilson. 'I said at one point that there was never a dull moment with you. I'm not usually known for understatement.' He walked to the door and opened it. 'I'll be in touch.'


WILSON HAD INVITED Moira to join him for breakfast in the

hotel. 'It doesn't sound so convincing when it's laid out like that,' he said when they were seated.

'There's a logic, but it's hard to grasp the scale. You can understand the CC's reluctance. You've already put Davidson, Davis and me out on the limb with you. It's beginning to bend a little and if the CC adds his weight, we might all fall. He wasn't in the hallway to see Grant hanging from a noose. He doesn't know how devious McCann can be.'

'But he's right on one point. If we went public with what we have, we'd be laughed out of it.'

They ate silently for a few moments.

'You're losing faith,' Moira said eventually.

'They're clever buggers. Rice and Carlisle are dead. So is Grant and the investigation into his death gave them time to cover up the corruption. I don't think Carlisle's story is a fantasy. McCann is the Queen and the Judge was her husband. Carlisle was probably the Politician. Rice was a pawn in their game, as were their contacts in the Housing Executive. They were expendable. There was a fear that Carlisle's cancer would go to his brain and he might talk. But that's just what I suspect. What I can prove is something else entirely.'

'If the CC cuts our legs off, is it finished?'

'What do you think? This business runs on resources and we don't have any. There could be something in that mass of paper Feinstein gave you, but we'll never know until someone with the right expertise looks at it. Even then it may lead nowhere. Maybe in ten years' time someone will stumble across a piece of evidence that shows we were right. All I know is that I'll still be thinking about this case when I'm in the hospice.'

# CHAPTER FORTY-FIVE

Jack Duane had spent an uncomfortable night on a camp bed in the incident room at Dundalk Garda Station. The thought of letting Flynn walk out of the station and into Feeney's clutches gave him nightmares. He had a quick breakfast in the cafeteria and was contemplating another run at knocking sense into Flynn's thick skull when the duty sergeant called him to the front desk.

'Flynn's solicitor has been on the blower,' the sergeant said. 'He's on the way over and he wants his boy ready to go.'

'Shit, how long have we got?'

'Five minutes.'

'Delay him.'

Duane went to the incident room. 'Where's Sergeant Guiney?' he asked a young detective.

'He was here a minute ago.'

'Get your coat. I've got a job for you.' Duane turned and tapped DG Hearney on the shoulder. 'You too. DI Flynn is about to leave the station and I want you two to tail him. Discreetly mind. I assume you've both done surveillance work.'

The two young officers nodded.

'I want to know where he is every waking moment. Someone will try to lift him. When that happens, don't stop them but make sure you follow them to wherever they take him. Tell the duty sergeant to assign you an unmarked car and get on your way. And I want to be kept informed of every development.'

The two young detectives rushed out the door and Duane slumped into one of the chairs at a free desk. Flynn was his only lead and the fool was about to place himself in mortal danger. If Feeney decided that Flynn had to die, it would be a short drive to a bog hole and Flynn would never be seen again. One of the officers from the duty desk opened the door and motioned to Duane to come outside.

Duane found Flynn's solicitor in the reception area. 'You're not doing your client a favour.'

'My client begs to differ.'

Flynn walked out from the cell area.

'Daragh, don't do this,' Duane said. 'You're safer here.'

'I have to stick my hand in the wound,' Flynn said. 'The DPP will crucify me. What do I have to lose?'

'Your life.'

'That's not worth much. I've already made a right royal fuck-up of it.'

'What about your wife and children?'

'They'll be better off without me.' Flynn took an envelope containing his personal effects from the duty sergeant and signed the clipboard that was proffered.

A lightbulb went off in Duane's head. So that was Flynn's game. 'You want them to kill you. This is a suicide mission isn't it? Remember the photos of Lennon. It won't be quick, and it won't be easy.'

'I'm still a serving officer and innocent until proven guilty. If anything happens to me, Angela will get a lump sum and my pension. Maybe there'll be some atonement in that.'

'That's mad. Help us bring Feeney down. We'll get the

corruption charge squared with the DPP. You can have a life with Angela and the kids.'

Flynn held out his hand. 'When I started out in the force, I didn't for a minute think it would end like this.'

Duane took his hand. 'But it doesn't have to end like this.'

'Thanks for trying, Jack.' Flynn nodded at his solicitor and they both walked out of the station.

Duane remembered Sydney Carton's line from *A Tale of Two Cities*: 'It's a far, far better thing that I do, than I have ever done'. It was a load of bullshit. Life was about survival. There was very little nobility in death at the hands of criminals like Feeney.

COLEMAN CLOSED his phone and sat down behind his desk at Feeney's Builders Providers. 'They've cut Flynn loose.'

Feeney smiled. 'Then you know what you have to do.'

'For God's sake, Tommy, the man has obviously kept his mouth shut. And you can't go around killing a garda inspector.'

'Who says I can't? The man's mind has gone. He's run once so maybe he'll run again. Except this time, he'll run to the bottom of a bog and never be found again. Flynn can put us in prison and I'm not having that.'

'He knows next to nothing about our business.'

'At a minimum he can put the finger on us for bribery and corruption of a public official. Duane would be all over us like a rash.'

'Duane has no jurisdiction up here. And if the fools in Westminster get their way, they'll succeed in breaking the link between the PSNI and the Garda Síochána.'

'That'll be the day. My contacts in Dublin tell me the guards are working themselves up for a major operation against criminality in the border area. We can't afford any slip-ups.'

'You should have thought about that before you topped that poor wee Lennon boy.'

Feeney was out of his chair and had his hands around Coleman's neck in one movement. 'Nobody welshes on Tommy Feeney. You get this straight in your head. I run things here. If I let some eejit stand up to me, I lose respect. You're gone soft. Mind I don't turn my attention to you.'

Coleman was spluttering and Feeney released his grip.

'McCluskey is watching Flynn. As soon as possible, I want him to lift Flynn and make sure that he disappears for good.'

# CHAPTER FORTY-SIX

Wilson replayed the meeting with Baird over and over in his mind when he returned to the station. He'd been right to bring the CC on board, but he didn't think that he had done justice to the work that Davidson had done. The cover-up of Carlisle's death had been almost perfect. The coroner's verdict of suicide should have closed the affair. But he had to go playing detective. Davidson's police work had exposed much of what happened. The future evolution of the case was now in the hands of the chief constable. Even with increased resources, Wilson wasn't sure he could unearth enough evidence to satisfy the DPP. McCann and her friends had been very careful. There was a knock on his door, and he looked up to see O'Neill standing outside. He motioned her in.

'I just got the call log from Lennon's mobile phone company.' She put two sheets onto his desk. 'He wasn't a prolific user of his phone. On the day of his death, he made only two calls and received one. One of the calls he made was to the same number as the call he received.'

'And you've checked whose phone that is.'

'It belongs to Dáithí Ó Brádaigh.'

'Now, that's interesting. Good work.'

O'Neill left the office and Wilson called Duane. 'We just turned up something interesting.'

'What?'

'On the day of his death, Lennon made two phone calls and received one.'

'Busy man.'

'Exactly. The number for one of the calls he made and the one he received is listed to Ó Brádaigh.'

'So what's your theory?'

'When I interviewed Ó Brádaigh, I found him very unclear and evasive. I'd say if you did a polygraph on him the needle would be all over the place. The business about rezoning part of Lennon's land was pure bullshit. Let's agree that we have Feeney marked as the man behind the murder. I think that Lennon was having some sort of problem with Feeney. He went to Ó Brádaigh in the hope that his local councillor could intervene on his behalf and got nowhere. Then on the day he died, he called Ó Brádaigh and told him that he was going to the police. Ó Brádaigh called back and said that he'd fix things with Feeney. That's how Lennon ended up in Inniskeen. I don't think there was any other reason for him to go there late at night. Except maybe that he'd been sold out to Feeney. Ó Brádaigh was possibly the only person that could lure him there.'

'It's a theory that fits the facts. Feeney and Ó Brádaigh are on the same side politically. A lot of Feeney's old comrades are Ó Brádaigh's bosses. How are you going to prove it?'

'I'm going to invite Ó Brádaigh to Newry PSNI Station for a little talk.'

'Ó Brádaigh has important friends, Ian. He's going to make some calls when he gets your message and ten minutes later your superiors are going to receive some calls. If he refuses to speak, or if he sticks to the bullshit story, there's very little you can do about it.'

'It's worth a try. Why don't you come up and watch the fun?'

'Normally I'd be only too happy to oblige, but we have a little drama of our own on here. I've had to let Flynn go. The stupid bastard has decided to get himself murdered. That way he won't be discharged from the force and his wife will be entitled to a lump sum and his pension. He thinks it's the only decent thing he can do for her and his kids.'

'It's not the first time it's been done. I assume you're keeping an eye on him.'

'More than one. Feeney has people watching as well. It depends who'll blink first. Feeney isn't famous for his patience.'

'You're risking a man's life, Jack.'

'He's doing that all on his own. I tried to talk him out of it.'

'I'm going to pick up Ó Brádaigh. I'll get back to you.'


WILSON AND GRAHAM were about to exit the station when Wilson heard the duty sergeant call his name. He turned and saw the sergeant pointing upwards. 'Stay of execution, Harry. I'm wanted upstairs, but as soon as I'm free we're on our way.'


CS DAVIS LOOKED RELAXED after her break. 'Bring me up to speed.'

Wilson told her about the meeting with Baird and filled her in on the latest development on the Lennon case.

'How will it turn out?' she asked.

'I don't know.'

'In a couple of weeks, we might all be packing our personal effects into boxes.'

'That thought had already crossed my mind. There'll have to be a reason.'

'Wasting everyone's time might just about do it. Where's the mobile phone?'

'DS McElvaney has it.'

She tapped a few keys on her computer and turned the screen to face him. 'Six messages from the DCC in the past two days. Each one angrier than the one before.'

'McCann must be getting antsy.'

'You think it's about her.'

'I know it's about her. I think she's pissed because she left a hole, even though the phone alone won't convict her. What happens next will depend on whether Baird mentions our meeting to Jennings. I've sowed the seed. If Jennings gives up the phone or swaps it out, Baird will know that we're on the level.'

'Can you get McCann?'

'I don't think so. It may be possible only if we locate Jackson and he's ready to flip. But we'll need something to induce him.'

'What about the attack on Davidson?'

'We have no proof Jackson was involved. The two men wore balaclavas. Peter thinks it was Jackson, but a good barrister would tear him to bits on the stand.'

'We're just tilting at windmills.'

'And pissing a whole lot of people off. We need someone to get nervous enough to make a big mistake.'

'We're not talking about your usual clients here. People like McCann don't go to jail for murder.'

'There's a first time for everything.'

'You've put a lot of eggs into your basket and unfortunately one of them belongs to me.'

'I wish there had been another way.'

'So do I. Keep in touch.'

# CHAPTER FORTY-SEVEN

Dáithí Ó Brádaigh wanted to be anywhere but Crossmaglen. He'd been reading up on Ian Wilson and everything he'd learned confirmed his own observation. Wilson was a dangerous man to lie to. And that was what he had done. Under normal circumstances, Ó Brádaigh would have hopped on a plane and headed south for some spring sunshine. But the local elections were around the corner and it would be very noticeable if he disappeared. Blowing town wouldn't necessarily hurt his chances of re-election though, as he was lucky to be in a borough where his election was virtually guaranteed. On the other hand it was his curse to be in the same borough as Tommy Feeney. Belfast had instructed him to assist Feeney in every way possible. That meant setting up that poor bastard Lennon and lying to the police. Neither of which sat well with him. Feeney was a ruthless criminal and the time when such people had the benefit of political support because of their past affiliations needed to end. Ó Brádaigh hoped he was going to be elected to Stormont whenever the political parties stopped playing silly buggers and decided that they were grown-ups rather than squabbling children. Leaving a political vacuum had only opened the door to people like

Feeney. Ó Brádaigh had a clear agenda for the afternoon and was contemplating slipping away early when he saw a car pull up outside the office. Wilson got out of the passenger side. Ó Brádaigh stood up quickly and went to the bathroom.

Wilson pushed in the door in time to see Ó Brádaigh's back disappearing into the rear of the office. His first reaction was to send Graham around the back to cut off a possible means of escape, but he resisted the impulse. If Ó Brádaigh ran, it would confirm Wilson's theory that he was involved somehow in Lennon's death. He stood in the office and waited.

Five minutes passed before Ó Brádaigh emerged from the rear. 'Superintendent, I wasn't aware that we had a meeting scheduled.'

'We don't. I was in the vicinity and I decided to drop in.'

'You don't strike me as the kind of man who just drops in. Still, you're here now. How can I help you?'

'You could begin by telling me the truth.'

'Are you suggesting that I've lied to you?'

'I am.'

'I take great exception to that.'

'Be that as it may. I'm of the opinion that you lied to me on my last visit here and that your lies had a very detrimental effect on my investigation into the death of Brian Lennon.'

'You can think what you like but what can you prove?'

'I'd like you to accompany me to Newry PSNI Station for a formal interview.'

'I'd like to call my solicitor.'

'You're free to do so.'

'Please wait outside.'

Wilson and Graham left the office. After ten minutes, Ó Brádaigh joined them and Wilson saw the figure of Michael Coyle heading in their direction. 'Your solicitor?'

Ó Brádaigh nodded. 'We'll meet you in Newry. I'm not travelling in a police car.'

'Let's go, Harry,' Wilson said. 'I'll call Newry on the way and have an interview room prepared.'

Newry PSNI Station looks like a medieval fortress. The buildings are surrounded by a high yellow-bricked wall, which is topped off with a steel barrier. It doesn't exactly fit the new softer image of the PSNI.

The duty sergeant led Wilson and Graham to an interview room with recording equipment already set up.

'We're giving Ó Brádaigh plenty of time to get his story straight,' Graham said.

'There's a faint possibility that he's been telling us the truth,' Wilson said.

There was a knock on the door and the duty sergeant ushered Ó Brádaigh and Coyle into the room. The two arrivals sat in the vacant chairs facing Wilson and Graham.

'Do the honours, DC Graham,' Wilson said when they were seated.

Graham turned on the recording equipment and introduced the participants. He looked at Wilson, who nodded. Graham said. 'You do not have to say anything. But it may harm your defence if you do not mention when questioned something which you later rely on in court. Anything you do say may be given in evidence.'

'The caution is a bit excessive,' Coyle said.

'Not at all,' Wilson said. 'Impeding a police murder inquiry is a serious offence.'

Ó Brádaigh and Coyle looked at each other.

Wilson removed a paper from his pocket and put it on the table. 'I am showing Mr Ó Brádaigh a copy of a call log from Brian Lennon's mobile phone for the day of his death. There are two calls relative to Mr Ó Brádaigh. The first a call made by Mr Lennon at midday and the second a call received from

Mr Ó Brádaigh at six-fifteen in the evening. Could you please tell me the contents of those calls?'

'I don't remember,' Ó Brádaigh said. 'Lennon probably called to ask what was happening with his request for rezoning. I don't remember if my secretary or I took the call. The evening call was probably me replying.'

'The call at midday lasted for ten minutes,' Wilson said. 'I hardly think that Lennon was on the line with your secretary for that length of time.'

'Maybe I took the call and we discussed his request some more.'

'Did you take notes of the call?'

'No.'

'Do you record calls?'

'No.'

'Then we have no proof of what was discussed.'

'No.' Ó Brádaigh drew a large breath.

'Would you like to know what I think?'

'Yes.'

'I think you lied to us about why Lennon came to you in the first place. I think he was having a problem with Tommy Feeney and that was not a good situation to be in. He came to you to arbitrate and possibly save his life. You probably tried to talk Feeney down, but he doesn't walk away easily, and you failed. But worse than that, you and Feeney are joined at the hip.' Ó Brádaigh raised his hand to object, but Wilson waved him away. 'Feeney told you to set up Lennon the next time he called and that's what the two calls were about. The first from Lennon was asking you how you got on with Feeney. The call back from you sent Lennon to his death in Inniskeen.'

Ó Brádaigh shot to his feet. 'That's not true. I'd never condone murder.'

'I believe you,' Wilson said. 'But you didn't know that the plan was to kill Lennon. You thought you were setting him up for a beating, or maybe a kneecapping. You were sold a pup, but that's what people like Feeney do, they use everyone around them.'

Ó Brádaigh sat down. 'There isn't a word of truth in your theory. I've come here in good faith and I've answered your questions. Now, I'd like to go.'

Coyle rose from his seat. 'If you need to speak with my client again, contact me first.'

'Conscience is a terrible thing,' Wilson said. 'You start off by rationalising what you did. But soon you realise that rationalisation is all bullshit. You know that you've been used and made an accessory to murder. Everyone I speak to says that Brian Lennon was harmless. Being involved in his murder is going to haunt you till the day you die.' Wilson watched as Ó Brádaigh stood unsteadily and Coyle and he went to the door.

'Boss?' Graham said.

'Let them go, Harry. Ó Brádaigh won't be sleeping so well tonight.'

# CHAPTER FORTY-EIGHT

Davis put the evidence bag containing the mobile phone and the file of statements on Jennings' desk. 'This is the evidence that DC Davidson collected on the preliminary investigation into Jackie Carlisle's death.'

Jennings picked up the file of statements and thumbed through them. 'Davidson did this investigation off his own bat?'

'More or less. He found the anomaly that despite the visit from the hospice being cancelled, Carlisle received the shot of morphine that killed him ostensibly from a male nurse. He was looking retirement in the face and didn't like it.'

'We should have held on to Davidson.' He put the file down and picked up the plastic bag containing the mobile phone. 'The coroner has already passed judgement on Carlisle's death. The final injection was self-administered, and the death was suicide. A sad end to a spectacular political career.' He tossed the evidence bag onto the desk. 'Any alternative theory appears rather flimsy. Especially in the light of the coroner's verdict.'

Priceless, Davis thought, coming from a man who had

never led an investigation in his entire career. 'It was significant enough for someone to nearly kill Davidson.'

Jennings picked up a file from the side of his desk. 'I took
the liberty of examining Davidson's file.' He handed it to her.
'He was what they call a "colourful character". Some of us
wondered whether he was on our side or with the opposition.'

Davis flipped through the pages and smiled. 'Colourful'
was a mild description of the antics that Davidson got up to on
occasion. She handed the file back. 'He was a first-class
detective.'

'Leave this with me. It won't break the chain of evidence.'

'I would prefer to return it to the station.'

'Thank you, chief superintendent. Considering the political sensitivity, I'll review the evidence personally and let you
know whether I agree to you continuing the investigation.'

'Of course.' Davis stood. 'I'll tell Detective Superintendent
Wilson to await your decision.'

Jennings gave her a smile that would befit a reptile about to
eat a rodent.

Davis swivelled and headed for the office door. She felt an
urgent need to wash her hands. A shower would have been
preferable, but she was going to have to spend the rest of the
day with a peculiar smell in her nostrils.


JENNINGS WATCHED Davis leave the room. Her distaste for
him was obvious. He put the blame on Wilson. Whatever the
chemistry between him and Wilson, people were always
forced to take one side or the other. In general, women took
Wilson's side and Davis was no exception. He thought he
should be feeling the warm glow of victory, but he wasn't and
that bothered him. He had managed to obtain the phone as
requested by McCann. It would be easy to replace it with
another and incinerate the original. Nobody was about to
believe that the DCC was capable of interfering with

evidence. One reason for his disquiet was his belief that Davis had been holding something back. He may never have interrogated a prisoner, but that didn't mean he hadn't developed a sense for when people were lying to him. People like him, an only child with a dysfunctional childhood, developed a second sense in dealing with others. He didn't believe in the psychobabble surrounding 'tells' and people looking to the right or left or up and down. The Americans had developed that and they were beginning to see the error of their ways. What was Davis holding back? It had something to do with turning his apparent victory into defeat. He picked up his phone to announce his success to Helen McCann but replaced the handset. Perhaps it would be better if he kept the news to himself for the moment. A bun fight between McCann and Lattimer was in the offing. He hadn't yet decided whose side he would come down on. If he selected Lattimer, he would have to ensure that McCann would be comprehensively defeated. Otherwise, he would go the same way as Carlisle. Lattimer wasn't the murdering type. Interesting days, he thought, as long as one is prepared for every eventuality.

# CHAPTER FORTY-NINE

F lynn was staring at the television screen but seeing nothing. He knew that a team of detectives at Dundalk station was busy trawling through his bank and credit card statements. They would be speaking with his bank manager and his mortgage lender. That would expose the level of his gambling and his debt. They would dip into the minutiae of his life. They would find his betting accounts and examine his betting record. The evidence would point clearly to him being corrupt. Why the hell should he care? In a few hours or a few days, he would be dead. Feeney would already know he'd been freed and would not want to risk him changing his mind and telling everything he knew.

Flynn had hardly slept the previous night in the cell. Around three o'clock in the morning, he had formulated his plan for 'suicide by criminal'. It sounded so right at the time and even later in the morning when Duane had interviewed him. It was only when he entered his own house that the full impact of the decision hit home. As a father, he wanted to see his children grow to maturity. He had a duty to care for them. He had failed miserably so far, but his plan would turn that around.

He moved to the window and looked out. There were plenty of parked cars, but they all appeared unoccupied. What if he had misjudged Feeney? What if his plan was a bust? He believed Duane when he said that the DPP was prepared to go the distance with him. The country was flooded with drugs and the gangs in cities like Dublin, Cork. Limerick and Galway weren't short of filling an amenable garda's pockets with cash. Hauling a bent copper like him over the coals might give other police officers pause for thought. What use would he be to his wife and children serving ten years in prison? He looked along the line of cars. Where the hell are Feeney's men? He wished they'd get on with it.

Detective Garda Johnny Murray was also wondering what was taking so long. He and DG Meg Hearney were parked one hundred and thirty metres down the road from the Flynn residence. They'd already been on station for four hours and there hadn't been hide nor hair of any of Feeney's goons. In fact, Mount Street was as quiet as a graveyard. Murray had reported back to Duane and given the inactivity had requested his superior to set up a rota to continue the surveillance. This was the part of the job that most coppers hated. They had watched the solicitor drop Flynn at the front door and depart. Flynn had gone inside and hadn't stirred since.

Michael McCluskey and his companion were parked at the opposite end of the street from the police officers. He didn't agree with Feeney's strategy, but he knew his boss too well to voice any disagreement. Dealing with bent coppers was always a tricky business. Killing one was even trickier. McCluskey hadn't been happy about killing young Brian Lennon either. And he knew he wasn't the only one. There had been some grumbling in the minibus on the way back from

Inniskeen that he hadn't experienced before. All the men at the farmhouse had been with Tommy for years. They'd followed him through thick and thin and were at his side during the so-called Troubles. Some, like himself, had spent years behind the wire with him. But things were different now. They were no longer fighting for a cause. Back then they considered themselves soldiers. Now they were common criminals. But a man had to provide for his family. 'In for a penny, in for a pound' had always been his motto.

He looked at his watch. Flynn had been inside for four hours. He could snatch him from the front door but there was a risk that he would resist and some old biddy sitting in a window across the street would witness it. Better to wait until Flynn showed himself. He pulled a flask from a bag and poured himself some tea. He hoped he wouldn't be there for the night. His wife was already giving him shit over the Inniskeen business.

## CHAPTER FIFTY

Wilson had been tempted to head back to Belfast as soon as they finished with Ó Brádaigh but instead had ordered Graham to take them to Dundalk. They made straight for the incident room, where they found Duane working at a computer. He finished up as soon as Wilson and Graham entered.

'I think we know how Lennon ended up in Inniskeen.' Wilson sat on a free chair.

'Tell me,' Duane said.

'The local councillor, Ó Brádaigh, set him up.'

'You have proof?'

'I think it went down as I guessed. Ó Brádaigh and Feeney are connected politically. The new politicians aren't allowed to forget the old operators. Feeney tells Ó Brádaigh what to do. I don't think the councillor is happy about it, but he's received his instructions from above. Except, Ó Brádaigh didn't sign up for murder. It's more likely that he thought it was going to be a punishment beating. But I'm still in the dark on the reason why Feeney wanted Lennon dead.'

'People like Feeney don't need a reason. Do you think Ó Brádaigh might have been the man who made the 999 call?'

'We recorded the interview with him in Newry.' Wilson took a USB drive from his pocket. 'Run a voice-print on it and see if there's a match. And while you're at it, why don't you do the same for the guys you busted on the raids? They all work for Feeney. Maybe one of them was in Inniskeen and didn't fancy what went on.'

'It's worth a try.' Duane looked at his watch. 'Meanwhile, Flynn has been free for nearly five hours now and has been holed up in his house since his solicitor dropped him off. I have two young detectives on him, but they'll need to be relieved soon. My superiors are fretting about the cost of twenty-four-hour surveillance. The DPP won't allow me to arrest him as apparently we don't have enough hard evidence. We've subpoenaed his bank and credit card statements and as soon as we can show he was spending more than he was earning we can drag him in again.'

'What if he can't put Feeney in the frame for Lennon's murder?'

'They're going to crucify the poor bastard. That's if he's still alive. He's still counting on Feeney killing him.'

'That's mad.'

'I don't think he's thinking clearly.'

'In the meantime?'

'We wait. I'll have the voice-print done and maybe we'll strike lucky, but I wouldn't count on it.'

'We can't let Feeney get away with murder.'

'It wouldn't be the first time. He's got money and he's got political connections, north and south.'

'Who'd be a copper?'

Ó Brádaigh lifted the cup to his lips and spilt some of the contents on his desk. His hands hadn't stopped shaking since he'd looked up the sentence for conspiracy to murder. He had no idea that Feeney intended to murder Lennon when he'd called the poor bugger and set up the meeting at Inniskeen. Maybe he should have guessed. Feeney didn't like to take no for an answer. But killing Lennon was way over the top. The simple truth was that Lennon had come to him for help in dealing with Feeney and he had betrayed him.

A life in politics had turned him into a complete shit. If he were to succeed in becoming a member of the Northern Ireland Assembly, he would have to toe the party line and that meant sucking up to people like Feeney. The old guard were dying out but not fast enough for the younger generation. He stared at the phone on his desk. By rights, he should call Belfast and tell them about being interviewed by Wilson. He could just imagine the reaction. Whatever way he looked at it, his glittering political career was over. Perhaps Coyle was right, and Wilson wouldn't be able to prove that he was part of the plan to murder Lennon. He wouldn't like to bet ten years in prison on that. But you didn't cross someone like Feeney without considering the consequences. Ten years in prison would be no walk in the park, but it was a damn sight better that becoming a corpse. His hand hovered over the phone. Belfast and Dublin were the bosses. It was their job to come up with a plan. That plan would certainly involve covering Feeney's arse. When were they going to realise that it was time to put the old guard out to grass? Feeney wasn't a patriot; he was a criminal. His time had come and gone. Just because he was part of the struggle thirty years ago didn't mean all his sins were absolved. He picked up the phone. Please God let someone with half a brain consign Feeney to his fate.

FLYNN SWITCHED off the television and went to the window. Some children were playing directly outside and screaming like banshees. If his children were here, they'd be right in the middle of them. A tear crept out of his right eye. He wiped it away and looked down the road. Feeney's men were out there somewhere. What were they waiting for? A fucking gilt-edged invitation. Why the hell hadn't they just knocked on the door and taken him away with them? They were probably waiting for darkness, but in the meantime, he could feel his resolve weakening with every hour that passed. There might be another way out of his problem. All he had to do was find something that would put Feeney behind bars, clear his debts and leave him as a police officer.

Who was he kidding? Eight corrupt members of the Garda Síochána had been locked up over the previous year and another three guys – a superintendent, an inspector and a sergeant – were helping with enquiries into information leaking to an OCG operating in Limerick. So, continuing as a police officer would be out of the question. Feeney had bested better men than him and been backed up by major political figures, so Feeney wouldn't be going to jail. And there was no prospect of a hundred thousand euro dropping into his lap to allow him to pay off his debts. There was a full house on the table, and he was holding a pair of twos. Why wouldn't Feeney's men just come and put him out of his misery?

# CHAPTER FIFTY-ONE

Wilson wished he was back in Belfast, ensconced in the Crown waiting for Reid to show. Instead, he was hanging around Dundalk Garda Station, marking time in the hope that something was about to happen. He wasn't the only one. Duane was in constant motion like a caged animal and there was an atmosphere of expectancy in the incident room. Graham had refused the chance to return to Belfast alone, he had been a copper long enough to feel the vibe. The only interruption to the silence was the intermittent reports from the detectives watching Flynn. All was quiet in Mount Street.

THE WORKERS LIVING near Flynn had been arriving home in bunches since five o'clock, the children had been called inside for their tea and silence had descended on the street. Dusk fell at six o'clock and a light drizzle that had threatened all after-noon began to fall. McCluskey continued waiting for Flynn to leave his house. He and his companion, Durkan, looked at each other and smiled when the rain began to fall. McCluskey would have preferred to pick up Flynn at around midnight, but Feeney had ordered the job done as soon as possible and the rain would make that easier.

Flynn stood at the window. He didn't know how long he'd been standing there. He'd watched his neighbours returning from work. On another day he would have been just like them. Open the door, give the kids a hug and the wife a peck on the cheek, talk about his and her day, help the kids with their homework, watch six upper-class twits on TV discussing how they intended to wreck the lives of honest working men. All very normal and humdrum, except when the light went out and his wife retired to bed and he entered his secret life. How many of his neighbours had a secret life? Were they all as squeaky clean as they looked? Mortgage paid up to date, no overdue bills lying around and no debts to a criminal with a reputation for burying his mistakes. What would they think when the media reported that the highly respected detective inspector living on their street was a diseased gambler who leaked information to a criminal gang and left his wife and children destitute? Raindrops began to beat against the window, and he watched the water stream down in rivulets. Out of the corner of his eye, he saw a car door open and a man he had seen with Feeney get out. He took a deep breath. It was time. It would be over soon. As anticipated, Feeney was going to claim his pound of flesh.

Murray and Hearney chatted like a young courting couple and watched the evening scene unfold. They had been on station for eight hours and the time was dragging. Murray had asked to be relieved on several occasions, but Duane had told him to sit tight and stop bitching. The drizzle was turning to outright rain and the drops played a military tattoo on the roof of their Skoda.

'Shit,' Murray said. 'I have a date tonight.'

'Lucky you,' Hearney said. 'I was looking forward to an evening at home with a pizza, a few glasses of wine and the latest episode of *Grey's Anatomy*.'

Murray turned and looked at her. 'I thought for sure that you had a boyfriend.'

'I did have, but I kicked the bastard to the kerb when I heard he'd been texting my best friend.'

'Maybe we can go for a drink some time?'

'Yeah, that'd be okay.' She hated surveillance, but she was happy for the chance to get to know Murray better. 'Movement from a parked car at the end of the street. Turn on the wipers.'

Murray cleared the windscreen in time to see two heavily built men exit a car and walk in the direction of Flynn's house. He picked up his walkie-talkie. 'Papa, two men approaching Flynn's house.'

'Report back if they enter.' Duane's voice was sharp. 'If they pick him up, you follow. If you lose them, both of you will be looking for a new job tomorrow.'


As SOON AS Duane put down the walkie-talkie, he unlocked his desk drawer and took out a Sig Sauer P226 automatic pistol. He put it in his jacket pocket and turned to Wilson. 'It's going down. You and Graham stay here and hold the fort.'

Wilson shot to his feet. 'You've got to be joking. Harry can stay here, I'm going along.'

'Boss, where you go, I go,' Graham said.

'Not this time, Harry.'

'I think you should stay too, Ian,' Duane said. 'It might not look too good if a detective superintendent in the PSNI was injured in a garda operation.'

'Maybe I was never in that operation, just like you weren't in Ballymacarrett.'

'Do you have a weapon?'

Wilson shook his head.

Duane opened the drawer again and handed Wilson a Walther P99.

'Do you have an H and K MP7 in there by any chance?' Wilson asked.

'Very droll,' Duane said.

'Maybe you should call up an armed response unit?'

'We may not have the time.'

'What if your guys lose him?'

'I've confidence in Murray and Hearney.'

'I hope it isn't misplaced. Feeney and his gang are no schoolboys.'


MURRAY PUT down the walkie-talkie and turned to Hearney, who had been watching the scene at Flynn's door through binoculars.

'What do we do if there's any rough stuff?' Hearney asked.

'The same thing Attenborough does when he's filming a lion killing a zebra. We watch and follow. Duane will be right behind us and we leave all the decision-making to him.' Murray flipped the ignition and the motor of the Skoda came to life. He was playing Mr Cool for Hearney's benefit, but his stomach was churning inside. If this whole business went to shit, there was a good chance that he and Hearney would carry the can.


MCCLUSKEY WAS ABOUT to put his finger on the bell when the door opened.

'What took you so long?' Flynn already had his coat on. 'Don't give me some bullshit about Tommy wanting to have a word with me. I know why you're here so let's get on with it.'

McCluskey stood back in surprise. He and Durkan

exchanged a look. They'd expected to have to use force to get Flynn to go along. Something wasn't right about this scene. McCluskey looked around the street. It was a quiet as the grave. His first reaction was to abandon the plan, but he didn't want to risk Feeney's anger.

'For God's sake, get a move on or we'll be soaked.' Flynn gave a high-pitched laugh. Being worried about getting wet when you're about to be murdered was too ridiculous.

Flynn locked the front door and slipped the key into his pocket. The three men strolled down the street. To the onlooker, they might be three friends heading out for an evening at a local pub or on their way to watch a football match. There was nothing unusual as McCluskey opened the car door and invited Flynn to take the passenger seat. Durkan was already in the rear.

DUANE HAD an unmarked police car waiting outside the station. He took the wheel and Wilson sat in the passenger seat.

'Any idea where they'll take him?'

'Somewhere quiet where the body won't be found.'

'That's not very specific.'

'There's a lot of empty country out there and these guys know every inch of it like the back of their hands. We have to stay cool and hope that we get there in time.'

MURRAY TOOK A DEEP BREATH. Two suspected members of an OCG were abducting a detective inspector right before their eyes and they were doing nothing. But it had to be said, Flynn wasn't exactly resisting. He waited while the car carrying Flynn pulled out and headed for the exit to the estate, and then he followed.

.  .  .

McCLUSKEY WAS THINKING that it was a perfect night for what they had in mind. He would have preferred to be taking Flynn north, but Feeney wanted everything done south of the border. He glanced at Flynn, who was staring straight ahead. The lift had been too damn easy. He'd been here before, but it wasn't anything like this. He made his way to the R178 heading west. Their destination was only ten minutes away in clear traffic. They had planned on Flynn being resistant, so they chose the nearest wetland, which was Glebe Bog. It wasn't the largest bog in the country, but it was suitable for their purpose.

'Where are we heading?' Flynn asked.

'Need to know,' McCluskey replied. 'All you need to know is that we'll be there shortly.'

'It'll be quick?'

A shiver ran down McCluskey's back. He'd lifted many men in his time and most of them soiled themselves at the thought of what was waiting for them. This Flynn character was treating his death like he was heading for a picnic. Something was very badly off and McCluskey had no idea what. He put his hand into his coat pocket and felt the reassuring weight of the pistol.

MURRAY AND HEARNEY were nearly two hundred metres behind the car carrying Flynn, with Hearney continually relaying their position to Duane, who was nearly five kilometres behind. They passed through the village of Kilcurly and Murray reduced speed when he saw the car they were following pull onto a grass verge at the left-hand side of the road. He was obliged to pass them and continue down the road before stopping beyond the next turn.

'What do we do now?' Hearney asked.

'Where's Duane?'

'A few kilometres back.'

'Fuck it.' Murray switched off the engine. 'You stay here. I'll go back to see what's going on.'

'GET OUT,' McCluskey cut the engine as soon as the road was clear of traffic. 'We walk from here.'

Flynn was desperately trying to get his bearings. They had passed Kilcurly. Why had they stopped here? Then it dawned on him. They were a stone's throw from Glebe Bog. They were going to kill him and bury him in the bog. If it all went to plan, he would never be found. This wasn't part of his plan. His body needed to be discovered. His wife and kids couldn't wait seven years to have him declared dead. 'Wait a minute.'

McCluskey stopped, put his hand in his pocket and took out his gun. 'What's the problem? One minute you're telling me to get on with it. Now you want to wait a minute. Make your fucking mind up.' He brought the gun up to Flynn's head. 'What are you up to?' He turned to Durkan, who also had a gun in his hand. 'This fucker is up to something. Check the road.'

Durkan went out to the middle of the road. 'It's clear in both directions.'

'Get the spade from the boot,' McCluskey said.

Durkan took out the spade and walked back to McCluskey and Flynn.

'Let's go,' McCluskey shoved Flynn in the direction of the bog.

Flynn didn't move.

'I said let's go.' McCluskey waved the gun in Flynn's face. 'I'll do you here if you don't.'

'It can't go down like this,' Flynn said. 'Shoot me here and leave the body on the road.'

'That's not the plan. Now get a fucking move on into the field.'

'No, do it here and leave me. I'll still be dead.'

'You're fucking mental.' McCluskey pointed his gun at Flynn's head. 'Get into that fucking field.'

'Or what?'

Durkan, spade in hand, stood beside McCluskey. 'What the fuck is going on here? We need to get off this road.'

Flynn said. 'Do it.'

MURRAY HAD SLIPPED into the field bordering the road and made his way back towards the parked car that had contained Flynn. Crouched behind some bushes, he strained to hear what was being said. Flynn and the man facing him appeared to be having an argument. Murray stiffened when he saw the gun. He had no weapon. A second man was carrying a spade. Murray couldn't remember anything in his training to cover this situation. He badly needed a piss.

DUANE RACED through the village of Kilcurly and was speeding west when he saw that a car had parked ahead on the left side of the road. He quickly assessed the situation. Flynn and his abductors stood beside the car. He recognised one as McCluskey and he was holding a gun.

MURRAY STOOD up from his hiding place. 'Police officer, put down the gun.'

The man holding the gun turned in his direction. He saw the gun pointing towards him and dived to his right. There was a bang and he felt a burning sensation in his left shoulder. He hit the soft earth and didn't move.

Duane drove onto the verge and he and Wilson were out as soon as the car stopped. They'd seen McCluskey turn and fire the gun. They didn't know why or at whom. Duane drew a bead on McCluskey. 'Drop the gun or I will blow your fucking head off, I mean it.'

McCluskey turned and saw two men pointing guns in his direction. He dropped the gun.

'Everybody on the ground,' Duane said. 'That includes you Flynn.'

Wilson and Duane walked towards the three prone men.

'You'll not walk away from this one, Michael,' Duane said. He looked up when he heard someone running towards them.

Hearney arrived breathing hard. 'Where's Johnny?'

Duane and Wilson looked at each other.

'He went through the fields,' Hearney said. 'I heard a shot.'

'I'll go.' Wilson vaulted the wooden fence and started moving along the hedge. He found Murray lying in the long grass. 'Call an ambulance, now,' he roared. He checked Murray's pulse and it was strong. There seemed to be only one wound. The bullet had ripped through Murray's left shoulder. Wilson was no doctor, but he doubted Murray would be using that arm for a while. He took off his jacket and covered Murray with it.

The young man moaned and his eyes opened. 'What happened?'

'You've been shot. But not fatally.'

Hearney arrived beside her colleague. 'Johnny, are you all right?'

'The super thinks I'll survive.'

Wilson watched as she kneeled beside her stricken part-ner. There was a little more concern there than he'd neces-sarily expect between work colleagues. He left them together and made his way back to the road.

'The ambulance is on its way,' Duane said. 'And so is trans-port for our friends here.' The three men were still prone but had been handcuffed.

'You're a bastard Duane.' Flynn lifted his head. 'You should have left me to die.'

'I'm a garda officer and as such I'm sworn to preserve life, even when that life doesn't wish to be preserved.' Duane held his hand out to Wilson. 'I'll take the Walther if you don't mind. We don't want it to go missing. I already signed a chit for it.'

'What's next?' Wilson asked.

'Next we have a long talk with McCluskey and his friend here. We can play the prisoners' dilemma. The first one to tell all gets the lightest sentence.'

# CHAPTER FIFTY-TWO

Feeney had heard about the fuck-up outside Kilcurly and had taken his anger out on the furniture in Coleman's office. The scene was one of devastation.

'What do we do now, Tommy?' Coleman asked.

Feeney rubbed his forehead. He needed to think but for the moment he couldn't see beyond the red mist. 'It's a cluster-fuck. McCluskey and Durkan have been arrested. McCluskey has shot and wounded a garda officer. They'll be charged with kidnapping and attempted murder. The charge sheet will be as long as your arm. And you can bet Duane will lean on them. McCluskey and me go back a long way, but who knows what he'll say if they threaten him with a long custodial sentence. He might roll over on the whole operation.'

'McCluskey is a sound man,' Coleman said. 'He'll do his duty.'

'He'd better. If he doesn't, there won't be a hole in Ireland big enough for him to hide in.' Feeney gave the remaining side of Coleman's desk a kick and his foot pierced the thin sheet of plywood. 'What happens if he flips on Lennon?'

'That's not worth thinking about.'

'We should start working on a plan.'

'Maybe we should have had a plan in the first place. The poor fucker did no harm.'

'No harm.' Feeney covered the distance between him and Coleman in two seconds and punched Coleman so hard he knocked him off his feet. 'The fucker welshed on me and nobody does that. I had an option to buy that poor excuse for a farm from his oul fella. It was mine and he wouldn't sell it to me.'

Coleman got up slowly and felt the welt rising on the side of his jaw. 'You could have negotiated with him.'

'I own this country.' Feeney brought his face close to Coleman's. 'I negotiate and people will think I've gone soft.'

'You've lost the run of yourself. Whoever said power corrupts knew what he was talking about. Look at you now. You're attacking your oldest friend. There was no need to kill the Lennon boy. The farm was failing. In a few weeks or months, he would have been at your gate begging you to buy him out.'

'McCluskey is going to flip. I can feel it in my water. Better men than him have turned on their comrades. It doesn't matter, they have nothing concrete on me. It'll end up as hearsay.'

'Do you really believe that?' Coleman rubbed the side of his face. 'When Duane came up here to investigate Lennon's murder, you should have seen the writing on the wall. When Wilson arrived from Belfast, it was time to go to ground. Belfast and Dublin want to get rid of us and you've handed it to them on a plate. Flynn was a distraction. All they knew was that he was passing on information. They would have hauled him over the coals and given him jail time. Big fucking deal. Your desire to get rid of him has opened up the can of worms we're looking at now.'

Feeney slumped into a chair. 'Our friends will stand by us.'

'I wouldn't be so sure of that.'

. . .

'It's going to be a long night,' Duane said as he sipped his tea in the cafeteria at Dundalk Garda Station. 'Maybe you and Harry should get yourselves back to Belfast.'

'And miss all the fun, I don't think so,' Wilson said. 'I've been on to Steph and, while she's not over the moon, she's decided to have some me-time, whatever that means.'

'McCluskey and Durkan are stewing in the cells. If I had my way, Flynn would be sectioned to the funny farm, but Dublin won't hear of it. At least the mad bastard's suicide plan came to nothing.'

'What about Murray?'

'He's in Louth County Hospital and the official description is stable. They dug a .22 out of his shoulder. I suppose he won't be using his left arm for a while.'

'Is Hearney in attendance?'

'She is.'

'How soon do we start on McCluskey?'

'You have no jurisdiction here, so there is no we. You can watch in the TV room, but do not jeopardise our case by getting involved. I've scheduled a preliminary interview in fifteen minutes. His brief has been informed. If you want my professional opinion, he'll play dumb until he realises the gravity of his situation and then he'll give us what we want. It might take time.'

'McCluskey's got form. What about his pal?'

'He appears to be a newbie so maybe he'll crack first.'

'Maybe he knows nothing.'

Duane stood. 'Let's find out.'


Ó Brádaigh put the phone down and looked around the office. He'd known that politics was a rough profession when he put his name forward for the council. But he'd had no idea how rough it really was. He had worked his arse off over the past four years representing his constituents. How many hours had he spent helping fill in forms for the elderly and sick so that they could avail of the help they were entitled to? That should be remembered. The instructions from Belfast were clear. He'd had no brief to help Feeney on a personal matter. That was one hundred per cent down to him. The fact that he was instrumental in setting up a murder had put him beyond redemption. He was to resign his council seat immediately, citing family reasons. The party hierarchy would be very pleased if he would just piss off. Feeney was the cause of his downfall and there might be worse to follow. The word was out that there had been some sort of fracas south of the border and one of Feeney's henchmen had shot a garda. It was the end of a trail of crumbs that might lead back to him. For now, he was lamenting the end of his short political career. Soon, he might be fighting to keep himself out of prison. He had one last job to do for the party. Then he had to decide whether to wait for the police to follow the trail of crumbs or to step forward and admit his role in Lennon's death. He switched off the lights and closed the office door for the last time.

'FUCK OFF.' Feeney started to close the door.

'I just got off the phone with Belfast,' Ó Brádaigh shouted.

Feeney stopped and opened the door again but didn't invite Ó Brádaigh in. 'And?'

'You're on your own. They're fed up with you and they're cutting you loose. You can expect no help this time.'

'We'll see about that. After what I've done for the cause, do you think I'm going to let them walk away and leave me in the shit?'

'I'm only the messenger.'

'Okay, you've given the message.' He started to close the door again.

'You don't understand. You're dead to them. You're an embarrassment.' The door slammed in Ó Brádaigh's face.

Ó Brádaigh walked back to his car. He'd gone into politics to help people and the system had corrupted him. Feeney was the source of all his problems. He'd been used by a brute and a criminal and he'd complied because he thought it would please his superiors. He felt dirty and he realised that he deserved everything he got. If he went to the police, Feeney would never forgive him.

# CHAPTER FIFTY-THREE

Duane and Guiney sat across from Durkan and his solicitor, Michael Coyle, in the interview room. Durkan was stooped over the table and his bulk pushed Coyle into a wide left position. Duane thought he looked like a guy you brought along when there was heavy work involved. Right now, he was somnolent and didn't look threatening, but Duane could well believe that an ordinary individual would be intimidated by his presence. Duane nodded at Guiney, who switched on the recording equipment and went through the well-practised rigmarole.

Durkan's head shot up when Guiney read the charges. Coyle put a comforting hand on his left forearm.

'Surprised?' Duane said.

Durkan remained silent.

'We know your friend McCluskey is the brains of the operation,' Duane began. 'It will help your case if you tell us everything you know about what went down this evening.'

'No comment.'

'Kidnapping, conspiracy to murder a police officer and the attempted murder of another police officer. You're looking at a long stretch. McCluskey is in the next room. He's been down this road before and my guess is that he's going to shop you. Do yourself a favour and tell us what you know.'

Durkan glanced sideways at Coyle, who was busy writing in his notebook. 'No comment.'

'You've never been to prison. It's not fun. You're a big lad and you probably think that you can handle yourself in any situation. Well, you're wrong. Some of the men inside are animals. They'll chew you up and spit you out. Who told you to lift Detective Inspector Flynn and bring him to Glebe Bog?'

Durkan hesitated slightly. 'No comment.'

'For God's sake, man, you were witnessed kidnapping Flynn and driving him to the bog. Your companion shot and wounded a serving police officer. We have the gun and we have the bullet. The jury will be out for less than five minutes before they find you guilty.' Duane could see sweat forming on Durkan's forehead. 'It's a no-brainer.' Duane looked at the file in front of him. 'You're twenty-five now. You'll go down for twenty-five years for this, which means you'll be out when you're fifty. Cop on, we're giving you first chance to help us. Take it and we'll help you.'

'I want to talk to my solicitor,' Durkan said.

It was the first fissure in the wall of silence and Duane knew that it wouldn't be the last. Durkan would get them McCluskey, but only McCluskey would get them Feeney. He looked at Guiney, who declared the interview suspended and switched off the recording equipment.

'We'll be back.' Duane stood and he and Guiney left the room.

'Get the duty sergeant to prepare a charge sheet for Durkan. We'll stick with kidnapping for the minute and add other charges as they arise.'

Duane went into the TV room where Wilson was lying back with his feet on the desk. 'He'll crack.'

'For sure.' Wilson sat up. 'But he took his orders from McCluskey. Is that where you're going next?'

'I think we should both have a word with Flynn first.'

'How long do you intend to hold him?'

'We have proof that a known criminal has put a hit on him. I'm keeping him in protective custody.'

'And what does Flynn say to that?'

'Let's find out.'

THE SMALL NUMBER of officers who constituted the night shift occupied only two tables in the cafeteria. Duane, Wilson and Flynn sat at a table at the far end of the room. Flynn's eyes were red-rimmed and the skin on his face was pale and waxy. The grey fringe around his temples had encroached further into his fair hair.

'Your plan didn't quite work out.' Duane sipped his tea. 'Feeney doesn't play by anyone's rules.'

Flynn resembled a balloon with all the air let out.

'It's over,' Wilson added. 'You getting buried in a bog wouldn't do your wife and children much good.'

'You'll go down,' Duane said. 'The preliminary examination of your bank statements and your online betting accounts showed cash flows inconsistent with your salary. If you help us, we'll help you. You'll be out in a few years and you can start to put your life back together. You'll never be a police officer again, but there are other ways you can play a positive role.'

'I am so bloody tired,' Flynn said. 'Okay, I'll give you Feeney. He paid me off personally a half-dozen times.'

'That's a good man,' Duane said. 'What about Lennon?'

'I'm sure Feeney ordered it, but I have no proof. I can't help you there.'

'We'll take a statement in the morning.' Duane nodded at a uniformed officer standing beside the cafeteria door. 'Take DI Flynn back to his cell.'

'You'll have a hell of a job nailing Feeney on a corruption charge,' Wilson said as soon as the door closed on Flynn.

'It's a start.'

'He'll delay until he sees how Brexit turns out. The case will be down here, but he lives in the north.'

'We'll chip away at him. The days of these warlords are over. Thirty years of madness had to leave behind some rubbish to be cleaned up. That's our job.'

'And a right shit job it is.' Wilson said as his phone buzzed.

'Reid already getting lonely?' Duane asked.

Wilson read the message from Baird: *Tomorrow. Same place, same time.* 'I wish. I need to go back to Belfast tonight, but I'll wait and see how you get on with McCluskey.'

'Then we better get to it.'


McCluskey was picking his nose and didn't bother to look up when Duane and Guiney entered the interview room. Coyle was in attendance once more. Guiney did the preliminaries.

'Mr McCluskey,' Duane began. 'You are still under caution. We are currently preparing a charge sheet for you that will include the attempted murder of a police officer, conspiracy to murder a police officer and possession of a firearm. Other charges are likely to follow. Do you understand the charges?'

'No comment.'

Duane looked at Coyle. 'Please tell your client that he has to respond that he understands the charges to be put to him.'

Coyle whispered in McCluskey's ear.

'Do you understand, Mr McCluskey?' Duane repeated.

'Yes.'

'You've had a busy time. What with the Lennon murder, the assault on Keating and tonight's events, you're a bit of a one-man crime spree.'

'No comment.' McCluskey looked concerned.

'I was trying to tot up the number of years you'll go down for, but I ran out of fingers. This is the big one, Michael.'

McCluskey remained silent.

'You can do yourself some good by telling me why you and Durkan abducted Detective Inspector Flynn from his residence this evening?'

'No comment.'

'In that case, I will be adding the charge of kidnapping to your sheet. Do you understand?'

'The crazy bastard came willingly.'

Coyle looked sharply at his client.

'You may have some difficulty getting a jury to believe that. Why did you drive DI Flynn to Glebe Bog?'

'No comment.'

'When you were arrested, you were in possession of a Ruger SR 22 pistol. We have checked and this is an illegally held firearm. How did you come by this firearm?'

'No comment.'

'You may be interested to know that DG Johnny Murray is in a stable condition in Louth County Hospital and that the doctors removed a .22 bullet from his shoulder. I have no doubt that a ballistics test will show that that bullet came from the pistol you had in your possession. Do you deny shooting Garda Murray with the intention of killing him?'

'No comment.'

Duane leaned back in his chair. 'I know you think you're a hard man.' A thin smile creased McCluskey's lips. 'But you're facing a series of capital charges here, any of which will put you behind bars for up to twenty-five years. That means you'll be in your seventies the day you walk out of Portlaoise Prison. Your wife will be a stranger and your kids will be away. I know your solicitor will deny it, but I think your colleague Durkan will turn state's evidence. For that, we'll be lenient with him, while you'll draw the full ticket. Now, if the shoe were on the other foot.' He could see that McCluskey was taking a greater interest in the proceedings. 'We know you were only following orders. It's not like the old days when there was a proper chain of command. This time it was one man's impulse, and he'll walk free while you go down. That's not fair. You shouldn't be the only one to feel the pain. The first one who signs up to help us will get the best deal.' He looked at Coyle. 'When you take your solicitor's advice, remember who he really works for.'

'I resent that, chief inspector,' Coyle bristled.

'Sorry, Mr Coyle, it's just remarkable that nearly every time we have one of Feeney's men in for questioning, you seem to be their solicitor.'

'I'm here representing Mr McCluskey.'

'I'm sure you are.' Duane turned to McCluskey. 'You're going down for shooting DG Murray, but if you help us, we'll make sure you get the lightest sentence possible. And you'll be in witness protection when you get out.'

There was a pregnant silence.

'I think you have a lot to reflect on. Out in your seventies, or a lot sooner and a new life.' Duane nodded at Guiney, who closed the proceedings.

Before Duane and Guiney reached the door, McCluskey was already in deep conversation with Coyle.


WILSON MET them in the corridor outside the interview room. 'Good job.' He slapped Duane on the back.

They started back towards the incident room.

'It'll take a few more conversations, but you have a good chance to turn him,' Wilson said. 'I bet he asks for a new solicitor tomorrow. Harry is having a snooze on the camp bed. It seems a shame to wake him, but I need to get back.'

'I hope you don't find Reid *in flagrante* when you get home,' Duane said.

'You have a twisted mind.'

'So people tell me.'

'I have a meeting with the chief constable early tomorrow and I'm not sure of the outcome.'

'You could always come and work for us,' Duane said.

'I'll take that under advisement.'

In the incident room, Wilson shook Graham awake. 'Home, James.'


DUANE AND GUINEY had walked them to the station door.

'I like working with them,' Guiney said as they watched their car pull away.

'They're not bad guys,' Duane said. 'For northerners.'

# CHAPTER FIFTY-FOUR

Wilson met Moira in the lobby of Benedict's Hotel.

'You look tired,' she said.

'It was a long day yesterday. I'll tell you about it later. Let's go up.'

'Room 205?'

The receptionist watched them as they entered the lift. Wilson felt like saying 'it's not what you think'. But the receptionist would have said an older man entering the lift accompanied by an attractive redhead could mean only one thing.

Wilson had woken in the early morning having had a dream that he was stark naked in a room full of his peers. He was desperate to cover himself, but nobody appeared to be taking a blind bit of notice of him. As soon as the meeting with Baird was over, he'd have to find out what the dream signified.

Baird opened the door to them and shook their hands. Wilson looked beyond the CC and saw ACC Craig Humphreys sitting watching Sky News. Humphreys turned off the TV as Wilson and Moira arrived.

'You know ACC Humphreys,' Baird said.

'We've met.' Wilson shook Humphreys' hand. The handshake was firm. Humphreys was a thirty-year man and close to retirement. He had a reputation for being honest and had climbed the career ladder on merit. Wilson introduced Moira.

'Let's sit,' Baird said. 'Moira, you can have the chair and us old fogies will manage on the bed. I've asked Craig to come along because of his experience. I have no desire to expand the group wider.'

'I think the ACC will add value to the discussion,' Wilson said.

'Good,' Baird said. 'First off, I'm not going to make the investigation public. I've looked at the evidence that Davidson developed and while I agree that he did an excellent job, I don't think that there's enough to conclude that Carlisle was murdered. That doesn't mean, however, that I'm going to close the investigation down.'

Wilson said. 'We have a positive identification of Jackson wearing a white nurse's jacket in the area on the morning that Carlisle received the overdose. Davidson found no evidence that Carlisle obtained the morphine on his own.'

'You have enough to pick up Jackson,' Humphreys said.

'If we could find him. He disappeared after Davidson was assaulted. We have a photo of him at Rosslare about to board a ferry to France and we have a glimpse of him in a photo taken at Helen McCann's villa in Antibes. We've issued a European Arrest Warrant for him, but so far, the French police haven't been able to locate him. We have reason to believe that he was in Belfast recently and that he's changed his appearance.'

'I made an enquiry with Special Branch about Jackson,' Humphreys said. 'They said that he simply disappeared.'

'We all know CS Bob Rodgers,' Wilson said. 'Jackson wouldn't have undertaken an operation without his approval. And Special Branch has become a law unto themselves.'

Wilson noticed the look that passed between Baird and Humphreys. They knew Rodgers as well as he did, and they

knew what he was capable of. It was possible that Rodgers was
the Policeman in Carlisle's story.

'You're treading on very thin ice here,' Baird said. 'We're
not talking about only a murder but about a conspiracy under-
lying it. And that conspiracy involves members of the PSNI.'

'It's not just one murder either,' Wilson said. 'It's multiple
murders. And it's ultimately about corruption and money.'

'Craig and I have discussed this and we're in agreement.
You've uncovered enough evidence to warrant further investigation, but we want it kept in-house. I'm personally very
worried about the consequences of making any of this investigation public. You're aware that Kate McCann is likely to
become the highest law officer in the land as soon as the
incumbent retires. The implications of her mother being put
on trial could be devastating.'

'There are also implications for the force,' Humphreys
added. 'We can't have the public thinking that rogue PSNI
officers are running around killing people.'

'Of course not, all that is in the past.' Wilson's own father,
a sergeant in the RUC, had been involved in the death of two
innocent boys. The guilt of that involvement had led to his
suicide.

'The bottom line is that you can continue to investigate
with my approval,' Baird said. Two officers will reinforce you,
one from Professional Services, who will examine the corruption aspects, and one from Fraud, who will examine the papers
DS McElvaney obtained from her American friend. You will
report to ACC Humphreys.'

'Can I ask for a particular officer from Professional
Services?' Wilson said.

'Who would you like?'

'DS Lucy Kane,' Wilson said.

'Any other requirements?' Baird asked.

'DS McElvaney will lead the investigation,' Wilson said.

'With you as SIO,' Baird said.

The implication was clear. If the investigation proved to be a disaster, Wilson would pay the price. 'Agreed.'

Baird stood. 'We don't need to meet again. Craig will keep me informed.' He put on his cap and went to the door followed by Humphreys. He turned and faced Wilson. 'Good luck, Ian. I have a feeling that you're going to need it.'

Baird and Humphreys left.

'No coffee today then,' Wilson said.

'Austerity,' Moira replied. 'What was that?'

'A major ass-covering operation. Humphreys will be retiring soon so he's the perfect fall guy for the CC if it all goes to shit. Of course, I'll take the major blast from the shit shotgun, and a couple of pellets will hit those around me and that will almost certainly include you.'

'He doesn't think that we can nail her?'

'He's pretty sure that we can't, but he has to cover all bases. He knows that we're holding some circumstantial evidence and, if we are diligent and extremely lucky, we might find some concrete evidence that will make the crap we have relevant.'

'You don't sound too hopeful yourself.'

'We live in a world where a twenty-year-old kid gets sent to jail for stealing a leather jacket and where corporate raiders and bankers rip off millions and retire gracefully to enjoy their offshore assets. I'm as sure as I can be that McCann ordered the murder of Carlisle. I have doubts that we'll ever put her behind bars for it, but I live in hope that we will. In the meantime, we will use the extra resources that we've been given to go over what we have.'

'That's why they call us the plod.'

'Exactly. I gave up looking for flashes of brilliance years ago.'

'I feel the same about Hills as you feel about McCann. I know he torched the car but there's no proof.'

'You might hit on a vital piece of evidence next week or

next month, or in a decade's time. It's the nature of the job. You're a first-class detective, Moira. You're going to have a career in the force if that's what you want. Just don't forget, there'll be a price to pay.'

'What price is that?'

'That's the thing, we don't know until we have to pay it.'

## CHAPTER FIFTY-FIVE

As soon Wilson and Moira entered the station, the duty sergeant nodded in the direction of a bench at the rear of the reception area.

Wilson turned and saw Dáithí Ó Brádaigh staring into space. He walked over to the councillor.

'Mr Ó Brádaigh.'

'What, oh!' Ó Brádaigh came out of his trace and looked up into Wilson's face. 'Superintendent Wilson, I wonder if we could have a word.'

'Certainly.' Wilson sat down beside him.

'I'd like to make a statement.'

'Concerning?'

'I may have inadvertently played a part in the death of Brian Lennon.'

'We'll have to record your statement, have it typed up and then signed. Is that okay with you?'

'Yes.'

Wilson arranged for Graham to join them and then led Ó Brádaigh to an interview room.

'DS Graham would you do the honours?'

Graham started the recording equipment and did the preliminaries.

'Mr Ó Brádaigh,' Wilson began. 'Perhaps you should explain how you inadvertently played a role in the death of Brian Lennon.'

Ó Brádaigh hugged himself and looked down at the table. 'Brian Lennon came to me some months ago and asked me to help him with a problem. His father was recently deceased and one of his neighbours claimed that he had an option to buy the Lennon farm. Brian and his father were close, but he had no knowledge of the option. I advised him to negotiate with the neighbour. He told me that he had already tried, but the neighbour was adamant. He was very upset. The farm was losing money, but it was one of the last pieces of land in the area owned by a Lennon. He felt he would be letting his ancestors down by selling. I told him I would speak to the neighbour. Can I have a glass of water, please?'

'DS Graham will fetch one for you.'

Graham left and returned with a bottle of water and a glass. Ó Brádaigh filled the glass and drank.

'I spoke to the neighbour and found that he was intransigent. He had already arranged to buy the land and he wanted the deal to go through. I passed this information to Brian. A week or so later, the neighbour approached me. As you surmised, Lennon was talking about going to the police. Feeney couldn't have that, he asked me to telephone Lennon to set up a meeting with him at a deserted farmhouse in Inniskeen. To my discredit, I agreed and set up the meeting.' Ó Brádaigh filled a second glass and drank.

Wilson waited for more, but Ó Brádaigh was finished. 'DS Graham, would you do the necessary?'

'Dáithí Ó Brádaigh, I am cautioning you that you do not have to say anything. But it may harm your defence if you do not mention when questioned something that you later rely on in court. Anything you do say may be given in evidence.'

'We'll have the statement typed. Do you agree to be interviewed?' Wilson asked.

Ó Brádaigh nodded.

'For the tape, please.'

'Yes.'

'Do you wish to have a solicitor present?'

'No.'

'Who is the neighbour in question?'

Ó Brádaigh hesitated. 'Tommy Feeney.'

'Thomas Feeney asked you to arrange a meeting with Brian Lennon at the farmhouse in Inniskeen where his body was found.'

Ó Brádaigh hung his head. 'Yes.'

'And you are now aware that you were complicit in the murder of Brian Lennon?'

'I had no idea that he was going to be murdered.'

'What did you think was going to happen?'

'I thought that he would get roughed up.'

'Perhaps kneecapped?'

'Yes, something like that.'

'So, you knew that Brian Lennon was going to be violently assaulted and you went ahead?'

'Yes.'

'Why did you lie to us before?'

'I can't discuss that.'

'You mean you don't want to discuss it. Why tell us the truth now?'

'My conscience is bothering me.'

'Interview suspended at nine-forty-five.' Wilson turned and nodded at Graham, who stopped the recording.

Wilson stood. 'Hang on a bit here. Would you like some tea?'

'Yes, please.'

'I'll have some sent in.'

. . .

WILSON WENT to his office and phoned Duane. 'We caught a break but how big a one I can't really say.' He proceeded to tell Duane about his interview with Ó Brádaigh.

'It moves us along the road but not far enough,' Duane said. 'It's a he said/she said situation. We need someone who was present and who received their orders from Feeney. The interesting point is that Ó Brádaigh named Feeney. That means his political protection has been lifted.'

'What about McCluskey and Durkan?'

'Both men were fed a healthy breakfast. I've been granted a remand on them for a week and I'll keep plugging away.'

'What about the phone call?'

'We voice-printed the men we arrested during the raid but didn't find a match. We did a voice-print on Durkan last night, but it'll take a while before the results come back.'

'So what's next?'

'I've got McCluskey and Durkan in this morning and we'll see if a night in the cells will make them more talkative.'

'What about young Murray?'

'He'll pull through.'

'Keep me informed.'

'Will do.'

Wilson thought they had pushed Ó Brádaigh as far as he would go. The question of whether to pursue a charge of wasting police time would require the approval of the DPP. He'd let Ó Brádaigh have his tea and then cut him loose. There was a risk that he'd run to Feeney and beg his forgiveness, but that risk was minimal. Ó Brádaigh knew what Feeney was capable of.

Wilson looked at the mass of documents on his desk. The running back and forth over the border had seriously affected his administrative output. He'd just opened the latest budget file when Davis's assistant called to say his presence was required in Davis's office.

. . .

DAVIS LOOKED WORRIED. She indicated her empty visitor's chair as soon as Wilson entered. 'I've had a call from ACC Humphreys.'

'I thought you might.'

'I've already given Jennings the phone and a copy of the evidence Davidson collected.'

'I assumed you had.'

'So Jennings knows what you have.'

'He's the DCC. We couldn't keep the investigation confidential forever. And he has every right to examine what we've been up to.'

'I thought you'd be pissed.'

'I am pissed, but only because I don't think the DCC can be trusted. The whole business was a long shot. The coroner's report was in. No one was looking at murder. Maybe we've all had our heads up our collective arses. You're the one who should be pissed at me. I've put all our careers on the line. If we're lucky, I'll be the only one to go down.'

'We have to make sure that doesn't happen. How is Jack?'

'Struggling to put Tommy Feeney away. How are things at home?'

'I'm moving out again.' She was holding back the tears.

'Have you told your family?'

'No, but I think it's for the best. We tried counselling and it just proved that things are over between us. There's too much resentment concerning my job and me. The children are grown up and they'll soon be off on their own.'

'We all sacrifice something for the job. For some it's the family, for others it's their moral principles.'

'What have you sacrificed?'

'A father, a mother, a wife and a lover, and I'm probably not finished yet. Don't put your entire store in Jack. I'm very fond of him, but he's not Mr Steadfast where women are concerned.'

'Maybe that's what I need now.'

'Sit down and talk to your family. Keep the channels open. I made the mistake of cutting my mother off and I deeply regret the lost years.'

'I'm keeping you from your work.'

'I'll tell Jack that you asked after him.'

'Do that.'

# CHAPTER FIFTY-SIX

Duane stared at the TV image of McCluskey sitting in the interview room. He thought Durkan would have been the first to fold, but he'd been wrong. McCluskey looked like a guy who hadn't slept a wink. His head was down and his arms were splayed on the table in front of him. There was no sign of Coyle. Duane opened the file in front of him. McCluskey was fifty-two years old. Considering the charges against him, he'd be over seventy by the time he left prison. He turned to Guiney. 'Let's do it.'

McCluskey's head came up when Duane and Guiney walked into the interview room. 'How's the boy in hospital?'

'You won't be facing a murder charge,' Duane said. 'Be grateful for small mercies.'

'You're still under caution.' Guiney switched on the recording equipment and did the preamble.

'I understand that you made a request that your solicitor should not attend,' Duane said.

McCluskey rubbed the stubble on his chin. 'Yeah, he's

Tommy's man. I need to look out for number one now. What can you do for me?'

'It depends on what you've got to offer.'

'I can give you the distillery and the fuel operation.'

'Not interested in the minor stuff. What about the Lennon murder?'

McCluskey shifted uneasily in his chair.

'We know you were in Inniskeen,' Duane lied. 'I want the names of all the others, and I want to know how it went down.'

'And what do I get?'

'I told you already that you'll have to do time for the Flynn business and the shooting of Detective Garda Murray. But it'll be a light sentence.'

'If I finger Tommy, I'll need witness protection.'

'That'll be arranged as soon as you're discharged from prison.'

'Can I trust you?'

'I'm the only game in town.'

'Give me a pen and paper.'

Duane looked at Guiney, who handed McCluskey some paper and a pen. McCluskey wrote a list of names on the page and passed it back to Duane. 'I'm not going to be popular after this gets out.'

'Coleman wasn't there,' Duane said as he read the list. 'I don't believe it.'

'Coleman drove the minibus and collected the clothing and the weapons.'

'Where are they now?'

'Where do you think they are?'

'We know why Feeney wanted Lennon dead. Were you there when he gave the order to kill him?'

'No. Coleman told me to gather a crew. The lads thought it was a punishment job.'

'Was it? Did you just go too far?'

'The instruction was given that Lennon was to die.'

'Stay here.' Duane turned to Guiney. 'Close it down for the moment.'

Guiney closed the interview and switched off the recording equipment.


'FLYNN WANTS TO SEE YOU,' Guiney said as they walked back towards the incident room.

'First we get these names on the wire to Wilson. I want all these men picked up today. Put Flynn in a room. I need a break and the fucker can wait.'


'YOU BASTARD.' Flynn shot to his feet as soon as Duane entered the room. 'You set me up, you fucker. You've ruined my life.'

'Sit down and shut the fuck up,' Duane pulled up a chair and sat opposite Flynn. 'I did nothing to you that you didn't do to yourself. Sure, I could have held you in custody. But your solicitor would have had you out sooner or later.'

'You used me.' Flynn slumped in the chair. 'Why didn't you let them kill me?'

'Because, unlike you, the oath I took when I passed out in Templemore meant something to me. We promised to the best of our skill and knowledge to discharge all our duties according to the law. That's what I do every day. Because of you, McCluskey has just given us the names of the men who beat Brian Lennon to death. I despise bent coppers, so I have no regrets about using you to expose Lennon's murderers.'

Flynn put his head in his hands. 'Feeney will never kill me now. You've beggared my wife and kids.'

'No, you've beggared your wife and kids. Unfortunately, there's no law against that. If there were, it would give me immense pleasure to charge you under it. But there is a law against a member of An Garda Síochána leaking information to an OCG. And I'll make damn sure that you pay the price for that.' Duane stood and went to the door.

A uniformed officer was standing outside. 'Take former DI Flynn back to his cell,' Duane said. He turned to Flynn. 'You belong to the DPP now. Professional Standards is sending someone up from Dublin to talk to you. Don't ask to see me again. And don't for God's sake talk about your wife and kids in my company, because if you do, I won't be answerable for my actions.'

# CHAPTER FIFTY-SEVEN

W ilson had set up a small office at Newry PSNI Station. The local uniforms had brought in the five men whose names had been transmitted by Duane. Wilson and Graham had picked up Coleman. Most of the men worked for Feeney in some capacity. The duty sergeant at Newry had processed them and each had been assigned to a separate cell at the station. Duane arrived in the early afternoon.

'I've applied to have the five men extradited.' Duane was seated in Wilson makeshift office. 'The DPP has agreed to charge them with murder, which should expedite matters.'

'What about Coleman?' Wilson asked. 'He didn't swing a pickaxe handle, but he organised the murder and he was there to clean up. He's also the link in the chain that leads to Feeney.'

'The latter might be wishful thinking. Feeney and Coleman have been joined at the hip for years. They've soldiered together. It's a bond that transcends brotherhood.'

'If Coleman is convicted, he'll probably never see the outside of a prison again. That's a lot of pressure to bear.'

'You think he'll give Feeney up?'

'McCluskey gave him up.'

'You're right. We've got to go the distance. Feeney's pals have deserted him. He had a bloody good run. But it's over. Now, you get to interview Coleman and I get to watch.'

COLEMAN STOOD when Wilson entered the interview room.

'Sit down, man,' Wilson said. He had no respect for the men he had to put behind bars. When he came across some-body who had taken the life of another human being, they appeared diminished in his eyes. It was the opposite of the American Indian contention that the killer absorbed some of the soul of the man he killed. Wilson found most of the killers he'd dealt with to be soulless. Coleman might be the exception. There was light in his blue eyes and a level of sensitivity.

Graham did the necessary and as soon as Wilson heard the tape running, he began. 'You've been cautioned?'

'Yes.'

'Do you wish to have a solicitor present?'

'No.'

'Do you know why you're here?'

'I have no idea.'

'We have every detail of what happened at Inniskeen. Michael McCluskey has placed you there and as soon as we explain to the other five men who took part in the murder of Brian Lennon the predicament they're in, they'll finger you too. You asked McCluskey to put the crew together, you gave the instructions, you collected the bloody boiler-suits and pickaxe handles and you drove the minibus.'

Coleman stared straight ahead.

'Dáithí Ó Brádaigh has confessed to his role in setting up Brian Lennon. So, we are simply dotting the i's and crossing the t's. Where are the boiler-suits and pickaxe handles?'

'I don't know what you're talking about.'

'We've got search warrants for the shop and the storeroom

and for your address. If there's anything left, even a scrap of wood with Lennon's blood on it, we'll find it. We won't need it to put you away, but it'll be another nail in your coffin.'

'Do you have a question?'

'How can you be loyal to a man like Feeney? He'd sell his grandmother for a fiver. Aren't you disgusted to be part of an organisation that sells fuel that screws up people's car engines and rotgut that ruins their insides?'

'You're forgetting the cigarettes that are full of carcinogens.'

'Thanks for reminding me. Are you proud of what you've done?'

'I've never liked the taxman.'

'Don't be flippant.'

'Was it our fault that the politicians on both sides of the border set up regulations that permitted unscrupulous men to make money by moving goods from one side of the border to the other? That's without considering the whole question of whether there should be a border in Ireland at all.'

'We're not talking politics here. We're talking about taking a young man's life.' Wilson got another lightbulb moment. 'It was your voice on the 999 call, wasn't it?'

'No comment.'

'We'll do a voice-print and prove it. Did you think they could get to him in time?'

'No comment.'

'You didn't want him to die, did you?'

'No comment.'

'We have a circumstantial case against Tommy Feeney. He's an affliction in this area. He thinks he's above the law. He told me that he was the law. Who told you to set up a crew to administer a beating to Brian Lennon?'

'No comment.'

'Did Feeney tell you to arrange the murder of Brian Lennon?'

'No comment.'

Wilson looked at Graham, who terminated the interview.

'We'll be charging you with murder. I don't think we'll have any difficulty proving your involvement. I hate to see an otherwise decent man go down instead of a blatant criminal, but it is what it is. Think about it.'


'WHAT NOW?' Duane asked when Wilson joined him. 'We have the gang that committed the murder and the man who organised it. We've dealt Feeney's organisation a blow and we've put him in a bad situation with his friends. All in all, I'd say it was a reasonable day's work.'

'Get your jacket,' Wilson said. 'We've one more call to make.'


FEENEY OPENED THE DOOR. 'FUCK OFF.' He started to close the door.

Duane's shoe stopped the door from fully closing. 'Not this time, Tommy. The real fucking law has arrived.'

Wilson jerked the door open. 'Thomas Feeney, I am arresting you for being involved in the unlawful death of Brian Lennon. You do not have to say anything, but anything you do say will be taken down and used in evidence.' He took a set of handcuffs from his jacket pocket. 'Put your hands out.' Wilson put the cuffs on Feeney's outstretched hands. 'These cuffs might pinch a little and I hope to God that they do.' Wilson pulled Feeney across the threshold and closed the door behind him.

'Do your superiors know you're doing this?' Feeney asked.

Wilson ushered him in the direction of the police car.

Feeney spat at Duane. 'That bastard has no jurisdiction here.'

Duane wiped the spittle off his face and rubbed it on Feeney's cheek.

'That bastard was never here.' Wilson opened the rear door and pushed Feeney into the seat.

'I'll be out before you have the papers written up. And then I'm going to dedicate my life to getting you both fired.'

'Your time has gone. It's a pity you didn't recognise it before you had Brian Lennon killed.' Wilson slammed the car door.

'He's right, you know,' Duane said. 'He'll be out as soon as his solicitor gets to Newry.'

'I've done my job,' Wilson said. 'You can extradite him. Coleman will come around, but it may take time.'

Duane opened the car door. 'We work well together.'

'Aye, we do. Or should I say, we did.'

'The politicians may screw around with the border, but we'll find ways to help each other out.' They shook hands. 'It's been a pleasure, Ian.'

# CHAPTER FIFTY-EIGHT

W ilson tried to put the money behind the bar, but Duane had beaten him to the punch. It was the prerogative of the SIO, so Wilson put his money back in his pocket. It was Duane's show. The rear of the Crown was packed with off-duty officers from Dundalk Garda Station. Meg Hearney was standing in the middle of the group. Duane sat in a corner whispering in Davis's ear. Graham and O'Neill stood together, and Moira was nowhere to be seen. Wilson was heading for the bar while Reid made for the group of gardaí.

Duane looked at Wilson and gave him the thumbs-up sign. Wilson interpreted the signal as confirming that Coleman had flipped. Jack would no longer be part of the investigation. He would leave the mundane job of collecting evidence to lesser mortals. There was a similarity with Reid's approach to her work. After she had completed her examination of the corpse, she walked away from the table and left her assistant to do the tedious job of closing-up. He envied them both.

'Is this like those Irish wedding parties where the two families refuse to mingle?' Reid said. She looked at Graham and O'Neill. 'Harry, Siobhan, come down here and show our guests some northern hospitality.'

Wilson put a gin and tonic in Reid's hand. 'Where did I find you?'

Reid raised the glass. 'Look who just walked in.'

Wilson turned and saw Moira entering with a man he hadn't seen before. Her face was lit up like a beacon. The man was nearly as tall as Wilson but younger. He was casually but tastefully dressed in a white blazer and blue jeans.

Moira joined Wilson. 'Boss, I'd like you to meet a friend of mine from Boston. Frank Shea, this is Ian Wilson.'

Shea put out his hand. 'I've heard a lot about you.'

Wilson shook. 'You have the advantage over me.' He stared at Moira. The look on her face told him everything he needed to know. 'You're welcome, Frank. In this company I hope you know how to drink and sing.'

'Count on it.'

Wilson turned and looked at the group. This might be the last time he would attend such a celebration. The thought left him feeling empty. He looked at Reid and saw that she was staring at him. She must have seen something in his face. He forced a smile and held his drink aloft. 'Raise your glasses to Jack Duane, the best SIO I've worked with.'

'Here's to you too, Butch,' Duane toasted Wilson.

Reid left the group and walked to Wilson's side. 'Now that the brofest is over,' she said. 'Let's get on with the party.'

————

I HOPE that you enjoyed this book. As an indie author, I very much depend on your feedback to see where my writing is going. I would be very grateful if you would take the time to pen a review on Amazon. This will not only help me but will also indicate to others your feelings, positive or negative, on the work. Writing is a lonely profession, and this is especially true for indie authors who don't have the backup of traditional publishers

.  .  .

PLEASE CHECK out my other books on Amazon and if you have time visit my website (derekfee.com) and sign up to receive additional materials, competitions for signed books and announcements of new book launches.

Dear Fee is a former oil company executive and EU Ambassador. He is the author of seven non-fiction books and fifteen novels. Border Badlands is the eleventh book featuring Ian Wilson and the Belfast Murder Squad.

Derek can be contacted at derekfee.com.

## AUTHOR'S PLEA

I hope that you enjoyed this book. As an indie author, I very much depend on your feedback to see where my writing is going. I would be very grateful if you would take the time to pen a short review. This will not only help me but will also indicate to others your feelings, positive or negative, on the work. Writing is a lonely profession, and this is especially true for indie authors who don't have the backup of traditional publishers.

Please check out my other books , and if you have time visit my web site (derekfee.com) and sign up to receive additional materials, competitions for signed books and announcements of new book launches.

You can contact me at derekfee.com.

# ABOUT THE AUTHOR

Derek Fee is a former oil company executive and EU Ambassador. He is the author of seven non-fiction books and sixteen novels. Derek can be contacted at http://derekfee.com.

Printed in Great Britain
by Amazon